MW01225133

# BREATHLESS

by

Steven J. Conifer

*Breathless*
© 2011 by Steven Conifer

For my parents.

I should scorn to shiver with terror at the thought of annihilation. Happiness is nonetheless true happiness because it must come to an end, nor do thought and love lose their value because they are not everlasting.

- Bertrand Russell
*Why I Am Not a Christian*

Well, I picked up a rose and it poked through my clothes
I followed the winding stream.
I heard the deafening noise, I felt transient joys
I know they're not what they seem.
In this earthly domain, full of disappointment and pain
You'll never see me frown.
I owe my heart to you, and that's sayin' it true
And I'll be with you when the deal goes down.

- Bob Dylan
"When the Deal Goes Down"

# PART I:

# diagnosis

# 1

As he had for several nights in a row, Dennis Arbaugh now awoke, cold and shivering, from a vivid and recurring dream in which he stood upon the summit of a great mountain, the sole survivor of a brief but gruesome holocaust. In the dream he was always naked save for a flimsy swatch of burgundy cloth tied to his waist by a string, concealing his genitals much as the fig-leaf concealed Adam's in modern Genesis pictorials. There blew invariably a gale so powerful as to threaten his balance, and he would sway precariously there on the precipice, to and fro, never quite toppling, his single garment flapping with violent, audible force. The peak was snow-swept, the sky above a uniformly dour gray, rife with clouds like barren continents. There was to the scene, and to the dream itself, a kind of spurious tranquility, a feeble repose which enveloped the very molecules in the air; but underneath, and not far underneath, there was a profound disquiet, a resignation too heavy and authentic to be tempered or borne, and yet too raw to be other than embraced. The overall effect of the dream was singularly unnerving, and drove sleep from his mind with a ferocious efficiency, now as before, at quarter past three on the morning of his fifty-second birthday.

With no thought of the woman fast asleep beside him, he threw back the sheets and sat bolt upright, his arms flailing in the dark, the old delirium squarely upon him. Tears streamed unnoticed from his eyes, and he breathed in quick, trembling gasps, his chest hitching as his lungs clamored for air. Slowly the image of the mountain receded, its contours blurring and blending with the darkness of the room. The image of the cloth was more stubborn, persisting well into his second minute of full wakefulness, the deep-red hue branded on his mind like an ancient bloodstain. He closed his eyes and pinched the bridge of his nose with his thumb and forefinger, trying desperately to banish it. At last it faded, and when it did he leaned back against the headboard and exhaled once, very slowly.

He wiped tears from his face with the back of his hand and glanced down at his wife, a nebulous lump buried in a tangle of linen. She had barely stirred. She had never done otherwise. The same thing had happened on five consecutive nights, and not once had it woken her.

## 2

Slumber was slow to return, painfully slow, and each night it seemed a little slower and more painful than the last. This time it would be four o' clock when at last he drifted off, and the forty minutes he spent staring at the ceiling and listening to the sound of his wife's muffled breathing were extraordinarily dark and lonely ones.

There was a word he had learned a long time ago, perhaps in college: "asymptote." It was a term of mathematics, and he supposed any application of it to the concrete world inevitably clumsy and inapt, but during those terrible intervals he could not help but recall it. He had a vague idea that it referred to a certain kind of line or curve or some relationship between the two, but the definition he assigned it in the privacy of his own mind was this: "a progression which infinitely approaches but never quite reaches termination." Such were precisely the blank, fretful spaces between the conclusion of his dream and the onset of a shallow, uneasy sleep: creeping progressions of time which slogged tediously forward but seemingly never expired. And in a sense, he supposed, they did *not* expire, for so long as he was awake the arrow remained in flight, moving futilely and imperceptibly closer to its target.

And of course there was the physical pain as well. The headaches, the vomiting (a recent phenomenon), the incessant cough which left his lungs so bruised and throat so raw that to form words was at times a monumental burden. There were stretches, some of them mercifully quite long, during which these manifestations subsided (that was how he thought of them already, as manifestations of something far more permanent and foreboding), and for those he was thankful. For the last week or so he had enjoyed just such a reprieve. His physical suffering during the nightly spells between dream and dreamless black had so far been confined to a mild nausea and dull headache. He was particularly grateful for this, though in the wake of the dream, in the midst of the weird, free-floating anxiety it always induced, it was hard to be grateful for anything.

Each morning at seven o' clock the alarm would sound, and he would rise groggily and plod into the bathroom. There he would sit on the toilet and wish for a cigarette - still, still, after six months without a single draw, he would wish for a cigarette - and scan through bleary eyes the headlines in yesterday's Seattle *Times*. He did this mostly to wake himself up and get his brain working. More often than not, in fact, he had already read the articles in their entirety over the previous evening's supper.

This morning was such an instance: when his eyes flitted over the headline which blared "Seattle Smokers Moving Forward With Class Action Suit Against Stevens & Brent," he recalled at once the ominous account thus denoted. He pushed this thought away, very consciously, and trained his eyes on a less conspicuous headline he had apparently missed between forkfuls of pork and carrots: "Woodstock-Style Music Festival in the Works for Oregon Town." The subhead read: "A-List bands to gather in Corvallis this summer to benefit cancer research." Some of the bands named were The Rolling Stones, The Eagles, and Fleetwood Mac. Tom Petty and Bruce Springsteen were each to perform solo.

*Cancer research*, he thought. *Might be a little late for that, fellas. Where I'm concerned, anyway.* He made a half-hearted effort to squeeze something out as he scoured the newspaper for something, anything, without significance to his troubled lot.

And then came his wife's voice through the bathroom door: "Dennis? Are you all right?"

"Yes," he said.

"Headache?"

"Small one."

"Did you throw up?"

"No."

Long pause, then: "I'll put on some coffee."

*Yes, coffee... that'll help. Always does. Do you believe that I'm dying, Rachael? Will you at least consider the possibility? Or can't you? Is it beyond you?* "Okay," he said.

Another pause, this one slightly longer. "Happy birthday, sweetheart."

"Uh huh. Thanks."

He waited, listening for footsteps, praying that she would say no more. When at last she retreated, he sighed gratefully and went back to his paper. But now his concentration was broken, and a moment later he gave up. *Fifty-two*, he thought. *You ancient bastard. Where did the time go? Everyone wonders and nobody knows.*

He pushed his bowels again, grunting hard enough that she could no doubt hear him, and produced nothing but a slimy perspiration on his brow. He had been eating quite little these past few weeks but often felt the need to shit - and was nearly as often incapable of doing so. Loss of appetite was a symptom, he knew (he'd been reading lots of medical encyclopedias just lately), but he had come across nothing in the literature about incontinence. Not yet, anyway. He still had a few hundred volumes to leaf through.

"Dennis?" Her again. Always her.

"Yes?"

"How did you sleep, hon?"

*Don't call me that, you bitch.* "Fine."

"Huh?"

He growled under his breath, spoke louder this time: "Fine! Fine!"

He waited, listened. No response. Maybe this time she'd learned her lesson. *Don't hold your breath*, he thought, and almost laughed. It was probably best that he didn't: it hurt like hell to laugh, like a knife scraping his rib cage.

He would see the doctor today, he decided, and then he would see Sarah. He would end it. It was going to end, anyway. Better that it do so on his terms than hers, or life's. Life had its own set of terms, he knew, and they were often cruel, seldom moored by anything so pristine or exalted as justice. That, he supposed, was what made them so difficult to accept.

"Dennis?" She was in the kitchen now. He could tell by the distance of her voice.

"Yes?"

"Are you going to see Dr. Ravini today?"

"Yes."

"Did you say yes?"

"Goddammit!" he shouted. "You know it hurts me to shout!"

"Then don't shout."

"Then don't fucking..." His words trailed off. He rolled up the newspaper and swatted the wall with it - once, twice, three times in rapid succession. The act rather winded him, and he rocked on the toilet, panting. Tears prickled at the corners of his eyes.

*Why do you do it to yourself, Dennis?* It was her voice, in his head. It had lived there too long but he was helpless to evict it. He imagined he would hear it right up to the end, and perhaps (God help him) even beyond that. For this he despised her.

"Coffee's ready," she called.

*Fuck you.*

He flushed the toilet, although there was no reason to, and at great pains lifted himself to his feet.

"Are you going to work?" she asked him as she handed him the mug. It was his mug, the one that said, "LAWYERS MAKE THE BEST LOVERS." She had presented it to him for some birthday during the Paleolithic Era, back when he'd loved her, or at least not despised her. But it did not bother him to drink from it. To do so actually warmed his feelings for her a little, roused in him a sort of dim nostalgia for a past otherwise distinctly alien.

"You know I am, Rachael."

"I don't know why."

"Of course you do."

"Because the case was assigned to you."

"Not *assigned*. Partners aren't *assigned* cases. They either take them because they want to or a senior partner *asks* them to. And Fred McDiarmand asked me to take this one. Me and Mark Critchfield."

He carried his mug to the table and sat down. He heard the raspiness in his breath, that thin, reedy hiss laden with phlegm and inauspicious tidings, and the faint rattle in his chest. Where once such omens had aroused in him horror and revulsion, now they elicited only anger and impatience. He wished he could take more satisfaction in this minor triumph, and supposed he would, were he not so acutely aware of the childish terror which lay underneath, at the roots of those doughtier sensibilities.

He marshaled what little strength he had and inhaled slowly, deeply... and then let it out: *Hissssssssss*, tinny and coarse and nastily damp. *Like releasing the air from a balloon buried under a pile of gravel,* he'd once reflected with grim amusement.

"Dennis?" She took a step toward him, then stopped cold. She knew better than to come any closer. "Are you-"

"I'm... fine."

A grimace of doubt rose in her features, just the expression he had learned in the past month to dread and detest. The cowardice it bespoke, the weakness and fragility and fear... why were such things so repugnant to him? Whatever the reasons, they inspired in him feelings somehow more onerous and offensive than the quiet panic he carried inside himself. "But why-" she began.

"Because it's important," he said. "Billions of dollars are on the line. And it's just that simple."

Now her vague grimace contorted itself into a rancorous frown. "They're not *your* billions of dollars."

"What the fuck," he asked, "is the relevance of *that*?"

"They know you're having health problems."

"They think I've had migraines... and a touch of bronchitis."

"That's all you *have* had," she said.

He looked at her, began to ask how often migraines and

the flu made you puke up blood, but then she averted her eyes and he judged such a question superfluous. Besides, he had not yet told her about the blood; as much as he hated her he could not bring himself to do it, to frighten her in the way that such a revelation would.

"Anyway," she said, "they'd certainly understand if you... what's the word? *Recused* yourself?"

He sipped his coffee, craving a smoke again. "You don't know what the hell you're talking about," he said, "so please, quit talking."

"You'd think they wouldn't even *want* you to work on a case like this, if you really do have... I mean, since you think you have..." She stumbled hopelessly, then took his advice and shut up.

He eyed her with a resentful sneer. "I thought it was just migraines and bronchitis, sweetheart?"

"It is," she said quickly. "I'm sure it is."

"I'm sure it's not."

She met his gaze for a moment, then lowered her head. "I'm going to take a shower."

"Sounds like a marvelous idea."

At first she didn't move, just stood there with her back

against the stove, chewing on her bottom lip. He ignored her and cracked his knuckles, a habit of his which he knew irked her fiercely. Finally she stomped off, perfectly frazzled, and he said a silent prayer of thanks that he was alone again.

## 3

*You're too hard on her,* he thought, and, yes, he supposed that was true. Sometimes, when particularly annoyed with her, he could almost convince himself that she deserved it. But he knew, and when in a more rational state of mind grudgingly acknowledged to himself, that she did not. She was weak, yes, and contemptible in many ways - she could be as careless and thoughtless and shallow as the worst offenders - but she had done nothing to merit the wrath he so often unleashed upon her. Certainly, at the very least, she had never been unfaithful to him, so far as he knew.

He stood, relieved to discover that the phlegm which had settled on his chest overnight was finally starting to loosen a little, and carried his cup of coffee over to the big picture window in the living room. Not only was a large portion of Lake Washington visible through this window, but it offered, as well, a virtually unobstructed (albeit distant) panorama of

Mount Rainier's western slope. Today, with the weather being so nice, he fancied he could pick out a fishing boat about a mile off-shore, a minuscule ballerina twirling slowly on a vast blue stage, a curtain of great white-gray rock behind her. The view was glorious, to be sure, though nothing compared to the one they had at their cottage in New England. He had always been a man who thought the sunrise far more beautiful than any sunset, and yet he had chosen to take up permanent residence on the West Coast rather than the East.

*What a paradox you are, Dennis*, he thought, and allowed himself a wan smile.

This right here, this was what he wanted and needed: peace and quiet and a view of still waters, and time plenty for reflection. He thought his mood would improve considerably under such conditions, that he might even achieve something like happiness. That would be nice. He would prefer to die without all the bitterness and animosity which had weighed on him so long. He would like to be free of such chains, and to explore the possibility, while perhaps there was still time, that he was not an abject moral failure in life, that he had done some deed or possessed some trait that might, in a pinch, be called upon to redeem him. He would prefer not to die with a heart as black as his lungs.

He watched the skiff vanish on the horizon, sipped his coffee, and allowed his thoughts to turn to more practical matters.

One such matter was that of his appointment at noon with Dr. Ravini. He had told the girl on the phone that he thought he might have bronchitis, maybe even the beginnings of pneumonia, and left it at that. When would you like to come in? she had asked after a brief silence. As soon as possible, he had said. How's ten on Tuesday? she had asked. No, it would have to be during his lunch hour; he would be in court all morning and had a meeting with the partners at one-thirty. All right, then, how about noon on Thursday? That would be fine, he'd said, as long as it wouldn't take more than an hour. She had assured him that it wouldn't. Very good, then, Thursday at noon it is. Okay, Mr. Arbaugh, see you then.

So bright, so sunny, so youthful and chirpy and sweet. Why should she be anything else? he had asked himself. She's probably all of twenty-five, perhaps newly engaged, already planning a family in her own mind if not with the express endorsement of her fiancé. No health problems, no real regrets, certainly no thoughts of old age and the long sleep thereafter. Nothing but sunshine and laughter and steak sandwiches. Good sleep, good eats, good sex, nice life.

"Dennis?"

He turned and saw her standing in the doorway to the living room, clad in her customary bathroom attire: pink satin bathrobe, fuzzy pink slippers, white towel around her head. He was still by the window, still clasping his forgotten coffee mug in his right hand, its contents now lukewarm. He looked down at it, as if wondering where it had come from, and then back at his wife.

"Yes?"

"The shower's free," she said.

"We have three full bathrooms, darling. There's always a shower free."

"Well."

"Any hot water left?"

"There should be."

"There won't be," he said, and returned to the kitchen to dump his coffee in the sink.

"Dennis."

"Yes, hon?"

"Why are you being like this?"

He stopped halfway across the kitchen, her words somehow penetrating the fog that had, in the previous month or so, grown up around his brain like a moss. When he emerged from the kitchen a moment later, his expression was sincerely contrite. "I'm sorry," he said.

"I don't want an apology," she said. "I just want to know why you're acting like a giant asshole."

"It's complicated."

She went to him and ran her hand along his cheek. It felt wonderfully cool on his skin, and for a moment he closed his eyes and relished it; but then he found himself shying away from her. "Dennis? Sweetheart? Tell me what's wrong... please."

*Don't be kind to me*, he thought. *I can't stand it when you're kind to me.* "You know what's wrong," he said.

"Oh, honey, you don't honestly believe it's..." She glanced down, then met his eyes again. "Do you?"

"Cancer, you mean?" There. He had said it. He had said the awful word.

She nodded as if the act caused her great pain.

"Yes," he said. "I do. I *know* it is."

She sighed, hiding her fears, as always, behind a veil of exasperation. "How could you possibly know something like that?"

"Because there's nothing else it *could* be."

"You're not a doctor."

"No," he said, "I'm not. But the diagnosis fits with everything I've come to expect from life. For it to be anything else would be bad form."

He brushed past her and went upstairs to take a long, lukewarm shower.

## 4

*The old red Chevy pick-up rumbles around a curve and jostles him in his seat, but he doesn't react, doesn't say a word, just tightens his grip on the seat and digs his heels into the floor-well and keeps his mouth shut. Familiar scenery blurs past them on both sides, the Chevy's brakes whine in protest of the hard turn while the engine growls contentedly, and he distracts himself by trying to pick out individual trees and the budding leaves on their branches, and imagining how long they must have stood there, in the same place, never moving, with no aim or ambition but to grow bigger and bear the winters.*

*He steals a brief glance at his father, with whom he has not shared a meaningful conversation in perhaps five years, although he has lived at home all his life. There seems little point in trying to pursue one now, or even in making an off-handed remark about the weather or the potholes in the road and how the government will never get around to fixing them. His father would no doubt greet the comment with silence, as he greets most everything Dennis says. He seems to put no stock in even the most reasonable of his son's utterances, perhaps deeming them a product of total inexperience and thus unworthy of serious consideration. Besides, something is bothering him. Dennis can sense it, he can always sense it when his father is upset, and he knows better than to pry.*

*And then, out of nowhere, a thought arises in his mind like a bright figure from a thick gloom*: All these dreams and unfulfilled longings... what to do with them? Where to put them?

*What dreams? What longings? He is almost too embarrassed to acknowledge them even to himself, though they are, he knows, perfectly respectable. But they are unrealistic and a tad banal, perhaps, and he buries them for the thousandth time deep within himself, where they might behave themselves and cause no discernible trouble.*

Besides, that's no thought for a twenty-year-old to have, *he then thinks, chastising himself for looking back and regretting his failures prematurely.*

Yes, yes, because regrets are for the old, not the young; they are for those whose shortage of time is too blatant to ignore, who cannot still convince themselves that there is time yet to set right what is wrong and carry through on old plans.

*They take another sharp turn and his father's Chesterfields slide off the dashboard, landing in Dennis's lap. Dennis replaces them on the dashboard in silence and folds his hands together, gazing out the window at a field with no awkward secrets and nothing to say.*

*He has been smoking since the previous March, but his father doesn't know that.*

**5**

"Mr. Arbaugh?"

He looked up from his magazine, a six-month-old issue of *People*. He had been staring for almost ten minutes at an article about Terri Hatcher, whom he had never heard of, without reading more than a paragraph. The woman was giving him a practiced smile from which all traces of humanity had been systematically expunged, presumably by just such mindless routines as this.

"Yes?"

"Come on back."

He rose, not smiling, and followed the nurse into one of the examining rooms.

"How high?" he asked the nurse as she unstrapped the arm-band.

She hesitated. "A little high."

"How high is a 'little'?"

"One-sixty over one-oh-five."

"That sounds bad."

She shook her head. "It's nothing to be alarmed about. It's your weight I'm more concerned with."

"I've lost some, yes."

She glanced down at some paperwork in a manilla folder. "Thirty-six pounds in six months, according to your chart. Have you been dieting, Mr. Arbaugh?"

"No. But I've not been eating as much as I used to."

"How long has your appetite been..."

"Diminished?"

She blushed a little, embarrassed by her ineloquence. "Yes."

"Six to eight weeks, maybe. I ate like a horse after I quit smoking, but then I tapered off."

"When did you quit smoking?"

"Right after my last appointment with Dr. Ravini."

"Six months ago?"

"Yes."

She closed the folder. "That's wonderful, Mr. Arbaugh. Do you feel better now that you've quit?"

"No," he said. "Worse, actually."

"Oh."

"I want one all the time. A cigarette, I mean."

"I understand."

He arched his eyebrows. "You smoke? Or used to?"

"Me?" she said, as if the idea were patently ludicrous. "No, never. But my father did."

"He... passed away?"

"Yes, last year."

"From?"

She looked at him, a sudden anxiety stealing over her

features. "He... had a heart attack," she said.

*You're lying.*

"Oh," he said. "I'm sorry."

She smiled at him, this time with real warmth. And a disconcerting pity. "The doctor will be right in," she said.

"Okay."

She left the room, and he immediately began to cough.

Dr. Baskhar Ravini was a short, balding man with small eyes and round, wire-rimmed spectacles. Though considerably heavier, he did not look entirely unlike Ghandi. He had been Dennis's physician for thirteen years, and so was well acquainted with his medical history. He was also well acquainted with the fact that he had smoked like a fucking chimney for thirty-four years.

"Dennis," he said, closing the door behind him. "How are you feeling today?"

"Fine," he lied. "Good."

"You are good?" the doctor echoed.

"I am."

Ravini grinned, pressing his stethoscope against Dennis's chest. It was a skeptical, knowing little grin, the sort you see on the face of a friend you're unwisely attempting to bullshit. "Then why did you come to see me today, Dennis?"

"I have a cough. A bad cough."

"You have a cough?"

"Yes."

"Breathe in, please."

He inhaled.

"And out, please."

He exhaled.

"And in again."

Deeper breath this time, extraordinarily painful.

"And out."

He heard his own chest rattle as he exhaled once more.

Ravini fixed him with his eyes, which were grave despite his lingering smile. "I am hearing substantial congestion in your lungs," he said.

A flutter of panicky fear bloomed in Dennis's stomach. "How substantial?"

Ravini stopped smiling, but did not hesitate as the nurse had when Dennis had asked about his blood pressure. "Enough to concern me."

"Do you think it's bronchitis?"

He shook his head. There was an almost artful somberness to the gesture, as if all this were playing out in some bad TV drama whose ending was predictable from the outset. "No," he said. "Bronchitis is essentially mucous build-up on your chest. This is concentrated in your lungs."

Dennis wiped his arm across his forehead, suddenly very warm. "Emphysema, then?"

*Just ask him, for Christ's sake. There's no point in dragging it out, is there?*

"I cannot make a diagnosis on so flimsy a basis, Dennis."

"Well, what more do you need to do?"

"Many things," said the doctor. "A chest x-ray, a sputum cytology, things of this nature."

"A... sputum what?"

"Cytology. A deep-cough sample of mucus from your lungs, to be tested for foreign bodies."

He blinked. "What sort of... foreign bodies?"

Ravini groped bootlessly for a moment, then said it: "Cancerous cells, for instance."

"What else?"

"Mostly just that."

Dennis nodded. It seemed appropriate. "When?"

"I will do that in a moment. And I will arrange for a biopsy, if it turns out that one is needed. But first I must complete the exam, and ask you some questions."

"Okay."

Dennis's idea that this was all taking place in a movie, or perhaps a radically new but somehow more horrifying breed of nightmare than what he thought of as The Mountain Dream, was in that instant firmly cemented. From that point on, everything felt distinctly surreal, his own words seemed to originate from someone else's voice, and he only half-believed the reality violently thrust upon him. Yet, at the same time, a deeper part of him remained entirely and authentically unsurprised. He was not a religious man by any stretch of the imagination, and did not normally subscribe to such airy concepts as psychic intuition, but he had foreseen all of this with uncompromising clarity and sureness. At first he had dismissed the knowledge as mere cynicism - even when he had told Rachael of it, presenting it as a kind of darkly poetic prophecy, he had still not really *believed* it - but now he realized that he really *had* known, and that all the tests Dr. Ravini intended to run would be little more than expensive formalities.

"Dennis?" Ravini asked. "Can you answer my question, please?"

"Sorry... what question? I didn't hear you."

"Has there been any blood in your stool? Or have you coughed up any blood?"

"No," he said. He took a long, shuddery breath. "There's been no blood in my stool."

"Have you coughed up any?"

"No."

"Dennis?" the doctor pressed, furrowing his brow.

"A little."

"How much is 'a little'?"

"Well," Dennis said, "enough to concern me, I guess."

Ravini nodded, coasted across the room on his stool, and removed a tongue depressor from a glass jar. On his way back he said, "Dennis, you are a witty man, did you know that?"

"I know," Dennis said. "My wit, in fact, is my one good quality."

Ravini snickered. "Open up and say 'ahhhh.'"

"Ahhhh."

*  *  *

He got as far as the parking lot and threw up. The urge came upon him suddenly, and he scarcely had time to bend over before his entire breakfast (waffles and French toast made lovingly from scratch) met the pavement with a quiet *splat*. He had barely picked at the meal, yet felt as if he were heaving up every last nutrient in his body, and produced enough vomit almost to believe that he had. He could see a few of the pecans from the pancakes floating on top of the slime, whose queer organic colors shone brilliantly in the sunlight, and, just beneath those, dark red filaments of blood. He gasped and jammed his eyes shut. For a moment he retched, half-expecting a tar-laden lung to emerge at any moment from his gaping mouth, and then his throat relaxed and his stomach began to settle.

He collected himself and stood up, looked around, saw no one. That was good. He didn't want anyone to have been subjected to so ghastly an incident. Once, as a teenager, he had found a dead body in an elevator in Memphis, Tennessee. The man had apparently shot himself while descending from a higher floor, perhaps in response to some unfortunate news received from one of the stock brokers in the penthouse office. When the doors opened on the ground floor and Dennis found him, he was slumped against the wall, still mostly erect, the blood-stippled gun lying at his feet with smoke curling up from the barrel as if from a genie's lamp. Most of his head was missing, splattered across the wall behind him in the crazy, tangled patterns of an abstract painting. It was an experience Dennis had never fully gotten over, haunting him at quiet moments and in countless dreams, though none recently and none quite as awful as the latest nightmare. If seeing someone blow blood-strewn chunks outside a doctor's office was even one-fiftieth as disturbing as stumbling upon a suicide, he wouldn't wish it upon the lowliest criminal.

He climbed into his Mercedes and drove back to work, though the car kept wanting to steer itself to the other side of town, toward Sarah's place in Kirkland.

Johanna, his secretary, was sorting through files on her desk, not looking terribly interested in any of them. She looked distracted, actually, maybe worried about him, or one of her kids. Her eldest son, he understood, had a slight drug problem. Perhaps it had escalated in recent days; God knew he had been too distracted himself to inquire about such trifling matters.

"Johanna?"

She looked up, and a guilty expression washed over her face, as if he had caught her goofing off on the job. It was equal parts odd and pitiful, and under other circumstances might have made him laugh. She was no older than forty, but the expression made her look sixty-five, exposing wrinkles ordinarily unseen. "Sir," she said.

"I'm back."

"Yes, sir. How did it go?"

He shrugged. "I'm dying."

She jerked her arm and knocked over a styrofoam cup, fortunately empty. "Pardon me, sir?"

Now he *did* chuckle, though on the inside he winced. "No," he said. "Pardon *me.* The joke was in poor taste. I'm not dying, Johanna. In fact, the doctor said I appear to be in excellent health. There's nothing wrong with me but a garden-variety chest cold, it would seem."

Relief flooded her eyes. "I'm glad to hear that, sir. Are you having a nice birthday?"

He nodded. "The best. Been busy?"

She glanced down at the files. "No, sir, not particularly. Mr. Shaffer called a little while ago."

"Oh?"

"Yes. He thinks his client wants to settle."

"His clients always want to settle. Either he takes bad cases or he has no backbone. Either way, he's a shitty lawyer."

She tried to smile and fell well short of it. "Yes, well... he's expecting your call. The trial's scheduled for next week, remember."

"I remember." He waved a finger at the files on her desk. "What's all this?"

"Oh." She cast a puzzled glance at them, as if she'd never seen them before. "Just getting some of your case materials in order."

"That isn't necessary, Johanna."

Short pause. "Sir?"

"Take a break. Go get some lunch."

"I've already eaten, sir."

"What did you have?"

She pointed to a box of Chinese take-out in the corner of her desk. "Um. Orange chicken, sir."

"Good choice. In any event, take a breather. You work too hard, Jo..." He exploded in a violent coughing fit, leaning against her desk for support.

"Sir? Are you all right?"

He nodded, struggling to quiet his lungs. “Fine. I’m fine.”

“That sounds like a very bad cough, sir.”

“Doctor didn’t...” He wiped his eyes, and then smiled at her. “The doctor didn’t think it was anything to be concerned about.”

“Good,” she said doubtfully. “That’s good to hear, sir.”

“Did Mark call? Or Fred?”

“Oh, dear. I nearly forgot.”

“What?”

“Mr. McDiarmand stopped by and asked if I’d arrange a lunch for the three of you. You, he, and Mr. Critchfield. Did you stop to eat on your way back from the doctor?”

He shook his head slowly, his muscles tensing. “No,” he said. “As a matter of fact I didn’t. I was going to get something on my way out. I have some errands to run over in Kirkland. I just came back to get my messages and, uh... tell you to take the rest of the afternoon off, if you want to. Did you schedule the lunch?”

“No, sir. I thought I’d better check with you first, to make sure you were available.”

“Well, did you tell Mark about my doctor’s

appointment?"

"Yes, sir."

"And what did he say?"

"He said to set the lunch as early as possible. I gather it's fairly important, whatever he wants to meet with you about."

He nodded. "Stevens & Brent."

"Should I make the arrangements, sir?"

"Um." He looked around. A paralegal named Sue was coming down the hall and stopped at the water fountain for a drink, a stack of papers bundled under one of her arms. She looked good in the skirt she was wearing, a low-cut red skirt that crept invitingly up her thighs as she bent to drink. Even in his present circumstances he noticed this, had to acknowledge this. Two summers ago he had tried unsuccessfully to sleep with her, though as far as he knew nobody at the firm had ever found out. Now a pang of guilt coursed through him to counter his lust.

"Yes," he said, consciously shifting his eyes back to Johanna. "Reserve a table at Prazzini's for quarter of two, then call Fred and Mark and let them know."

"Yes, sir."

He began to turn away, then stopped, remembering

something. “Oh, and Johanna?”

“Yes, sir?”

He jerked a thumb at the elevator across the room. “Go home and see your family, okay?”

“I appreciate that, sir, but I really should get these folders organized and -”

“What you should really do,” he said, “is go spend time with your husband and kids.”

“My husband’s at work, sir. And my kids are at school.”

“Be there to greet them when they get home, then, maybe cook them a little dinner. When was the last time you were able to do *that*?”

She blushed.

“Go ahead. You can be honest.”

“It’s been a while, sir.”

“I know,” he said. “And that’s my fault.”

“Sir?”

“Schedule the lunch and go home. Okay?”

“Yes, sir.”

He went into his office and closed the door, thinking of Rachael and Sarah and Dr. Ravini and the dead man in Memphis all at once, but mostly of his grown son, Sean, whom he had not seen in six and a half years.

## 6

*They're lying out by the lake on a wool throw blanket, under an ocean of stars, snuggling close to keep warm. There is no sound save that of their breathing, and the buzzing of cicadas, and the high, flute-like trill of frogs serenading potential mates. It's chilly, well into October, hardly the right season for young lovers to be star-gazing or getting frisky outdoors, but tonight they are doing both, and with the body heat building between them they barely notice the cold, only each other, the feel of their hands on their clothes and skin, cautiously but eagerly exploring. His pulse quickens madly with each new crevice and startling protrusion, territory which is only dimly familiar to him even now, five months after his seventeenth birthday.*

*Most of his friends lost their virginity last summer, he knows, and he feels mildly ashamed of his inexperience. There is an urgency and a desperateness to his advances of which he is too aware but helpless to contain, his body acting wholly of its own accord, undeterred by fuzzy qualms. He is like a traveler relentlessly pursuing some mythical destination, or a starship hurtling uncontrollably into deep space: he means to get where he is going, he will get there come hell or high water, he will get there and then he will know what -*

*"Dennis," she whispers, but he does not hear her. "Dennis," she says again, louder this time. Now he hears her but does not stop, fumbling with the clasp on her bra strap, wondering idly how girls ever learned to undo the damned things with such ease as they did, and only dimly does he realize that his hands are trembling. Not just trembling, actually, but* shaking, *like those of a drunk trying to lift the day's first Bloody Mary to his lips. And there is a pain deep in his middle, an aching-*

*"Dennis!"*

*He stops. "What?"*

*"For God's sake!"*

*"What?" he repeats, and the pain in his middle recedes a bit. His hands have begun to steady themselves. She pulls away from him. "What's the matter?"*

*"No!" she barks. "We're not having sex!"*

*"I didn't... why are you..."*

*"I know that's what you're trying to get me to do, Dennis, and it's not going to happen. Do you understand?"*

*He feels his temper rising and checks it, knowing that if he loses his cool he'll blow whatever slim chance of getting laid might remain for him. "I'm not trying -"*

*"I asked you to stop three times and you just ignored me. That pisses me off. Severely."*

*"You didn't ask me to stop."*

*"Yes, I did!"*

*"No," he says calmly. "You just said my name. I figured you were just getting into it, that's all."*

*"Well, I wasn't. I'm not." She scoots farther away and he curses her, curses himself. He should never have gone so fast; he should have known better, should have restrained himself. His friends often tease him about going out with a Catholic girl, warn him that he'll never see the inside of her panties unless he buys her a ring, but he feels deeply for her, suspects he might even love her.*

*"Why're you moving away from me?"*

*She scoffs. "Why do you* think, *Dennis?"*

*"I don't know, Mary. I don't even know why you're acting like this."*

*"Just forget it," she says, her tone leaving no doubt that she is thoroughly disgusted with him. "It's not like this is the*

*first time you've done that."*

*She's right: it isn't. He has tried twice before to sleep with her, neither time succeeding even in getting her shirt off. At least he got that far this time. This time he even got her pants off. He takes a fleeting, nebulous pride in this accomplishment before the guilt and remorse supplant it.*

*"I'm sorry," he says.*

*"Whatever. Can we please go home now? I'm cold."*

*"Mary," he whines.*

*"Dennis, I just want to go home. Okay?"*

*"I said I was sorry."*

*"Yeah, well, you're always sorry."*

*He inches closer to her, the blanket rumpling beneath him. "Come here," he says.*

*"No."*

*"Please come here." He gingerly slips an arm around her waist. She makes a token effort to remove it, but he holds it fast. "I'm sorry," he repeats. "Really." He feels her resistance waning, her anger melting, and a powerful relief surges through him. He messed up, but now it's all right; the damage has been repaired, the stuff that was broken fixed.*

*He begins to nuzzle the back of her neck and she sighs,*

*as much with pleasure as with lingering annoyance, and soon the latter subsides completely. They have come full circle, and things are as they were; all is well once more.*

*They lie there by the lake on the disheveled blanket, their bodies pressed tightly together, producing new warmth and friction. He feels the excitement again, the raw exhilaration, but this time he subdues it, and contents himself to savor the smell of her hair, and the softness of her skin, and the heat of her body. They lie there by the lake, the stars still shining but now forgotten, pale specks on a black dome, distant as the surly nightmares of old age.*

*He is right that he loves the girl, but he will never have her. He will take a different girl instead, a year later, and she will give herself to him freely, and he will feel none of the thrill or excitement that he did the night by the lake, when the air seemed to breathe and his head was filled with her scent and the challenge of the conquest proved too keen to surmount. Nor will he ever feel that way again, and through many lovers he will regret the feeling's absence.*

# 7

The restaurant was quiet, most of the lunch crowd having already filtered out. He spotted Fred and Mark immediately, bypassing the sleepy-looking host and going directly to their table. He'd gotten caught in traffic, and had called the restaurant and instructed one of the staff to tell them he was running late and to go ahead and order. By the looks of it the only things they'd ordered were drinks and a couple of house salads. Neither of them, he noted, was smiling, and Mark looked especially dismayed, his whole body sagging inside of his navy-blue blazer.

"Mark," he said, stretching a hand out. Without rising, Mark gave it a feeble shake, and Dennis then offered it to McDiarmand. "Fred." The Elder Statesman, as he was sometimes called, *did* rise, though not fully. His shake was much firmer than Mark's, but still devoid of any real vigor. Or maybe, Dennis thought, it was only the arthritis in the old man's hand; at times it was so bad that the poor bastard couldn't even hold a pencil. He took the only empty chair at the table, facing a window which looked out on Puget Sound.

"How are you, Dennis?" asked McDiarmand, whose salad appeared untouched. His martini glass, however, was almost empty (probably for the second or third time, Dennis imagined). "Happy birthday."

"Oh, thanks," he said. *Johanna must've mentioned it to him.* "Kind of you to remember."

"I never forget a friend's birthday, Dennis. How're you feeling?"

"Good. Excellent, in fact. Just got a clean bill of health from my doctor." He felt a cough rise in his throat and choked it back.

"Good," Fred said. "That's wonderful. See, that's what you get for giving up the coffin nails." He winked - and, finally, a hint of a smile touched his lips. But there was no warmth in it, only a cold appreciation of the subject's irony in light of their agenda.

Somehow, Dennis managed to smile back. "Yeah... I guess it is." He glanced at Mark, who had yet to speak, and who also, Dennis saw, had yet to touch his food. Eating, apparently, was the last thing on these men's minds.

He turned back to Fred, convinced that if he simply acted cheerful enough, whatever unpleasant eventuality presently awaited him would somehow just go away. "So what's up, fellas? Has there been some movement in the Stevens &

Brent case?"

At last, Mark spoke: "Yes," he said. "Oh, yes, indeed."

"Good or bad?"

Fred twirled his fork around his salad bowl, then let the handle fall against the rim: *clink*. "Judge Kramer just granted opposing counsel leave to amend their complaint, so as to add three hundred and six new plaintiffs to the ranks. Theirs is now officially a class action of galactic proportions."

Dennis felt his stomach drop, a vision of the corpse in the Memphis elevator flashing inexplicably before his mind. "Jesus," he croaked.

"Jesus doesn't appear to be on our side in this one, Dennis," Fred said blandly, pursing his lips. He was a man of slender frame and high, prominent cheekbones, with slack jowls and jagged yellow teeth. Often, as now, he worked his jaw between sentences, as if trying to get rid of a cramp or swallow something unwieldy. Even in the sunlight his skin looked dull and sallow and withered. "Nor anyone even remotely associated with Him."

"When did this happen?"

"Two hours ago. Probably at the very moment your physician pronounced you fit to continue the practice of law for another thirty years, much to his professional chagrin." His eyes flickered with an appalling smugness.

Dennis said nothing. He shot a glance at Mark, who had turned to face the wall. He looked pale and queasy, his face shiny with sweat, hair unkempt, tie crooked. He was a picture-perfect image of the hotshot lawyer who senses his career on the verge of imploding, personifying for Dennis the most obscene and repugnant qualities of their profession. *Shooting pigeons*, Mark sometimes called it, what they did for a living. It was his euphemism, Dennis supposed, for *fucking people in the ass to turn a buck.* Swell.

"Dennis?"

He looked at Fred. "Yeah?"

"Our client is facing potential damages of twenty billion dollars. Not to mention very considerable attorney's fees. Such a verdict would render the company permanently insolvent."

"Yes."

"Prospective clients tend not to trust law firms whose former clients went bankrupt with those firms' assistance."

"Right."

The old man speared a crouton with his fork and popped it into his mouth, chewed it, swallowed. For some reason, the sight of his Adam's apple bobbing filled Dennis with revulsion; the act seemed infused with a nasty, ambiguous symbolism, weighty and terrifying. When he spoke next he did so with a seriousness which was at once both perfectly sincere and wildly exaggerated: "We absolutely cannot afford to lose this case, Dennis."

"Absolutely not."

A waiter appeared at their table, pad and pen in hand. He was tall, skinny, effeminate, with blond highlights in his jet-black hair. "May I bring you something to drink, sir?" he asked Dennis. "A cocktail, perhaps?"

"Yes," he said without thinking. "A double gin and tonic, please."

"Yes, sir. Very good. And would you care to order an appetizer?"

"Not just now, thanks."

"Yes, sir. I'll be right back with your drink."

"You know our tack, Dennis," Fred continued, intolerably, interminably. "These people should have known better. The information was out there, widely disseminated for decades, even to the least connected and most poorly educated asshole on the street. And more to the point, S&B sent out letters to the vast majority of their customers, as many as they could reach, warning them of the increase in tar and nicotine. In short, nobody's ignorance was excusable. *Nobody's*." He tapped his martini glass with his fork for emphasis.

"It doesn't take a genius to figure out it's a bad idea to suck carbon monoxide into your lungs, right?" To his ears it sounded as if his voice were emanating from the other side of the world.

Fred leaned into the table, not quite grinning, but almost, almost. "Exactly," he said. "Warning labels on the packages, public-service announcements, and the warning letters aside, common sense alone suggests that repeated inhalation of the various ingredients in a standard commercially manufactured cigarette - carbon monoxide, as you say, formaldehyde, ammonia - constitutes decidedly imprudent behavior. The jury will already believe that, Dennis. Our job - *your* job, really - is to see to it that the other side doesn't brainwash them with so much propaganda that they *stop* believing it. Some truths are so simple that it's alarmingly easy to lose sight of them when presented with seemingly contrary data, especially of the highly complex, technical variety. And that's what opposing counsel will do, Dennis: saturate the jury with lofty scientific facts and statistics far beyond their modest ken. They'll call expert witnesses to reinforce their smokescreens - pardon the pun - and further obfuscate the *real* issue, which is that these unfortunate individuals made a conscious and deliberate *choice* to smoke, despite all the best, most reliable evidence and medical advice, and, later on, even despite its glaring ill effects on their own health. *That's* what you've got to home in on, Dennis, and hammer away at constantly throughout the course of the trial." He paused and took a sip of his gin. "You're up to the task, I'm sure."

Dennis thought a moment, then nodded. He wanted to throw up again. "Yes," he said. "Quite definitely."

McDiarmand gave Mark a hearty clap on the back. "As are you, Master Critchfield."

Mark jerked mildly in surprise. What assorted horrors, Dennis mused, must have been haunting his daydream! "I'll do my best," he said. "You know that, Fred."

"Of course I do." He looked back at Dennis, who grew suddenly, violently nauseous at the sight of the old man's face: it was that of a jackal, a devil poorly disguised, a cougar licking its chops at a mound of fresh meat, jaundiced and shriveled and hideously ugly. "I have no doubt whatsoever that the both of you will throw the veritable kitchen sink at this case. And that, ultimately, our client will leave the courtroom triumphant - and only a few million in the hole rather than tens of billions."

Before anything further could be said, the waiter arrived with Dennis's gin and tonic. He had never been more grateful for a drink in his life.

"Trial's set for Tuesday, July third. Can we be ready by then?"

"Sure," Mark said.

"Dennis?"

"Yeah." He looked at Mark, who had again averted his eyes. "July third should be fine."

"Excellent." McDiarmand gave a big *what-a-load-off* sigh and relaxed his shoulders, draining the last of his martini. "Shall we order, gentlemen?"

"Sure," Dennis said. "Let's order. I'm starving." He had not eaten a bite since breakfast and felt about as hungry as a stone.

"Mark?" asked Fred. "Ready to order?"

"Yeah."

"Great. Now, where's our waiter?"

A wave of dizziness overcame him then, and a surrealness much akin to what he had experienced in Dr. Ravini's office. Things suddenly appeared blurry, out of focus. A wild panic gripped him, his heart pounding furiously.

"I'll find him," he heard himself say. He gulped what was left of his drink and stood on wobbly legs. "I... excuse me, guys. I need to use the bathroom."

"Is everything all right?" asked McDiarmand, a striking absence of genuine concern in his voice. "You look a little... peaked, Dennis."

"Yes," he said quickly. "Fine. I'll be back in a jiffy."

"Well, what do you want for your meal?"

*I think I'll just munch on a dirt sandwich,* he thought. "The chicken primavera. And another drink."

He half-walked, half-stumbled to the restroom, eager to put the noises and faces of the dining room behind him.

Once there, he bent over the sink and splashed cold water on his face. It felt great. Wonderful, actually. The vertigo receded. His heart slowed. Shapes and colors returned to normal, and his thoughts made sense again. For a moment he had feared he might lose it, just start screaming at the top of his lungs (*that wouldn't be very loud, ha ha*) right there in the restaurant, in front of Fred and Mark and everyone else. He could not quite identify what had so abruptly and dramatically thrown him off kilter, but he supposed that, under the present circumstances, it could have been any number of things. Or, more likely, everything.

He looked in the mirror. He looked scrawny, pallid, and frightened, as if he had stayed awake for two or three days and then stuck his finger in an electrical socket. The image did not amuse him, for it was too accurate, too close to the truth. He shut off the water and dried his face on a paper towel from the dispenser on the wall.

As he turned to leave, a little boy of perhaps nine or ten came in. He saw Dennis and immediately looked away, as if his parents had trained him from young never to make eye contact with a stranger, especially when alone with one. He made a bee-line to the urinal farthest from Dennis and began to relieve himself.

*It's not fair,* Dennis thought. *I could have been him; he could have been me. There is no rhyme or reason, no overriding logic, no master plan; there is only chance, the sole cosmic constant. I want his life. I want my future to be open, my fate unsealed. I want to make the bad choices and do the stupid things all over again. I don't want to die, I want to be young. I want time to be slow again, I want unlimited tomorrows. I want a lifetime of unmade mistakes to stretch out in front of me, to infinity. It isn't fair and I want his life.*

He realized he was watching the kid pee, probably terrifying the poor tyke, and hurriedly vacated the restroom.

There was another gin and tonic waiting for him when he returned to the table. Fred was working on yet another martini. Mark remained as he had been, seemingly uninterested in both food and drink, huddled in his chair as if waiting for a meteor to crash through the window at any moment. There was something the matter with him, something more than just the prospect of losing the biggest case of his career. What it might be Dennis had no idea.

"I ordered for you," Fred informed him.

"Thanks." He took his seat, raised the glass to his lips, set it back down on the table. All at once the drink seemed decidedly unappealing.

"Are you all right?"

"Yes."

"You seem a bit... frazzled."

"I'm fine. Just hungry, I guess."

"I hope you're not doubting your abilities, Dennis. In the courtroom, I mean."

"I'm not."

"I've worked with dozens of attorneys throughout my thirty-seven years in the practice of law, and you undoubtedly rank among the best."

"I appreciate that." *Quit blowing smoke up my ass, Fred. Booze-induced flattery doesn't go far with me.*

"Same goes for you, Mark."

Mark stirred, nodded. "Thank you, Fred."

A wordless minute passed, and then another. Dennis sipped his drink restlessly, his mind turning again and again to the child in the bathroom. Mark made a half-hearted start on his salad. Fred nursed his martini, regarding them both with a sort of detached, mildly intoxicated curiosity. Dennis found it first irritating and then infuriating. He wanted badly to be somewhere else, anywhere else, away from all of it. He wanted to know what was bothering Mark so much. He wanted to see Sarah.

*Blond hair, blue eyes, no one so young and handsome ever dies.*

Their meals came, delivered by their chirpy, flamboyantly gay waiter. Dennis's chicken primavera was steaming, plentiful, and thoroughly unappetizing. He took two bites of it and set his fork down on the plate. Fred, engrossed in his shrimp scampi, took no notice. Nor did Mark, who was sulkily poking at his lasagna like a kid with meat loaf. Dennis cleared his throat. Still nothing.

He gazed at the glass holding Fred's drink, at the olive floating on the surface like a buoy, speared with a toothpick fringed with festive dark-pink trim. He looked closer, at the pinhead-sized red eye in the pit facing upward. A woman at a nearby table gave a shrill, haughty laugh pregnant with self-doubt. The sound of a dish breaking reverberated in the kitchen, followed by a startled cry and then an angry rebuke. A blender whirred to life behind the bar. He looked deeper still, at Fred's glass and then at the table, until the two blurred into one, and he saw only a muddled, formless splotch of colors.

And then the room got very small and very dark and very quiet, and he was alone. He was back on the mountain, rocking in the gale, his threadbare cloth whipping his thighs and genitals with mammoth fury. It was bitterly cold, the sun close to setting, the sky perfectly clear and the air still except for the lone column of wind that battered him. He was going to fall this time; the wind was going to sweep him forward, off the narrow ledge, and he was going to tumble down the face of the mountain, breaking all his bones en route to death. This time the wind would be too strong to withstand.

He heard people whispering and saw dim faces and braced himself for the plunge.

## 8

*"In life," announces Father Mooney, "one is required to make choices. And one is, of course, free at all times to make whatever choice he likes. God does not interfere. God does not* impose *a course of action on anyone, at any time, under any circumstances. Certainly God hopes that we will make the* right *choice, that the values He has inscribed on each of our hearts will inform and, indeed, ultimately determine the path we elect to follow. But let me reiterate:* God does not interfere with our freedom of choice - ever."

*As he speaks he intermittently taps his finger on the Bible lying open on the pulpit, sweeping his eyes back and forth across the congregation, pausing in all the right places for dramatic effect. It is hot, the church will not acquire air conditioning for another decade, and most of the parishioners are fanning themselves with hymnals or paper fans they have brought from home. Many of the women in long dresses are perspiring visibly. Dennis is sitting in the far back, next to an old man in a tweed coat who reeks of bourbon (or maybe it's scotch, he is not yet old enough to differentiate such odors) and appears to be sleeping. His red, puffy face glistens greasily with sweat, his bulbous nose full of broken blood vessels glowing like Rudolph the Reindeer's. The combined stench of alcohol and body odor is overwhelming, and Dennis will spend most of the hour leaning as far to his left as he can without drawing attention to himself.*

*"Many of us, on certain occasions," the priest intones, "naturally make the* wrong *choices. We are led astray by temptation. We opt to indulge appetites best suppressed, to engage in activities which, while immediately enticing, appealing to our baser impulses, we know to violate God's law. Which is to say, oftentimes we* sin.*"*

*Here the priest seems to look directly at Dennis, and while he knows that is absurd, that it is only his imagination, must be, he feels a sudden terror seize him, a monstrous guilt. His heart begins to pound. He shifts in the pew, catches a particularly pungent whiff of the old guy in the tweed coat and cringes, his eyes starting to water. His mother and father are seated beside him, his father directly to his left, and he can feel his eyes on him but dares not confirm this. Does his father know what he's done? Does Father Mooney? How could they? He was careful, so careful, didn't leave a trace of himself in that closet. So how could they know?*

*There is silence for a moment, the whole church is deathly quiet, and Dennis's panic swells majestically, a balloon on the brink of exploding. Now he is sweating like the bourbon-soaked man in the tweed jacket, and squirming deliriously in the pew, afraid that his bladder if not his heart will burst at any moment, convinced that everyone is looking at him even though they're clearly not, clearly they're all looking at Father Mooney, and he knows only a few seconds have passed but it feels like an eternity and he's going to lose it, he's going to soil himself right there in Mass and everyone will see and* his father knows what he's done, *it's impossible but he does, and so does Father Mooney, and-*

*His father leans over and whispers in his ear:*

*"Dennis?"*

*His dread climaxes, abates. He whispers back: "Yes, sir?"*

*"Sit still!"*

*"Sorry, sir."*

*"What's wrong with you?"*

*"Nothing, sir."*

*"Then sit still."*

*"Okay, sir."*

*It's all right, he tells himself. Nobody knows. His secret is safe. Nobody knows, and nobody's looking at him. It's all in his mind, of course. Just in his mind.*

*"Sin is unfortunate," Father Mooney continues, "and of course unavoidable for fallible men, but there is no sin too terrible to be forgiven, too awful to bar the offender from God's grace and prevent him from attaining eternal salvation. For God is merciful, and His forgiveness may always be sought, even for the most shameful and odious of transgressions. The Lord God shall damn no one who earnestly and sincerely repents. In chapter one of the Book of Luke, in 'Zechariah's Song,' the new father Zechariah tells his infant son, John the Baptist, 'You, my child, will be called a prophet of the Most*

*High; for you will go on before the Lord to prepare the way for him, to give his people the knowledge of salvation through the forgiveness of their sins, because of the tender mercy of our God, by which the rising sun will come to us from heaven to shine on those living in darkness and in the shadow of death, to guide our feet into the path of peace.'*

*"Penance makes that path possible, my friends. But the sacrament must be performed no less sincerely or earnestly than one can seek divine forgiveness itself, only in virtue of which sacrament is such forgiveness acquired. I therefore urge you, friends, to enter into it solemnly, to enter into it with humility and a constant, unflinching awareness of how righteous and awesome is our Lord who confers it. It is a gift, friends, which we do not deserve, but which God our Father grants us out of unconditional love for us, the love He demonstrated so powerfully by sending his only begotten Son to die on the cross for us, to atone for our sins. Who among us should be so foolish and self-glorifying as to refuse that gift, to flounder in the shadow of death rather than embrace the eternal light of redemption?"*

*Dennis swallows thickly and sits up straight, fighting back images of the letters he found in a shoebox in his parents' bedroom closet, the ones the Isabelle lady had written his father. There were five of them in all, each still in its plain white envelope bearing only his father's name (in big cursive red ink, he'll never forget that, he's sure of it), the shortest less than a page and the longest six and a half. The longest had been the last one, where she'd told him she wouldn't see him anymore, that it was over. He cannot say for certain but knows in his gut that his mother has never found them, might never find them, might never know unless he tells her. But he can't; he won't. It would devastate her. She would leave his father. Then he might abandon Dennis and his sister, and his mother might never find them. He would be forced to raise his sister on his own. They would be orphans. They would surely die.*

*He looks at his father, tears welling up in his eyes, tears he is ashamed of, and then looks away, no longer smelling the bourbon or sweat on the man beside him, no longer smelling or hearing or seeing anything, adrift in his thoughts, alone with himself.*

**9**

He stood on leaden feet, holding the edge of the table for support. "I have to go to the bathroom," he said to no one in particular.

"You just went five minutes ago," Fred noted matter-of-factly.

"Yeah," Dennis said. "Weak bladder, I guess."

"I hope that's not some sort of *condition*, Dennis." He smiled perhaps the ugliest smile Dennis had ever seen. "We can't have you rushing out of the courtroom every five minutes in the middle of a case like Stevens & Brent."

Dennis stared at him for a long time. "I can always just piss my pants, Fred. Nothing inspires confidence in a client like a lawyer with wet undershorts."

A single laugh rose above the din, that of an old woman seated at a table behind them. It was a rich, husky laugh, incredulous and admiring all at once. Dennis relished it.

He turned with his head raised high and strode past a chubby, ill-kempt maïtre d'.

When he got outside it was raining.

He got into his car and started the engine, put the gear in reverse. Then Mark appeared at the driver's-side window, knocking on the glass. Dennis put the gear back in park.

"Dennis?"

"Hi, Mark."

For a moment Mark just looked at him, rainwater beading on his hair. "Can you roll the window down?"

"Oh, sorry." Dennis rolled the window down about halfway.

"I thought you were going to the bathroom?"

"I lied, Mark."

Rivulets now coursed down his brow and cheeks. "Why?"

"Because I'm tired. And sick."

"What do you mean? Sick how?"

"You're getting wet, Mark."

"Is it the flu?"

Dennis shook his head. "No, it's cancer."

Mark blinked. "What?"

"I have *cancer*, Mark."

Mark's eyes slowly widened, his disbelief that of a child. "Holy shit, Dennis. Seriously?"

"Yes."

"When did you find out?"

"Today."

He shook his head disbelievingly. "Lung?"

"Yes, sir. The big L-C."

"Jesus Christ. And the irony, too, I mean -"

"Yep," Dennis cut in pointedly, "irony aplenty." He shot a glance at the entrance to the restaurant, convinced somehow that McDiarmand would come bursting out at any moment, hunting down both of them, maybe wielding a tire iron or something. He didn't.

"I'm sorry," Mark said.

"Me too. But listen, Mark... what's wrong with *you*?"

"What do you mean?"

"The way you were acting in there, you'd think *you* were dying."

"Oh..." He brushed water out of his eyes. "I'm just having some problems with Miranda, that's all."

"What kind of problems?"

"You know," he said, "the usual bullshit. She thinks I don't love her anymore."

"Well, why would she think that?"

"I don't know," he said. "I guess because I don't."

Long pause, then: "Mark?"

"I've been seeing someone else, Dennis. For three months."

"Oh."

"I'm ashamed of myself."

Dennis said nothing.

"I think I love her, though."

"Mark."

"I never felt this way about Miranda. Or maybe I did, at one time. Maybe I've just forgotten. But this woman... Dennis, this woman is special."

"I have to go, Mark."

"She's a lawyer in Portland."

"I really have to go."

"Where will you go?"

"I don't know. Home, I guess."

"Does Rachael -"

"Bye, Mark. Take care of yourself."

He rolled up the window, threw the car in reverse, and backed out. Mark simply stood and watched him, soaked now through and through. As Dennis drove off he glanced once into the rearview mirror, hoping he'd be gone, but he was still there, still standing in the rain, a navy-blue ghost beneath a damp chrome sky.

## 10

Sarah's was a two-bedroom apartment on the outskirts of Kirkland. She lived alone, simply using the spare bedroom for storage and the occasional guest. She'd get claustrophobic in a one-bedroom, she'd once told him. She kept the whole place permanently spotless. He always felt guilty when he used one of her dishes, felt compelled to wash it right away. She would scold him for this, insisting that he put it down, she'd get it later. He'd met her last fall, while shopping, ironically, for Rachael's birthday. She'd worked in a clothing store at that time. Now she was a waitress at a twenty-four-hour diner. She was intelligent and well traveled and well read, had done two years of college before dropping out to give birth to her daughter, a sophomore at the University of Arizona. She had never gone back to school, hoping to open her own restaurant one day. She never had. She was thirty-nine.

This afternoon, she answered the door in her work uniform, which puzzled him because she normally worked the third shift, from midnight to eight. If anything, he'd expected her to still be in bed.

"Dennis," she said, surprised but clearly not unhappy to see him. "What're you doing here?"

"Sarah," he said. He coughed.

"You okay? What's going on?"

"I'm fine. Why are you dressed for work?"

She grimaced, her trademark expression of confusion. "Cindy asked me to work her shift for her. She had to go out of town. She's gonna take one of mine when she gets back." She blinked, shook her head. "Dennis, what're you doing here? You never show up unannounced like this."

"Well, I've never been in a situation like this."

"A situation like what, Dennis? What're you talking about? I don't exactly have time for riddles right now. I'm running late as it is."

"Should I come back later?"

"I don't know. Is it important?"

"Yes. But I don't want to rush it."

She sighed, looked at her watch. "Come in," she said. "Take all the time you need. I'll call and have somebody cover for me until I get there."

He went inside and she closed the door.

"Because you're dying?" she said, making no effort to mask the skepticism in her tone. She sat on the couch beside him, a mug of coffee in her lap. "You're leaving me... because you're dying?"

He looked at her, baffled and plaintive. "You make it sound like an insignificant reason."

"You're not dying, Dennis."

"Of course I am. The doctor said I am."

"No, he told you that your lungs sound congested."

"Well, what else could it be?"

"I don't know. Bronchitis?"

"He said it wasn't that."

"Okay, then, chronic pulmonary... whatever you call it."

"Chronic obstructive pulmonary disease? COPD?"

"Yeah. That."

"Well, he didn't explicitly rule it out, but he didn't mention it, either."

"Dennis." She rose from the couch, went into the kitchen to freshen her coffee.

"What?"

"You're being ludicrous."

"This isn't exactly the reaction I expected."

"What reaction did you expect? Did you think I'd break down crying and beg you to stay?"

He began to shake his head, to tell her no, of course not, and then realized that that was *exactly* what he'd expected. "I don't know," he said. "But not *this*."

"Well, you won't get any tears out of me. But I *would* like an honest explanation."

"I gave you one."

She reappeared in the living room. "Oh, the 'you're dying' thing?"

"I am!"

"And you'd prefer to die without me?"

"No," he said. "I mean..." He sighed. "Sarah, Jesus."

"Yes, Dennis? Something on your mind?"

"Why're you being like this?" *Where have I heard that before?*

"Being like what?"

"Like *this*," he said. A whininess was creeping into his tone that he didn't like. "So... *ornery*."

She snickered. "Is that what I'm being? Ornery?"

"Yes."

"Well."

"I thought you loved me."

She sat down. "I *do* love you, Dennis. But if you want to

be a paranoid, self-obsessed asshole, you're going to make it hard to love you much longer."

He sighed again and put his head in his hands. "That's exactly what I'm trying *not* to be. It's what I've been all my life and I don't want to be it anymore." He lifted his head, looked at her. "I quit my job today."

"You did *what*?"

"I quit my job. I walked out of the lunch meeting I just came from, right after I told my boss to go fuck himself."

Her jaw fell agape. "Fred McDiarmand? You told Fred *McDiarmand* to go fuck himself?"

"Yes, I did."

She shook her head, threw up her arms. "Jesus Christ, Dennis, you really *have* gone insane, haven't you?"

"I'd like to think," he said, "that I just made the first sane choice of my adult life."

She frowned. "Including me?"

"You know I didn't mean it like that."

"There's a certain hollow ring to your voice, Dennis, that I could almost mistake for the sound of bullshit."

"Fine," he said, turning away from her. "Take it however you want. I don't give a shit. Believe it or not, some people actually consider cheating on your spouse to be immoral."

She set her mug on the coffee table and, looking straight ahead, said, "Get out."

He looked at her. "Huh?"

"Get the fuck out of my apartment, Dennis!"

"What's wrong with you?"

Her face was beet red. There were tears in her eyes, belying her promise. She no doubt realized this and resented him for it all the more. "You're a real piece of shit, you know that?"

"Please let's not end it like this."

"Go!" she yelled.

He made no move to get off the couch.

"Fine," she said, grabbing her car keys. She stood in a flurry and stomped to the door. "*I'll* go, then. But if this door isn't locked when I get home, and so much as a fucking *spoon* is missing, I'll hunt your ass down, understand me?"

"Sarah, wait."

"Good-bye, Dennis." She turned to leave, then paused and yanked something out of her purse. It was a small box wrapped in glossy, sky-blue paper. "Here, I almost forgot. Happy birthday." She tossed it at him, and he caught it.

"Sarah, please wait."

"No time, gotta go."

He closed his eyes and waited for the door to slam. It came a moment later, hard enough to rattle the frame.

"Bye, Sarah."

He sliced through the wrapping paper with one of his keys and removed the lid of the black cardboard box inside. "Cuff links," he said to the empty room, holding them up. "Neat."

He sat with the box in his lap for a long time.

There was a used-car dealership that he knew in Hunt's Point, almost exactly midway between Kirkland and Seattle. He went there, and went into the office to talk to the owner. A bell jingled as he opened the door, conjuring pleasant memories of his youth, the dark age before the advent of electronics.

The owner greeted him warmly, stepping out from behind his desk and giving Dennis's hand a vigorous shake. It put Mark's and Fred's to shame. "What can I help you with today, sir?"

"I'd like to purchase an automobile," Dennis said. "Something cheap but reliable."

"Cheap but reliable," mused the owner. He was a big, jolly, balding man in his mid- to late forties. His eyes sparkled when he spoke. "Sounds like every car on the lot."

Dennis smiled. "Perfect."

"Come on out with me," said the owner, leading him back outside. "Let me show you what we've got."

"That one," Dennis said, pointing to a burnt-orange Volkswagen Beetle. "That's exactly the car I've always wanted. Same color and everything."

The owner, whose name was Benjamin Price, followed Dennis's finger to the beat-up, rusted-out Beetle on the other side of the lot. "The Bug?"

"The Bug," Dennis confirmed, and laughed. He felt good, for some odd reason. Not quite liberated - he had never felt anything so grand as to merit *that* description, supposed only people in books and movies ever really did - but he felt infinitely better than he had when he'd pulled in here five minutes ago. He knew the feeling wouldn't last long and tried to savor it.

"Well, let's go take a look at 'er."

"All right."

Dennis followed him over to the car, his mind already made up that he was going to buy it, whatever the price, so long as the engine started.

"This baby's vintage," Ben said.

"Not an antique?"

"Not quite. Four more years. She's an '80."

"Damn. How many miles?"

"Hundred-five or so, I believe. Let me grab the keys from the office and I'll open 'er up, let you take a look at the inside."

"Thanks."

While Ben was inside retrieving the keys, Dennis circled the car, appraising it with the eyes of a mother seeing her newborn son for the first time, eyes that saw all of the beauty and none of the scars. He wanted it. He was going to have it. And then he was going to get the cabin, and some peace, and figure things out while he still had a chance. Maybe it was having a plan that had lifted his spirits, even more than the sight of the Beetle. He closed his eyes and relished the feel of the wind on his face, drifting so far into his thoughts that at first he didn't hear Ben rattling the keys behind him.

"She runs good," he said, "or did at last check, but she

needs some work. An oil change, for starters. And you might wanna get her fuel line flushed out. Nobody's driven her in a while."

He started and turned, saw Ben dangling the keys in front of him. "Okay," he said, taking the keys. "Thanks, let me take a look."

He opened the door and climbed into the driver's seat. Ben's estimate had been damned close to the mark: the odometer read "151,006." The interior was badly mangled, with long tears in the seat covers, deep stains on the floor carpets, and assorted bruises across the dashboard. The backseat was in similarly poor shape, one of the buckets a mere skeleton and one of the seatbelts missing its buckle. There were scratches on the door frames and cigarette burns above the windows. None of these defects had the slightest impact on Dennis's abiding love for the car. If anything, they only deepened it.

"See if she starts," Ben suggested. "I bet she will."

She did, too. On the first try, no less. The engine coughed and sputtered a bit, but within a second or two rumbled to full life obligingly enough. Dennis poked his head out the window, grinning like a kid on Christmas. "Can I give her a test drive?"

"Be my guest," Ben said.

He threw the car in reverse, backed out, and turned right out of the parking lot. He was gone for only three minutes, and was still grinning when he pulled back into the lot. He drove up to Ben and stuck his head out the window again. "Man," he said, "she runs like a dream."

Ben laughed. "They don't make 'em like they used to, huh?"

"You got that right."

"So what do you think? You want her?"

He cut the engine and got out. "Absolutely."

"Excellent, excellent."

He gestured at the windshield. "I see the sticker says $5,500. I have a 2006 Mercedes-Benz that cost me forty-six grand. It's yours, in exchange for the Beetle and, say..." He pretended to select a figure off the top of his head. The more casual he seemed, he'd decided, the better. "Twenty thou?"

Ben's eyes turned into tea-saucers. "How's that, buddy?"

"It's right over here," Dennis said, waving him along. "Come take a look."

Ben followed, perplexed but intrigued.

"Still in mint condition, except for a tiny crack in the

mirror in the passenger's-side visor. My wife must've done that somehow." He gave Ben an amiable, *you-know-how-women-are* smile and unlocked the doors from his key fob. "Not even five thousand miles on it. Her." He opened the driver's-side door and motioned for Ben to climb inside. "See for yourself."

Skeptically, Ben leaned in and examined the odometer. A moment later he backed out and righted himself, apparently satisfied. "4,891, as a matter of fact."

"Like I said."

Now, as Dennis had circled the Bug twenty minutes earlier, Ben proceeded to walk around the Mercedes, inspecting the exterior with a trained, discerning eye, hunkering down to get a closer look at the bumpers and wheel guards. When he got back to where he'd started, he nodded and said, "You'll need to let me drive 'er."

"Of course," Dennis said, handing him the keys. He smiled. "Be careful with her. She's been good to me."

Ben smiled back. "Don't worry about a thing. I'll be back in five minutes."

"Take all the time you need."

According to Dennis's watch, he was actually back in less than four minutes, and Dennis knew the moment he stepped out of the car that he'd be leaving with what he came for.

"This isn't exactly a routine transaction," Ben said as they sat down in his office, he behind his big formica desk and Dennis in the folding chair in front of it. "So you'll have to forgive me if I ask you some questions."

"Fire away," Dennis said.

"Well, first of all, why're you doing this?" Ben laughed, apparently caught off guard by the candor of his own question. "I mean, unless you're conning me, I'm getting one hell of a deal here. The Blue Book value of your vehicle is $41,000, and you're offering it to me in exchange for about $25,000. Pardon my skepticism, but that seems a little crazy to me."

Now Dennis laughed. "Yes," he said, "I imagine it does. And I do appreciate your curiosity here, Mr. Price."

Ben waved a hand at him. "Ben's fine."

"Well, Ben, to be completely honest with you, I'm in the process of making some major changes in my life. Money's no longer much of a priority for me. I've made plenty of it in my career as a lawyer, and now I'm looking to focus on other things for a while. I'm basically retiring, closing up shop and heading down to Oregon. I figure I'll find a little cabin tucked away in the mountains down there and hole up for a spell, just enjoy the peace and quiet and maybe do a little writing. I've always thought I might have a novel or two in me. There won't be much need for an automobile in that neck of the woods, I imagine, so the Bug will mostly be a novelty, and a means of getting out to do the occasional shopping and the like.

"I'm also aware of how irregular these circumstances must be, seeing as it's the customer who normally writes a check on a trade-in. My offer is designed to reflect that departure from standard practice. Now, this is an independent outfit, is it not? Not corporate-owned or part of a franchise?"

Ben nodded proudly. "That's correct, sir. I'm the owner and sole proprietor."

"Well," Dennis said, "I can think of lots of places I'd be less inclined to show charity to. That is to say, I don't mind at all making a contribution to your outfit, so long as you pledge to retain ownership rights and not sell out to any bigger fish who might cast their reel your way." He paused, suddenly craving a cigarette, his smoking-fingers actually twitching. "Your word's enough for me."

"You have it, Dennis. May I call you Dennis?"

"Certainly. I can't very well call you Ben if you can't

call me Dennis, can I?"

Ben shrugged affably. "I suppose not."

"So do we have a deal? I'm willing to sign whatever papers you need me to, contracts and so forth, attesting to the warrantability of the Mercedes and stipulating the conditions under which our negotiations here are null and void."

"Boy," said Ben with a smirk, "I bet you *were* a good lawyer, too."

"Among the best, I was told recently. I'd prefer to reserve judgment myself, however." He gave a little sigh and smoothed his pant legs. "Do you need some time to mull this over, Ben? If so, I can come back later."

Ben shook his head. "No need for that, buddy. My mother always told me I'd trust a man with a fin growing out of his back, but what the hell, you seem like an honest enough fella, and if I have it all in writing it won't matter much if it turns out I misjudged you." He stood and fished a key out of the desk drawer, carried it over to a filing cabinet in the corner. "Let me just grab those papers and we'll get down to business."

"Wonderful," Dennis said.

As he waited for Ben to unlock the cabinet and gather together the paperwork, Dennis reflected that he had just struck the first significant business deal in at least twenty years with which his conscience was entirely comfortable. Not only had it been honest and fair, it had been generous as well. So out of character for him was such a thing that he began seriously to wonder whether he had actually woken up that morning, or whether perhaps his nightmare had not simply woven itself into a quaintly poignant dream. Were it indeed real and not mere fantasy, he could not recall a day which had started out in one direction and ended in so radically different another as today seemed likely to. Nothing he had done since arriving at Prazzini's at quarter past two, he marveled, had been planned or premeditated in the slightest. He appeared to be acting now purely on instinct, allowing his gut to direct his movements and speech instead of his brain. The results, he decided, were exceptionally pleasing.

"Here we are," said Ben, plunking a batch of duplicate forms on the desk as he sank into his high-backed swivel chair. "This shouldn't take but twenty minutes or so."

"Oh, there's no rush," Dennis replied. He gave Ben another wide, sunny smile. "I have all the time in the world."

## 11

At twenty minutes past five, he drove off Benjamin Price's used-car lot in his newly purchased Volkswagen Beetle, which, he reminded himself, would not become an antique for another four years. He'd miss that joyous occasion by probably three and a half years, of course, but did not allow this fact to sour his good mood. Instead, he drove home with the windows rolled down and the radio on, turning the volume up when Roy Orbison started singing "Pretty Woman." If he could not be glad about what he had just done, he told himself, then what happiness could he expect to wrest from his six months of seclusion in the Oregon wilderness?

*Might be eight*, he thought. *You never know. If you can lay your hands on some drugs, shit, you might even push it to a year or more.*

Maybe so, maybe so. But for the time being, he resolved, he would not concern himself with such contingencies. He would simply make a start on his plans as best he could and take it from there. There was no point, after all, in worrying about how long he would live until he first ascertained what he was going to live *for*, what legitimate and valid and honorable purpose might be served by his rapidly dwindling time on planet Earth. It might well take him the remainder of his days just to figure that out.

He had devised no firm course of action in the event that Rachael should have returned from her weekly pilgrimage to the mall with her girlfriends (followed, typically, by dinner and sometimes a movie), partly because he had felt quite certain that she would not have - they would celebrate his birthday tomorrow night, he'd told her yesterday, since he'd probably need to work late on the Stevens & Brent case - and partly because he had been busy contemplating more pressing affairs. Still, he had worried a little that she might have forgone the outing entirely because of concerns for his health, or because he had failed to return the calls she had undoubtedly placed to his office in the hours after his appointment with Dr. Ravini. (If she had tried his cell phone, which he'd turned off before going into Prazzini's, she would have gotten an outdated message he hadn't yet bothered to replace, informing callers that he was tied up in court and to direct any urgent business to his secretary.) Fortunately, he saw as he turned into the driveway, her Lincoln Town Car wasn't there. Which meant, of course, that neither was she.

*What a lucky break*, he thought, trying his best to ignore

the little voice in his head that kept telling him a note was the coward's way out. Well, yes, maybe it was, but at the same time, he knew, he could say in a note what she never would have let him in person. Either her eyes would have stopped him or her mouth would. And in his anger and frustration he surely would have said things he would have later regretted, thus destroying this rare serenity he had found, and totally upsetting the profound if somewhat guilty thrill he had begun to experience at the thought of so abruptly and discreetly deserting everything and everyone familiar to him. It would kill his buzz, essentially, and he wanted desperately to maintain it; he had felt nothing so intense or exquisite in years.

*So much for not wanting to be a self-obsessed asshole anymore.*

"Shut up," he muttered, cutting the engine. "I did things today that I never thought I could do, made choices that in the past I would have trembled just to consider. I should be allowed this one thing. Just this one thing, dammit."

Obediently, the voice fell silent, and he went inside.

He wrote Rachael the following note on a yellow legal pad which he'd dug out of a kitchen drawer:

Dear Rachael,

I'm sorry to be telling you this by way of a note, but you weren't here, and if I'm going to do what I mean to do, then it has to be now. If I hesitate for even an hour, it will never happen. I know myself well enough to know that.

Telling you what I'm about to tell you, first of all, is without a doubt the hardest, most unpleasant thing I've ever done. But I could not bear the thought of leaving without giving you at least the bare beginnings of an explanation. We both know I'm dying - this afternoon Dr. Ravini all but confirmed that as certain. The only question now is how I'll choose to spend what little time I have left.

I've chosen to spend it alone, far away from here, away from everything that might distract me from my quest, which is to figure out who I am and what my life has meant, if anything, before I die. I won't disclose to you where I'm going, because, as hard as it must be for you to understand this, I don't want anyone to be able to find me. If I'm going to achieve anything like the kind of spiritual clarity I'd like to, it is absolutely imperative that I sever all ties to the life I've led up till now. And besides that, I'm not yet entirely sure myself where I'm going.

Something happened to me today, Rachael, something very weird and very powerful. I had some sort of epiphany, I guess. I quit my job and sold my car and told the woman I'd been seeing behind your back that I wouldn't see her anymore. (I cringed as I wrote those words, and cringe again, now, as I think how painful it will be for you to read them, knowing as I do how little you deserved so unforgivable a betrayal of your trust, not once but twice, and how much better you deserve than to hear about it in a fucking note.) Maybe I loved her and maybe I didn't, but I do love you, Rachael, even still - I know that must seem incredible, given what I've just said and how I've treated you lately, but please, for whatever it's worth, believe that it's true - and whether you ever decide to forgive me for it or not, I know I'll never forgive myself.

I don't know exactly what's happened to me, Rachael, but I'm glad that it has. I hated who I was, and can't stand the thought of leaving this earth as that man. I hope that someday you'll at least begin to understand why I've done this, and wish the best for me. But if not, please don't feel bad about it... I couldn't possibly expect anyone, least of all you, to understand such a thing.

If anyone asks, tell them whatever you like - that I'm away on business, that I went for treatment at the Mayo Clinic, that I'm off somewhere reliving my youth. It doesn't matter. The only people whose opinions of me I still care about are yours, Sean's, and my sister's. When Hope calls, tell her I went alone to Europe for a few weeks of R&R and that I'll give her a call when I return. And if by some remote chance Sean should ever ask about me, tell him the truth, and tell him that I love him very, very much.

All My Love Always,
Dennis

P.S. Maybe I'll call you once I get settled in at wherever it is I decide to go. I'm so sorry, Rachael, from the bottom of my heart. I love you.

He had felt himself on the verge of crying at several points throughout the letter but never had, and felt now that he *should* cry but could not. Rather than sad or mournful or repentant, he felt only bleary and drained, his emotions as well as his body exhausted. None of what he had done in the past six hours had seemed particularly real, and this latest affair seemed the least real yet. He scanned the letter quickly, mostly checking to see if he had omitted anything important and maybe in one last feeble attempt to wring some tears from his eyes, and then set the pad in the center of the kitchen table, displacing the basket of fake flowers Rachael kept there.

Then he went into his bedroom and started to pack.

He took with him only about half of his clothes and toiletries, mostly because he did not want to be there when Rachael got home but also because he thought she might fall apart if she found the house totally bereft of his things, full of bare closets with shirtless hangers and empty medicine cabinets and pillaged kitchen drawers. He would not so aggravate what was already certain to be a spectacular grief. He would not inflict upon her that final violence.

And so, with a suitcase in each hand and a blue drawstring tote bag flung over one shoulder, he stepped into the late-spring twilight beyond a door he now closed behind him for the last time, giddy at the prospect of his newfound freedom and guilt-ridden at the thought of all he was forsaking. He deposited his luggage into the trunk of his Beetle, got behind the wheel, and did not look back at the house as he descended the driveway.

At the junction of Ferncroft Road and the thoroughfare which would provide his escape, Rachael passed him in her Lincoln Town Car. It was almost dark outside and difficult to see her, but he was sure that she saw him at the last moment, her brow creasing ever so slightly in an expression of perfunctory disbelief.

He hesitated for a moment, just letting the Bug idle, watching the glare of his blinker in the rearview mirror - and then turned north onto the thoroughfare. He drove until he reached Interstate 5, then headed south, toward Oregon.

# PART II:

## t r e a t m e n t

## (round 1)

## 12

He stopped only once before getting to the motel near Portland where he stayed that night. He pulled onto the side of the road just before reaching a small truss bridge (having stopped for gas, he'd then decided to take a detour) and got out, carrying his cell phone in his hand. When, out of curiosity, he had turned it on a half-hour after setting out, he had seen that he had four messages and six missed calls, four of them from Rachael. Now he threw the phone over the side of the bridge, into the dark, shallow river below. He waited for the splash, heard it, and returned to his car.

In the wake of this simple act, only his driver's license and some assorted garments stood to remind him that he had woken up that morning in Seattle, a highly successful corporate lawyer with a wife and a mistress and a mere unconfirmed inkling that he was dying.

## 13

*There is near the cottage a lake not unlike the one he sometimes went to with Mary, his high-school girlfriend. The Arbaughs do not own it, but theirs is the only summer residence within a three-mile radius and, save for the occasional boater, nobody else ever uses it. They think of it as their own, certainly, especially Dennis and Sean, the latter of whom will turn ten next month. He is looking forward to the event with great excitement, as children tend to do, but with some nervousness as well. He cannot articulate the source of his unease but does not need to; he is getting older, and even children, Dennis supposes, can appreciate the significance of the affair. He is a deep kid, besides, keeps largely to himself. Sometimes this worries Dennis (it is unnatural, he thinks, for a child to be so withdrawn), but then he reminds himself that he was rather shy himself at that age and assures himself that all is well.*

*The boy has taken to fishing, a hobby Dennis enjoyed in his own youth but not nearly so much as Sean. He is delighted that the child has discovered a passion and so healthy a passion, and watches him now, with great affection, from the big white wrap-around porch they added to the cottage four summers ago. He is in a rocking chair his mother inherited from her father, and which he inherited from her. She has been sick lately, sleeps most of the time. Dennis finds she has been intruding into his thoughts quite a bit these last few weeks and tells himself he ought to call her, ought to visit her, actually, even if it means taking time off work.*

*Sean casts his reel and Dennis watches him, smiling a little. The boy is shirtless and bronze with tan, his bony legs dangling carelessly in the water, which shimmers now in that sublime, elusive way it does at early dusk. He has been down there on the dock for nearly an hour without so much as a nibble. Dennis admires his patience, wonders where he got it from.*

*Rachael is inside cooking dinner, a splendid feast no doubt fit for a family twice their size, everything from baked potatoes to fresh cod to buttered corn to sweet yams and seasoned pork chops. It will feed them for two days. He can smell it, the motley of enticing aromas, and his stomach growls volubly in anticipation. He loves his wife very much and has never been unfaithful to her, though he has thought about other women sometimes. Usually his guilt is enough to cut the fantasies short, however, and the idea of being with anyone else is virtually inconceivable to him. At moments like this it is completely inconceivable.*

*He gets up from the rocker, and the chair creaks but his bones don't. Nor do his lungs battle for air; he gets short of breath sometimes, same as any smoker, but it's nothing worth complaining about. He is only thirty-seven, and for the most part in the pink of physical condition. It will be another two years before he abandons his daily three-mile walk, and another four before he starts consistently ditching the gym in favor of the couch. Today, he feels stronger and better rested than he has in months.*

*He goes down to the dock, quietly so as not to disrupt Sean's concentration. Once there, he watches him a moment longer, his heart filling with love for the boy all over again. As a younger man he had not wanted kids, worrying that they would interfere with his career. Now he wonders how he survived so long without the child, and, dimly, what he might do if anything should ever happen to him. Rachael has been pushing for another in recent days, herself the fourth of seven children and of the unswayable opinion that it is cruel to withhold siblings from a child. Once, when particularly vehement about the subject, she went so far as to insist that only children are ten times more likely than children with brothers and Hopes to become serial killers as adults. Dennis had simply laughed and told her that he would give the matter some thought. He never had; as much as he loved Sean, he had no real hankering for another child. He still valued very much the work he did at the firm, and a wife and son seemed all he could handle in the way of a family.*

*"Hey, son," he says to him now, as he squats beside the boy at the end of the dock. "Gettin' any bites?"*

*"A few," Sean says in the hushed whisper of a serious fisherman, clearly worried that their chatter might scare away a potential catch. "None for a while."*

*"Well, keep at it."*

*"I will."*

*"It's just a matter of time."*

*"I know."*

*"You hungry? Your mother's put on a big supper."*

*"Dad," says the boy, giving Dennis a dirty look.* I'm trying to fish here, Dad, *the look says, and Dennis smiles, pretends to zip his lips shut.*

*He sits quietly with the boy for a minute or so and then leans over and whispers into his ear, "Come on up to the house in about ten minutes, all right?"*

*"Sure," Sean whispers back.*

*Dennis moves to stand up, and just then the boy's line goes taut, quivering with the tension. Whatever he has hooked, it is very big and intends to put up quite a fight. Dennis cries out enthusiastically and instructs his son to hold the rod steady* as he reels the line in, just hold it steady and don't let go, reel it in nice and slow so you don't snap the line, you got something big there, son, something big and mighty damn feisty. Sean, now smiling the wild, righteous smile of one who has triumphed over great adversity, faithfully heeds his father's instructions, reeling the line in with the automatic composure of a seasoned pro. Soon the fish emerges from the water - it is a large bass, at least a foot and half long and more likely a full two - flopping about on the hook with brainless fury, as if upset with itself for falling for such a dumb old trick. But it is too late now and it won't be freed until the boy who has caught it chooses to free it, which Dennis knows he will because he has a big heart and could not stomach the thought of killing it.

"Look at this fish, Dad!" he cries, excited in a way only children can be, so far as Dennis knows, and how lamentable a truth that is, how tragic and awful to know. The boy grabs the fish by its tail and displays it proudly, watching raptly as it continues to writhe under his hand, squirming in the cool air, slowly drying and struggling for breath.

"It's amazing," Dennis says, clapping the boy on the back. "You gonna throw it back?"

Sean pauses for a moment, thinking. He regards the fish

*with a profoundly mature consideration. Finally he renders his verdict: "Yeah," he says. "I guess so."*

*"Don't wanna keep it and eat it?"*

*"Nah. I don't really like fish."*

*That is not altogether untrue, but Dennis knows it is not the real reason, either. "All right, then. Throw it back and let's go eat some supper."*

*"Okay."*

*The boy holds onto the fish a moment longer and gives it a final once-over, still savoring his victory, the sweet fruit of his long toil, and then gently extracts the hook from its mouth and with a smooth, studied motion releases it into the lake. He watches it as it dives deep below the surface, eager to put recent perils behind it and return to safety; then he turns and follows Dennis up to the house.*

*Behind them, the sun begins to set over the lake, long, fire-red tendrils trailing in its path, the brilliant brushstrokes of some anonymous artist.*

## 14

He lay on the bed, atop the over-starched bedspread with its Oriental designs, looking from the ceiling to the draped window to the closet in which his two suitcases and tote bag sat like alien statues. Then he looked at the phone and began to reach for it, drew his hand back as if from hot coals. The phone was just as dangerous, he decided. If he picked it up he would call her, and if he called her he was liable to say most anything, and then to call other people and say most anything to them, too. Best that he kept to himself tonight, kept his thoughts in his head where they belonged, and slept on all the restless, nettlesome urges which danced through him in costumes of varied and deceptive colors. He must ignore them.

But he could not sleep. He was much too awake, for one, and for another, the dream would surely visit him if he slept, and he doubted whether he could handle it tonight. He felt too fragile and adrift, too unsettled. He did not quite regret his decision to do this, to take off in search of God knows what, but he did all of a sudden miss terribly his wife and the familiarity of his house, his bed, the cheesy flowered wallpaper of his bedroom and the scent of Pine Sol in the kitchen. If he was still awake, he supposed he would miss this latter even more in an hour or so, when normally he'd be poking his nose into the fridge for a midnight snack. Yes, if he dreamt the Mountain Dream tonight, he feared he might wake in the middle of it and plunge headlong into a permanent madness.

*So let me lie here, then,* he thought, *and think whatever thoughts I like or must, and if I have to stay awake all night to avoid the dream then I will, but perhaps if I've long forgotten about it by the time I fall asleep I won't dream it at all, and with the curse broken, never dream it again.*

A minute later he rolled over so that he was facing the nightstand, picked up the phone, and dialed his home phone number. *Only it's not your home anymore, you gave it up along with everything else when you packed your bags-*

The phone rang only once, and then he heard Rachael's voice in his ear: "Dennis?"

"Hi, Rachael."

"Dennis, where the hell are you? What the hell -"

"Calm down, honey. Everything's fine."

"Don't call me 'honey'! Where are you? Dennis, have you lost -"

"I'm in Vancouver, Washington, near the border of Oregon. At a motel."

Brief pause, then: "*Oregon?*"

"Yes, Oregon. At a motel." *You know, with a Bible in the drawer of the nightstand.*

"Why are you at a motel, Dennis? Could you please tell me what in the fuck you're *doing*?"

Such language was wholly unlike her, and to his surprise he found himself deeply bothered by it. "I left you a note," he said gently. "Didn't you read it?"

"Of course I read it!"

"Well, it told you what I'm doing, didn't it?"

"No!" she barked. "It didn't tell me a thing, except that... except that you've totally lost your mind and went God knows where with half your things!"

"I'm looking for something I won't find there," he said. It was a totally unrehearsed remark and sounded utterly stupid to his ears.

"And what's that, Dennis? Spiritual... what did you say in the note? 'Spiritual fulfillment'?"

"Something like that."

"What did the doctor say, Dennis? Please be sane for a second and just tell me what the doctor said."

He sighed. "That I'm going to die soon."

"Dennis."

"That's what he said!"

"He said you have cancer?"

"Yes."

"You're lying."

"I'm not lying, Rachael." He sighed.

"Dennis, please come home. You're just not thinking straight right now. We can get you some help. We'll figure this out. Please, sweetheart."

"This was a mistake."

"I know it was, Dennis. That's why you need to come home."

"No," he said. "Not my leaving. My calling you. *That* was the mistake."

There was a longer pause this time. "Oh, darling, you don't know what you're *saying*."

"Good night, Rachael. I'll call you whenever I get to wherever I'm going."

"Don't hang up, Dennis! Don't you hang up that phone!"

"Good night."

"Dennis!"

He returned the phone to its cradle and rolled onto his back, sliding his hands under the pillow, putting his eyes on the ceiling again, feeling much better now, much more like himself.

Sleep came shortly thereafter, before he had even undressed. He was not visited by the Mountain Dream or any other, and, in fact, enjoyed twelve and a half hours of dreamless, virtually unbroken sleep. It was broken at all only because, at some point in the night, he had stirred briefly and groggily removed his shoes and pants. When he finally woke completely seven hours later, at one o' clock in the afternoon, he had no recollection of having done it. For a while he had no recollection of his phone call to Rachael, either, or of selling his car, or of where in the hell he was. He just knew that he felt impossibly well rested, clear-headed, and relaxed.

Slowly the events of the previous day came back to him, but only his tiff with Sarah caused him any appreciable angst. Everything else - his scuffle at the restaurant with Fred McDiarmand, Mark's revelation of recent infidelity, his trade of one four-month-old Mercedes-Benz for one twenty-six-year-old Volkswagen Beetle, even his ill-advised communiqué to his wife - he registered all of it with perfect composure. Somehow, in the daylight, his brain recharged by half a day's sleep, it made total, unassailable sense, had an air of poetry and sweet finesse about it. It was not at all the irrevocable horror he had feared it might be, but instead a source of tremendous relief and gratitude. Quite fitting, he thought, for what was in all likelihood his last birthday.

He smiled, yawned and stretched, made a pot of coffee in the percolator generously provided by Herb's Hide-Away Motel. He turned on the TV as he waited for the pot to fill, scrolled through the stations, found nothing of interest, and turned it off. Then he went over to the big, wall-length window at the front of the room, drew the curtains back, and watched a family of four pile into their station wagon, no doubt bound for Highway 101 and, Dennis would have guessed, one of the innumerable beach resorts that lay along it. He expected a wave of envy to engulf him, a sense of longing for Rachael and Sean and their own romantic journeys eastward, but felt only the simple, rather puzzling tranquility with which he had risen.

And still, in the five minutes since waking, he had not coughed.

He closed the curtains and poured himself a cup of coffee. He raised the cup to his lips (it was plastic, with a tiny handle, made apparently for a gnome), then set it down on top of the television and went to the door. He opened it, unconcerned that he was dressed only in his boxer shorts, and retrieved the newspaper he knew he would find there: the May 22, 2006 edition of The Vancouver *Press*. (He'd been hoping for a Seattle *Times* or *Post Intelligencer* as well, but counted his blessings that he'd at least found a paper.) He bent, snapped it up, and carried it, along with his cup of coffee, into the bathroom.

He sat on the toilet for twenty minutes, reading the day's headlines as he drank his coffee and wished for a cigarette. At some point, he began to cough, and once he'd gotten started, once he'd unleashed the feral thing that lived in his lungs, he found it almost impossible to rein it in.

But eventually he did, of course. It left his throat bruised and battered, as it always did, but in no worse shape than usual. He would live; there had been no permanent damage.

*No permanent damage, just a touch of the ole L-C. Ha ha, Dennis, very funny. You kill me sometimes.*

He rose from the toilet, the forgotten newspaper sliding off his legs and onto the floor, and deposited himself in the shower. The water felt good on his body, warm and invigorating, and he ran it over his chest for a long time, letting it massage the muscles there, maybe eradicate some of the poisoned cells which lay beneath. He could fantasize, anyway, fantasize and pretend all he liked. What harm would it do? None, he supposed, kneading shampoo into his scalp. He rinsed it out and did it again, then slathered his body with soap for a second time. He was in no hurry, he reflected with some satisfaction, and he intended to enjoy, for once, the incomparable luxury of time.

After his shower he dressed, somewhat slowly, no longer quite as energized as he had felt upon waking, and began to pack his clothes. He was about to close the lid of his suitcase when a knock came at the door.

"Housekeeping!" cried a female voice on the other side, the lone word shimmering with a panoply of muddled but colorful accents.

"One minute, please," Dennis said.

"Housekeeping!"

"Just a *moment*," Dennis said, louder this time.

And, of course, a second later the door swung open, revealing a middle-aged woman of dark complexion, clad in a traditional maid's uniform and actually clasping, in her left hand, a feather duster. Her lower body was concealed by a badly dented metal cart, but from what he could see of her upper half, for her age she was extraordinarily well kept. She looked not only embarrassed but downright *astonished* to discover that the room was not yet bereft of the previous night's occupant. "I'm... so sorry!" she sputtered contritely, instinctively backing away.

"It's quite all right," Dennis assured her, and now *did* close and zip his suitcase. "I'm just about done here."

"Check-out time one o' clock!" she blared, not accusingly, but in her defense.

"My apologies," he said. "It must've slipped my mind. I'll gladly pay for the extra night."

"Me come back later?"

"Well, if that's what you'd pre-" He was interrupted by a rapid-fire series of coughs, phlegmy and full and raw.

"You... okay?" kindly inquired the maid.

"I'm... okay," he said, finding his breath, finding it, as he always had, at the end of a terrible spasm of self-perpetuating pain.

"Me... I come back later." She pulled her cart over the threshold and quickly closed the door.

He had frightened the woman; she had been afraid of the sound of his coughing, had perhaps detected the death-rattle in it. It was hardly subtle anymore, even to strangers, those who had been spared all but a passing exposure to it.

He sat down on the bed to regain his composure, and thought for a moment. He thought of Rachael, of the day he'd met her and how hard it had rained, later, in the evening. He thought of the funny little cloud in the sky that had looked like a gray armadillo, the one he'd been musing over right before he'd glanced into his rearview mirror and seen her dark-blue station wagon barreling toward him out of the gloom. He remembered his shock, the way his heart had leapt into his throat and time had frozen, his tongue turning to stone on the floor of his mouth, and the acrid taste of metal which had flooded his throat, that nasty precursor to panicky vomit. He'd experienced it before, though never like this; he'd experienced it in class, when faced with a particularly thorny question and he could feel his classmates' eyes on him, and of course the professor's eyes, and the sharp, stifling elongation of time that his silence seemed to produce. Now, though -

## 15

*Now there is no elongation of time, but rather an abrupt and drastic contraction of it, as if all the days and hours and minutes of his life were being sucked into a vacuum, crushed by the unforgiving gravity of some improbable blackhole. He sees again the gray armadillo in the sky, and supposes it will be the last thing he sees, at least in this world, with these eyes. He does not move his hand but rather watches it move itself, watches as it comes down like a sledgehammer on the center of the steering wheel, blaring the horn. He waits, then, for the sound of screeching tires, which he hears, and then for the deafening crunching of steel, the splintering of glass, the scream from his own mouth. He imagines there will be little left of the station wagon's front end, and even less of his boxy 1967 Volvo's rear, sturdy construction or none. Because the station wagon is simply moving too fast, too fast, and such destruction is as inevitable, he believes, as his death itself.*

*But while a moment later there does come the screeching of tires, there is no crunching or folding or twisting of steel, nor even a gentle collision. The station wagon grinds to a halt about two feet behind his rear bumper, sliding sideways in a rather graceful quarter-circle, like a pinwheel brusquely interrupted in mid-revolution. A breath which has been caught in his throat for however long - a year, perhaps? two? - now leaks out in a slow, uneven hiss, like air escaping a tire in sporadic bursts.*

*His eyes dart to the sky, searching frenziedly for the gray armadillo (as if it were to thank for sparing his life), but it is gone. Or it was never there. In the hangover of his terror, he finds it impossible to determine which. But there is no time to hunt for it now, as the driver of the station wagon is getting out, and she looks to be in far worse shape than he: there is no color in her cheeks at all, and the tears streaming down her face appear to him like equatorial rivers, surging without end.*

*Shakily, he reaches for the door handle and frees himself from the car. He steps out, onto the pavement, on what feel like wooden stilts, nearly losing his balance, and makes eye contact with the driver of the station wagon. She approaches him by a kind of hesitant stagger, unsure if he will be angry or merely frightened but certain that he will chastise her. And she strikes him, already, as distinctly the sort who takes badly to rebukes, whose world is shattered by the mildest censure. He is not sure if he meant to reprimand her in the first place, but certainly he will not do so now. On the contrary, he finds that his only reaction to her is one of pity; he has little inclination even to ask how she might have failed to notice that the traffic ahead of her was stopped. In fact - and he is more than a little surprised by his realization of this - he wants only to hug her, and to comfort her, and to let her know that he is all right, they are both all right, everything is just fine.*

*"Ma'am?" he says, but the word almost dies on his lips. He tries again: "Ma'am, are you okay?"*

*"I was looking at the sky," she says.*

So was I, *he thinks.*

*"I thought it was going to snow."*

*"Too early for that, I think."*

*"What did you say?"*

*"I said it's too early... for snow." He moves closer to her, unaware of the small crowd gathering on the sidewalk nearest their vehicles. Unaware of the drivers emerging from other cars, too. "Do you need an ambulance? Are you hurt?"*

*She shakes her head weakly. "No," she says. "Just... shook up."*

Shaken up, *he thinks, and wants to laugh at himself, at his preposterous obsession with grammar at a time like this. "You're sure?"*

*"Yes."*

*"Hey!" a man's voice calls from behind her. "Are you two okay?"*

*She turns to look at him, this man, and now Dennis can*

*see him over her right shoulder. He is tall and skinny, like Dennis, with shaggy blond hair and purple-tinted granny shades: a quintessential flower child. There are many of them in the world at this time, the hippie sorts, and Dennis will later wonder why he often felt so hostile toward them. It was not their politics, really, although by that point in his life he already considered himself fairly conservative. He would come to decide, eventually, that it was how their message of peace and love had often seemed subordinate to their hunger for attention, or how they had sometimes appeared to use that message as a pretext for irresponsibility. Really, though, it was probably more that he had never been invited to join them.*

*"We're okay," he tells the man. "Just a little... shaken up."*

*"You damn near got smashed to hell and back, brother!" the man replies, grinning more nervously than with amusement.*

*"I didn't see him," the woman interjects. "I didn't realize... the traffic. That it had stopped, you know?"*

*"You guys all right?" somebody - another female - now calls from behind Dennis. He turns and sees a middle-aged woman standing in the middle of the road, her eyes alternating*

*between him, the driver of the station wagon, and the ominous arrangement of their cars. Her hair, already graying, is tied in a bun, complementing perfectly her schoolmarmish dress. Dennis imagines this is the most dramatic and downright awful incident she has ever witnessed, and that she may well give up driving as a result of it, finding the subway or the bus far less risky.* Silly bitch, *he thinks, and wants to laugh again. It's his relief, he guesses, which is now coursing through him like the after-pangs of a powerful orgasm.*

*"We're fine!" he yells back, his eyes returning immediately to the young woman, the thin lady with long black hair and sea-green eyes... at least he* thinks *they're sea-green, they look to be so from where he's standing, but whatever their color, they are beautiful; that he noticed at once. She is leaning now on the hood of her station wagon, bent over a little with her hands on her knees, lank ropes of sweaty hair falling over the sides of her face. He wants to* see *her face, get a good hard look at it, and he still wants to hold her. He wants to hold her so badly now that he puts his hands in his pockets, as if afraid they might otherwise defy his better judgment and reach for her. He goes to her, approaching with delicate steps.*

*"Ma'am?" he says softly.*

*She looks up at him, her eyes still swimming with tears, dazed but reasonably alert. "I didn't see," she said.*

*"I know. It's all right."*

*"That was* so *close."*

*"Yes, it was."*

*She sees him now, really sees him, for the first time. She does not smile, but he does. "Are* you *all right?"*

*"I am," he says. "Honestly and truly. Perfectly unscathed."*

*"Thank God."*

*"Yes."*

*"What's your name?"*

*"Dennis Arbaugh. And you are?"*

*"Rachael Thompson." With endearing if somewhat pitiful self-doubt, she extends a trembling hand and he grasps it, his own far steadier. "Pleasure to meet you."*

*"Likewise," he says, "although I suppose the circumstances could be a little brighter."*

*She gives a wan but valiant chuckle, that of a true fighter, and he admires her for it instantly. "Yes, to say the least."*

*"Why don't we go over to that bus stop," he asks,*

*pointing to it, "and let you sit down for a few minutes, until you've calmed down a bit?"*

*"Okay," she says, then seems to remember that her car's blocking traffic, in fact a huge stream of it stretching so far that they can't even see where it ends; it disappears over a slope in the road some two hundred feet away. Remarkably, the cacophony of blaring horns has yet to commence. Perhaps the drivers are aware of what's happened and actually give a shit.* Certainly would make for a nice change, *Dennis thinks. "What about my car, though?"*

*"I'll move it," he says, and he does. He moves it as quickly as possible, to the parking lot of a BP station about seventy yards up the street. Then he goes back and retrieves his own car, parking it next to hers. When he returns a moment later, he sees that she is still sitting on the bench in the bus shelter, her hands in her lap and eyes cast downward. "Mind if I sit with you for a minute?" He speaks softly, so as not to startle her.*

*She looks up, sees him, and now finally manages something vaguely resembling a smile. "Please do." She gestures for him to sit, which he does.*

*"You doin' okay?"*

*"Yeah, I guess so."*

*"Still rattled?"*

*"A little."*

*"I understand."*

*"How about you?"*

*"I'm fine, thanks."*

*All the gawkers have moved on, he notices, and the traffic on Beltmore Avenue has resumed its steady, late-afternoon flow. No evidence remains of the near-collision that in all likelihood would have either killed or maimed him. There is now only the street as it has always been, and such tragedies are mere nightmarish visions. For the time being, at least, oblivion has spared them both.*

*He says, after a moment's consideration: "So where were you headed, if you don't mind my asking?"*

*"Home," she says, her voice a teary mumble. "I was coming home from class."*

*"You're a student?"*

*"Yes," she says. "Senior in British Lit."*

*"British Lit? Really?"*

*"It's silly, I know."*

*"It isn't silly."*

*"My parents think it is."*

*"What do parents know?"*

*Now she smiles widely enough to reveal some teeth... some very* white, *very* straight *teeth. "Everything, apparently."*

*"Nah," he says. "They just think they do."*

*"That's what they say about us."*

*"Us?"*

*"Yeah," she says. "Us kids."*

*"I'm twenty-five," he says. "How old are you?"*

*"Twenty-two."*

*He nods. "Ah, there you have it."*

*"Have what?"*

*"You stop being a kid at twenty-three."*

*"Really?"*

*He feigns a puzzled expression, scratches his chin. "Or maybe it's twenty-four."*

*She laughs, and what a lovely laugh it is: silky and vibrant, robust but unassuming, some heavenly blend of milk and honey. It is the sort of laugh, he realizes, with which a man is apt to fall in love much too fast. He grins impulsively.*

*"I never knew that," she says.*

*"Well, now you do."*

*She nods, and suddenly seems bashful again. "How about you? Where were you going when... well, where were you going?"*

*"Homeward bound, just like you."*

*"From work?"*

*"No, from class. I'm a third-year law student."*

*"Oh. Wow."*

*He realizes he has elicited a reaction he did not intend to - admiration - and laughs himself. "It isn't that thrilling or glamorous, believe me."*

*"More so than being an English major, I'm sure."*

*"I doubt it. At least you won't be corrupted by your profession. You'll teach, I assume?"*

*"I don't know* what *I'll do."*

*"Do you write?"*

*She nods. "A little. Poems and stuff." She laughs again. "No, not really."*

*"Ah, well. Give it time. You'll figure it out eventually."*

*"Yeah, if only I had till 'eventually' to figure it out. Six more months and I'm homeless. My parents promised to kick me out the day after graduation."*

*"Oh, come on. They'd really put you out on the street*

*like that?"*

*"In a second," she says, a coy expression coming over her face. "They wanted me to be a lawyer."*

*At this he smiles. He likes the girl's wit. He likes the* girl. *He clears his throat and summons what is for him uncommon courage. "Do you have an hour free... right now, I mean?"*

*She goes tense but he knows she won't refuse him. He gets the feeling she likes him, too. "Maybe. What did you have in mind?"*

*"Oh, just a cup of coffee and more stimulating conversation."*

*She crumples her brow and purses her lips, as if weighing some matter of utmost gravity. It is, like the rest of her, unbearably cute. "Could we make it a couple of beers instead?"*

*He laughs. "Absolutely."*

*What he will remember most clearly about the evening, other than her shyness and how pretty she looked and the gray armadillo in the sky, is that they made it to their cars just a moment before the rain began to pour, and lying awake beside her in his bed after making love to her, listening to the thunder retreat to some other, far lesser place, where life was far crueler and such things never happened, people never fell in love so quickly or lived inside a dream.*

## 16

There was another knock at the door, this one much gentler than the last. He rose to answer it, meaning to scold the maid for her obstinance, but froze in mid-step when a voice (female, but definitely *not* the maid's; this voice was far daintier, and had a southern rather than Hispanic accent) floated in from outside: "Hello? Anyone in there?"

Before he could answer, the door began to open. "Hello?" came the voice again.

"I'll be out of here in a goddam *minute*!" he yelled back, presuming the woman to be the day clerk, there to succeed where the maid had failed and oust him from the room.

"I'm sorry!" the voice called back, and the door immediately swung shut.

He went to it, opened it, and saw a woman scurrying away in the direction of the office, large, battered brown suitcase in hand. "Hey!" he called to her.

She turned, saw him, and blushed. She was thirty, maybe thirty-five, and attractive in a raw, unpolished sort of way. Her stringy, flaxen hair reached down to her waist, some of it spilling over her shoulders and modest bosom. She wore an inordinate amount of pale-green eyeshadow, and cowboy boots over tight denim jeans with holes in the knees.

"I'm *so* sorry about that, sir! They told me in the office that you'd just checked out and I could put my stuff in there! I only knocked because I noticed the Bug parked right outside the room."

"Oh, dammit, that stupid maid..."

"Excuse me?"

"The maid," he said. "She came by a few minutes ago and I told her I was just leaving. I guess she told the clerk I was on my way out and they just figured I'd run off with the key or something. In any case, I apologize for yelling like that. I assumed you were with the motel."

She shook her head. "No, I'm just a... a regular person."

He smiled. "I understand."

"So should I just come back later, or...?"

"Oh, no, no... just, uh... give me a second to grab my stuff and I'll be out of there." He waited for a response and got none. "Hold on for a second, okay?"

"Sure," she said, lowering her head.

He returned to the room, gathered his suitcase and a few assorted items from the bedside table, and went back outside. The woman was exactly where he had left her, standing with her head down and her suitcase swinging lightly from side to side. He studied her for a moment, intrigued by her sheepishness. Most of it was because he was a man, to be sure, but not all of it. He could tell there was something else at work here (one would have thought she'd caught him stark naked, she seemed so embarrassed), and he wanted to know what it was.

"It's all yours," he said.

She raised her head halfway, avoided his eyes completely. "Thanks."

"Where are you from?"

She spoke quickly, disjointedly, as though being tested: "California. I mean, my family lives in California now. Except for my aunt. She lives up in Vancouver. That's where I'm going. But we're all from Mississippi. That's where I grew up. In Biloxi."

He nodded, smiling. "I'm from Seattle."

"That's nice."

"My name is Dennis."

"Sheila."

He went to her with an outstretched hand, hoping she'd set her suitcase down and shake it, but she didn't. She just flashed him a pair of apprehensive doe eyes and continued to swing the suitcase back and forth, her body rocking in unison with it.

"Well," he said, "it's a pleasure to meet you."

"Uh huh. You too. I better go now."

"Okay."

He watched as she transferred the suitcase to one hand and brushed past him, plucking a duplicate key to the room from a pocket of her dusty jeans. He watched her unlock the door, and he knew she could tell he was watching her, that it was only making her more nervous, and he knew it was a mistake but he said it, anyway: "Say, Sheila, would you happen to have an hour free? Right now, I mean?"

She set the suitcase inside the room and turned but did not look at him. "Huh?"

"Would you maybe like to grab a cup of coffee with me? I mean, I know the circumstances are a bit odd, but -"

"No," she said. "I'm sorry, but I can't. Bye."

She slipped into the room and closed the door behind her. He stood for a moment, staring at it, then closed his eyes. A tremendous, wobbling sigh escaped him, his heart weighing like a stone. He wished in that moment that he were already dead.

The fellow behind the counter was the same man who'd checked him in the night before, was in fact the manager and sole proprietor of the establishment, Herb himself. He saw Dennis peeking over his newspaper and lowered it to the counter, bewilderment stealing over his features. A mug of coffee steamed beside a red marble ashtray in which a cigarette sat smoldering, cruelly neglected. *Go figure*, Dennis thought. *The son of a bitch is allowed to smoke and just takes it for granted, rubs it in the face of every ex-smoker who comes in here.*

"You're Mr. Arbaugh," the manager said. He was middle-aged, like Dennis, and almost completely bald. His eyes were small, listless ovals set deeply beneath his protuberant brow. His cheeks were hollow, gaunt, the skin slightly jaundiced. He looked rather like a cancer patient himself.

"Yes, I am."

"Sir, I thought you'd left an -"

Dennis waved smoke out of his face. "Do you always smoke in the office?"

"Sometimes," Herb said. He picked up the cigarette and lazily stubbed it out, then hid the ashtray below the counter. A thin tendril of smoke curled up around his face, as if from the barrel of a gun. "Anyway, as I was saying, I thought you'd left an hour ago."

Dennis scoffed. "An hour? I only spoke to your maid five minutes ago."

"No, sir," Herb said, and now sounded distinctly defensive, as if expecting a heated quarrel. He turned and pointed to the clock on the wall (a quaint affair which, in keeping with the motel's woodsy motif, sported a miniature hunting rifle for its minute hand, a shotgun for its hour hand, numerals carved from tree bark, and a bull's eye on its face; this complemented nicely, Dennis felt, the four artificial log-halves of which the counter's exterior was constructed). It indicated the time as approximately quarter-past two. The maid had arrived shortly after one. "Sixty-seven minutes, to be exact."

*What the hell? How is that possible? Was I really daydreaming all that time?*

"Our policy," the manager went on, "is to assume that guests who fail to check out within an hour of check-out time - that's one p.m. - don't intend to check out at all, and just took off with the key. So we change the lock on the door and bill them for it."

"You don't check first? To see if they're really gone?"

"Of course we do. Unless housekeeping tells us they've already left. Which is exactly what Camille told us *you'd* done."

"Camille?"

"Your 'maid,' as you called her."

"I apologize," Dennis said, "if I used an outdated nomenclature. I certainly meant no offense by it. And here, you can have your key back." He held it dramatically above the counter for a moment, pinching the brass blade between two fingers, then let it fall. The plastic paddle rattled noisily on the glass. "Camille misinformed you."

"How's that, buddy?"

"The maid - excuse me, the *housekeeper* - got it wrong: I hadn't yet vacated my room when she barged in on me and told me to get the fuck out."

"I'm sure she was much more polite than *that*, sir."

Dennis gave a dark, sour laugh. "You know, it's pretty funny that you care about what name we give them but you don't mind exploiting their labor."

Herb looked at him blankly.

"You know," Dennis said. A modest smile crept over his face. "Paying them their native wage."

At this, Herb scowled. "I beg your pardon, sir?"

"It's ironic, that's all." Now he gave the manager a big, toothy grin. "Hey, you have a good day now, ya hear?"

He had almost made it to his car when he stopped, bent, and coughed up (in addition to the usual ocean of phlegm) three perfectly dime-sized droplets of blood. They spangled in the mid-day sun like newly minted coins.

## 17

He finally got hungry about an hour after setting out and stopped to eat at a roadside diner in North Bonneville, which straddled the Oregon-Washington border. The diner itself was a bit of a dive but the back-patio seating afforded a glorious view of the Columbia River. He had seen large segments of it while driving along I-84, but as soon as he had really begun to savor it, it would snake its way behind a line of trees or the road would veer away from it or a truck would pass him on the left, replacing the natural beauty with a mammoth advertisement for whatever crappy product the truck was hauling. Now, though, his view of the river was complete and unfettered, save for the screen around the porch. He wondered that a restaurant as decrepit as the Columbia Gorge & Glut should boast so splendid an attraction (had he been less hungry, he likely would have kept driving until he'd found someplace with a more enticing outside).

While waiting to be seated, he had noticed several stacks of magazines on a shelf near the host's station: *The Oregon Trading Post* ("Thousands of Items Bought, Sold, & Bartered Every Day!"), *Guns & Ammo*, *Highlights for Children*, and *West-Central Oregon Real Estate* ("Serving Lincoln, Benton, Linn, Lane, & Hood River Counties"). He had slid a dollar and a quarter into the plastic box behind the stack of this last and taken a copy.

Riffling through it now as he waited on his tuna fish on rye with a side of "homemade slaw" (as the menu had billed it), he came upon a listing for a cabin overlooking Lost Lake on the north side of Mount Hood, near the eastern edge of Linn County. "Situated in the foothills of the Cascade Mountains," read the description, "the cabin features 3 BR's, modern kitchen w/ breakfast nook, 1 full bath, 1 ½ bath, 12' dock for fishing boats, hot tub in back deck, and private fishing pond.

BEAUTIFUL 2ND-STORY DECK!!! 4 hiking trails w/in 2 miles. Central air/heating, stone fireplace, working wood stove/electric stove. Unfurnished (except for washer/dryer, deck chairs, and stoves)." The asking price was $649,950, with both fifteen- and thirty-year mortgage options. By some act of Providence, or perhaps simple good luck, the home was for sale by owner.

*How about a six-month lease?* Dennis thought. *Six months for twenty grand up front. He'd take it. Anybody in his right mind would.*

A voice broke into his thoughts: "Tuna fish on rye?"

He looked up and saw a strikingly handsome young man holding his meal on a blue plastic plate, a dirty dish rag tucked into his pants. Obviously a busboy. Perhaps his waitress had gone outside to smoke. "Yes, that's me. Thank you."

"Not a problem."

Dennis looked out at the river, his mind returning to the cabin, and began to eat.

When the waitress brought his check, he asked her for two dollars' worth of quarters. She gladly obliged him, all the while sneaking peeks at the busboy. Dennis chuckled inwardly, and bristled with envy. Adolescent lust, he mused, was maybe the greatest thrill a human being could ever know, a drug like no other. He would never know it again, nor a thousand other pleasures. Soon he would know nothing but pain, as consummate and implacable as the river's grandeur.

He left the girl a ten-dollar tip (almost twice the cost of his meal) and went outside, to the phone booth in front of the restaurant.

He had circled the number with a pen, and dialed it now. The line rang three times before somebody picked up at the other end.

"Sam speaking."

"Mr. Jeffords?"

"Yes, this is Sam Jeffords. Can I help you?"

"Yes," Dennis said, then hesitated. "Well, possibly. My name is Dennis Arbaugh. I saw your ad for the cabin in a real-estate magazine."

"The cabin up Lost Lake?"

"That's right. I saw you were asking six-fifty for it."

"Yeah, and that's pretty firm, too."

"Well," Dennis said, "I have a rather particular request.

I'm not really looking to buy it, but just lease it for a few months."

"How many months?"

"Six."

"Six months?"

"That's right. With an option to renew."

"The place ain't furnished," Jeffords noted, as if worried Dennis might have breezed over the details of the description in the magazine. "Except for the washer and dryer, and the stoves. Wood stove and electric."

"Yes. I wouldn't need much. Just a couch and a desk and a bed. I'd be spending most of my time out on the front deck, I imagine."

"Well, as a matter of fact, I do have some furniture in storage, left over from a place I used to rent furnished and decided to sell a few years back. It's nice furniture. I might be able to cut you a deal on it."

"I'd appreciate that, sir."

"But I didn't really intend to rent it out," Jeffords said. "It's a big house, well out of tourist range."

"I realize that, sir. But I really like the looks of it and I think it would be perfect for my needs."

"What needs are those, if you don't mind me asking?"

"Well," said Dennis, "I'm planning to write a book."

"A book about what?"

He gave a self-effacing laugh. "*That* I don't know yet. I'm not exactly a professional writer or anything. It's just something I've always wanted to do, and I've finally decided to try my hand at it. I'm actually a lawyer."

"A lawyer, huh? You from Portland?"

"No, Seattle."

"I see, I see."

"I'm taking an extended hiatus from the firm in order to do this. In order to write the book, I mean. So I'm looking for six months of peace and quiet in a spot just like where your cabin is."

There was a brief pause on Jeffords's end of the line. Dennis was about to say something further when the man asked, "And you figure the scenery will inspire you to write something, huh?"

"Yeah," Dennis said. "Somethin' along those lines, anyway. And if not, if it's a total bust, then what the hell, I'll just enjoy the solitude and treat it like a vacation. I've got plenty of money saved up for just such a thing."

"How much were you thinking in terms of rent?" Jeffords asked. *He's caving*, Dennis thought excitedly. *Just like I knew he would.*

"Actually, that's the best part."

"Say again?"

"I just finished a big case today and, well... I don't like to brag, Mr. Jeffords, but to be perfectly frank with you, I made out very nicely. I was thinking I'd offer twenty thousand dollars up front, if that's what it took to get the place for six months."

Dennis heard papers rustling, then: "Why don't we meet in person to discuss this, Mr... Arbaugh, did you say it was?"

Dennis brightened immediately. He knew he all but had it in the bag now. "Yes, sir. That's correct. And I'd be happy to meet in person."

"Should I bring a lawyer with me?" Jeffords asked.

For a moment Dennis thought he was serious, then realized he was cracking a joke. That was a good sign: Dennis was winning him over; he was lightening up; the ice was melting. Dennis laughed good-naturedly. "Ah, I don't think that'll be necessary first thing."

"Oh, I'm just makin' a little joke, pal. No worries. I've got a niece who's a lawyer, and she's one of the sweetest, most decent people I ever met."

Dennis laughed again. "Oh, good. So you won't hold my profession against me?"

"Nah," Jeffords said. "Not if you're anything like her."

"*That's* a relief!"

There was more rustling of papers, and then Samuel Jeffords asked him the question that effectively sealed the deal: "So, when would you like to get together?"

From North Bonneville, where Dennis had stayed the night (this time at a chain motel, his experience at Herb's Hide-Away all too fresh in his memory), he continued east on I-84, taking the Hood River exit and joining U.S. Route 35. Jeffords lived in Odell, a tiny hamlet about twenty miles from the cabin at Lost Lake. Presumably he lived in a cabin of his own. Dennis supposed he was a professional entrepreneur, probably rich by blood. With few exceptions, only those born into money could afford to undertake the sorts of business ventures that yielded significant profits, like buying and selling real estate. Indeed, Dennis reflected, for the most part, only those born into money could afford to make much of their own by *any* route.

The irony of this did not escape him, and in recent years

had even come to bother him a little. The older he got, the less persuasive he found his pat answer to the seeming unfairness of it all: those unaccustomed to large sums of money seldom spent it wisely, anyway. In the end, he feared, this was but a self-serving rationalization of simple greed. Nevertheless, he had cheerily gone about amassing ample stores of capital all his adult life, seldom sparing much for philanthropy, and feeling little or no guilt about it. These days, he tried simply to repress any thought of the matter, and, on the rare occasions that he couldn't, satisfied himself that the problems of the world were fundamentally insoluble and money donated even to the most reputable charities was probably diverted long before it reached its purported recipients.

It was pure bullshit, of course, but seemed to quiet those niggling doubts that occasionally vexed him.

Incidentally, Dennis was wrong about Sam Jeffords: his father had been a lumberjack, and had built the very home in which Jeffords and his wife now lived, a humble log cabin, all the way back in 1954, when Jeffords was nine. Jeffords himself had worked in the timber industry for over a decade before branching out into contracting work, first laboring as part of a firm and then going freelance. The cabin at Lost Lake had been his fifth project as an independent contractor. He had completed work on it in the latter part of 1981, but had made several renovations in the time since.

"It's both quaint and relatively modern," he told Dennis as he maneuvered his Jeep Wrangler down the dirt road that led to the cabin. "For instance, it has a wood stove as a novelty, and a conventional oven for convenience. And in the bathroom, you flush the toilet with a chain, like you did back in the old days, but the plumbing is state-of-the-art. You'll never be short on hot water, no matter how much you use. You could shower all day and not want for it."

"The water comes from the lake, I assume?"

"Yes, sir. And it's completely purified, fit for drinking as any you'd get in the city."

"Well," Dennis said, "just so long as it isn't well-water. I stayed at a cabin in Washington once on a ski trip and we had to shower in that stuff. You ever smelled well-water?"

Jeffords chuckled knowingly. "Oh, yeah. Awful, ain't it?"

"Yes, it certainly is. Smells like a wet dog and tastes like old pennies."

Jeffords laughed harder. "My!" he said. "I wouldn't mind reading that book of yours if you ever get it written."

Dennis smiled. The act required surprisingly little effort. "You'll get the very first copy. Signed, of course."

"I'll hold you to that. Although I'm not much of a reader, really."

"No?"

"Never had the patience for it, to tell you the truth." He shifted the Jeep into second and then third gear as they climbed a steep hill. "Now, my wife's a regular *junkie* for books. Mostly them trashy romance novels you see in drugstores. You can't tear her away from that garbage!"

"Mine, either," Dennis said. It wasn't particularly true (while Rachael had many less-than-admirable qualities, her taste in literature was for the most part unimpeachable), but he wanted to seem convivial. Any opportunity he perceived to ingratiate himself to this man and lubricate the impending sale he meant to take. "She's been devouring those Harlequin books ever since I met her in law school."

Jeffords shook his head. "I'll tell ya," he said. "Ain't women somethin'?"

"They sure are."

They crested the hill and Jeffords dropped the Jeep back into first. "Is she a lawyer, too?"

"My wife? No, no. She's a homemaker. She wanted to be a college professor, but after we got married and had a son, she decided to just stay home and raise him. We've never believed in daycare. It's no substitute for a parent."

"Mr. Arbaugh," Sam Jeffords said, "I couldn't agree with you more."

Of course he couldn't: Dennis had seen the faded Bush/Cheney bumper-sticker on the back of the Jeep; the American flag flown proudly over the front porch of the Jeffords ranch; the red-white-and-blue throw pillows on the couch in his living room; even the hardcover copy of Bill O'Reilly's *Culture Warrior*, jutting longwise out of a wicker basket mounted to the wall beside the toilet, the dust-jacket stained with a faint coffee-mug ring.

In point of fact, however, Rachael had taught high-school English for several years, and later worked in the registrar's office at a community college in Seattle. She had been wholly unemployed for no more than six to eight months of Sean's childhood, and although they had never commended him to a professional daycare service, they had made extensive use of several after-school programs. When Rachael had completely given up work shortly before their son left home, she had done so only because they no longer needed the money and the lure of daytime TV had proved too much for her ("Who wouldn't rather watch soaps all day," she had asked rhetorically, "than listen to college kids bitch about having to shell out six measly bucks for a copy of their transcript?").

Jeffords had said something and Dennis had missed it. A minor panic swelled inside him; he could not afford to appear inattentive. "I'm sorry, Mr. Jeffords. I saw a deer out the window and missed what you said. Could you repeat that?"

Jeffords didn't seem ruffled in the slightest. "Oh, deer's rampant through these parts. You'll be seein' a lot of 'em, if you decide to take the cabin."

"Lovely. I'm quite the nature-lover. So what did you say a second ago?"

"Oh, right." Jeffords rolled down the window and, to Dennis's horror, removed a pack of Malboro Reds from his shirt pocket. Either they hadn't been there while Jeffords was showing him around the house, or Dennis simply hadn't noticed the bulge in his pocket. "Mind if I smoke? My wife hates these things, thinks I gave 'em up three months ago. And I pretty much did. Now I just have one every once in a while, when I'm out on a job site or goin' to the store."

"No, no," Dennis said, trying hard to conceal his discomfort. "Go right ahead."

"Appreciate that." Jeffords tapped the pack against the dashboard until one of the cigarettes came loose, then clamped his teeth around the butt and drew it all the way out. He lit it with the Jeep's built-in lighter and extended the pack to Dennis.

He nearly took one, wondering as he often had lately why in the hell he bothered staying quit if he was already dead, then shook his head and politely declined the offer. "I quit six months ago, and if *my* wife ever caught me lighting up again, you can be sure I wouldn't be around long enough to write even the first *chapter* of my book. If you take my drift."

Jeffords let out a good, hard laugh. "I hear ya, pardner, I hear ya. It's a damned blue-eyed miracle that Kathy ain't smelled it on me yet. I keep waiting for the day."

"Mine's got a nose on her like a bloodhound."

Jeffords nodded, still grinning. "So did she not wanna see the cabin herself? I mean, she's gonna be living there with you, right?"

"Not initially," Dennis said. "She's gonna stay back in

Seattle for a few weeks, tie things up up there, and then hopefully join me down here. I showed her the photo in the magazine and she loved it, gave it her unqualified endorsement. As long I don't spend our life-savings on it, she said, any bid I want to make has her full blessing."

Jeffords smiled. "Sounds like you got a good woman there." He extended his hand and flicked ash out the window.

"Oh, yes," Dennis said. "The very best."

The photograph in the magazine had done the cabin a gross injustice.

It was beautiful, maybe the most beautiful home Dennis had ever seen. It sat nestled in a stand of towering spruce trees, which gathered like a regiment of soldiers on the mountain looming behind it. Those in the highest ranks kissed the open sky, presently a dazzling azure, with their delicate needles. The cabin's breadth was half that of a football field. On its front, a deck of perhaps a third that width jutted out from under a high gable roof, supported by broad stilts made of the same finished oak as the cabin's exterior. The stilts rose from the shallow waters of the inlet, buried deep in the lake's dense silt-floor. The deck itself was girdled by a lattice railing with diagonal slats, thwarting the eyes of any nosy boaters who might pass by. Dennis saw none at the moment; the area looked every bit as serene as the sort he had often fantasized about lately.

"My God," Dennis said, more to himself than to Jeffords. "It's gorgeous."

Jeffords smiled softly, as if regarding a child he had watched grow from young. "Ain't it, though?"

"I think the word 'cabin' might be a misnomer," Dennis observed. "Maybe 'lakeside palace' would be more fitting."

Jeffords nodded. "Yeah, I always was a lousy salesman." He turned to Dennis, one hand on the latch of the driver's-side door. "But then, if you like the inside as much as the outside, I can pull the ad first thing in the morning."

"I suspect," Dennis said, "that you'll be doing just that, Mr. Jeffords."

They exited the Jeep and made their way down the dirt driveway, a cloud of dust still settling behind them.

"I was going to get it paved," Jeffords commented, gesturing at the ground, "but I was afraid it might take away from the rugged feel of the place. The downside is, the dust collects pretty good on any car that's parked here for a while.

You can park a vehicle in the garage, of course, but the door isn't automatic so it's a bit of a pain. I told my wife this morning, 'This fella from Seattle will drive a car white as the driven snow, you just watch.'"

Dennis laughed, slipped his hands inside his pockets. He felt like whistling.

"When I saw you pull up in that orange Bug of yours, I said 'hallelujah,' right out loud."

"I'll bet." He couldn't have cared less about the dust. He couldn't have cared less about the thirty-mile drive to civilization, either. He had seen the house and immediately fallen head-over-heels in love with it. With its very sight he found himself infatuated; of its *locus* here in this remote corner of the world, with only the sounds of pine jays and woodpeckers to fill the daytime air, he was hopelessly enamored.

"Let's go in through the front," Jeffords said. They came to a set of five wooden steps built into the side of a ridge, from which lush green grass sprouted in abundance. "I want you to see the foyer first, get the complete picture."

"All right."

"You might even want to just stand in the doorway for a

second or two and face the lake, take it all in."

Dennis nodded. They had reached a short concrete path crowded on either side by tall, perky tulips. Flanking the front door itself, to the sides of a small patio (also concrete), were pink azalea bushes. "I'm eager to see the view from the deck."

"Oh, that's the grand prize. The last, best stop on the tour. You're not even gonna believe it." He looked at Dennis as he reached into his pocket for the door key. His eyes were alight with perfect satisfaction. "It'll leave you breathless," he said.

The door opened, with a very gentle creak, onto a capacious foyer with a wood-tiled floor. A crystal chandelier hung perhaps eight feet from the vaulted ceiling. Twenty feet ahead lay what appeared to be the living room, the carpet a very soft lavender, a window only slightly smaller than the picture window in his Seattle home looking out onto the big back deck and the forest of pines beyond. A few feet before the arched, open doorway to the living room, on the left side of the hallway, was another arched entryway, this one presumably to the kitchen. Off to their right, just a few feet ahead, was an ordinary door with a shiny brass knob, and another almost parallel with the kitchen. Already Dennis began to wonder what the catch was, how a place like this, on a piece of land so valuable, could cost so little. Something closer to seven or even eight hundred thousand dollars seemed more believable. Hell, maybe even a million.

"You want to see the kitchen or the bathroom first?" Jeffords asked him. "Or the laundry room?"

"The bathroom and laundry room are on the right?"

"Uh huh."

"Then I guess we'll start there."

And so the tour continued. They started with the laundry room (nothing fancy, just a regular white Maytag washer-and-dryer set), moved to the bathroom (as promised, the toilet was a pull-chain, the tank mounted high on the wall), then proceeded to the kitchen (long island counter, charming nook with a gorgeous view of the pond at the west side of the house, stout avocado fridge), and completed the downstairs portion with a brief survey of the living room (the stone fireplace, like the house itself, was far nicer than the black-and-white photo had suggested). "I've got a real nice leather couch you could put in here," Jeffords said of this last. "If you're interested."

"I might well be," Dennis replied.

"Shall we move upstairs?"

"Sounds good."

Another arched doorway gave passage to the staircase, which rose eight or nine steps before angling right at the landing. Bare white walls stood on either side, with a banister affixed to the one on the right. On the second floor, a wide, carpeted balcony of sorts, adorned with a railing "made outta pure maple wood," spanned the north and west sides of the house. In the center of the northern section was a door which, presumably, led to the deck. On either side of the door were two large, octagonal windows with thick wooden frames. Two doors stood, perhaps ten feet apart, along the western section. Immediately to the left of the stairs was a short wall with a recessed doorway, this leading to the smallest of the three bedrooms. Dennis barely noticed these latter three doors; his eyes were fixed on that center door, the one that presently concealed what promised to be among the most magnificent views on earth.

"I see you eyeing that door," Jeffords said with a laugh, following his rapt gaze. "And I can certainly understand why it would grab your attention. But trust me on this one, Mr. Arbaugh... you'll be glad you saved it till the end, if you can hold out."

"I'll try," Dennis said, making a conscious effort to turn his attention back to Jeffords. "But the pull... it's like a magnet."

Jeffords clapped him on the shoulder. "I hear ya," he said. He pointed to the recessed doorway on their left. "C'mon, lemme show ya what I call the 'Sunrise Room.'"

"I'm guessing there's a window in the east wall?"

"No wonder you won that case," Jeffords said, and in they went.

He opened the door, and stepped outside, and felt the sickness inside of him shrivel.

*Maybe*, he thought, *if I stay out here long enough, it will disappear completely.*

It was an absurd thought he could almost believe. The view was, indeed, majestic. Sublimely panoramic. Heavenly in its every respect. No, no, it was quite simply indescribable. As he stood there at the railing, leaning over just the slightest bit, his eyes sweeping across the great expanse of the lake and its million points of midday sunlight, he found that Jeffords was right: he could scarcely breathe for all the beauty which lay before him.

Mountains dominated the landscape, the nearest hidden

in trees and the farthest, the tallest, including Mount Hood itself, hulking, barren rocks with pockets of snow piled in their deeper recesses, largely shielded from the melting rays of the sun. Below, but for the occasional jumping of a trout or catfish, the waters of the lake were completely calm. The air was perfumed with the redolence of fir trees and spring flowers and, from far away, freshly burned charcoals. A bird, not yet retired for evening, sounded its shrill but pleasant melody from a nearby perch.

"I want the house," he said, his heart pounding in his chest. His voice was so quiet he could barely hear it himself.

"What was that, Mr. Arbaugh?" Jeffords asked from behind him.

He repeated the words, louder this time, as he turned to face Jeffords: "I want the house."

"Excellent. I'm glad you like it. And I'll gladly rent it to you. You seem like an honest man."

"I like to think I am," Dennis said. *But I know I'm not. Not as a rule, anyway.*

"You still want to see the fishing pond?"

Dennis smiled and nodded his head very slowly, as if cataclysmically stoned. "Of course I do," he said. "Absolutely."

They went back inside, and down the stairs, and out to the pond.

It could not have been more than forty feet across at its widest point, but the pond had somehow all the quiet, awesome beauty of an ocean, or of the lake itself. Three ducks (two female, one male) swam at one end of it, a white swan at the other. It sat in a small recess in the earth, at the foot of a knoll. A ring of shrubs, mostly blue holly bushes and Pacific dogwoods, circled the bank, punctuated by four large openings. In each opening was a curve-backed garden bench with black cast-iron armrests. A ceramic gnome sat to the side of one, grinning mischievously through his thick white beard. A dirt foot path led over the knoll and down to the nearest of the four benches. At the mouth of it, presently at their feet, was a small sign planted in the earth by a stick sharpened at the end, to which it had been glued. It reached Dennis's thighs, Jeffords's waist, and was tilted slightly to the left. The sign itself was a simple, two-by-two block of varnished wood, on which the words "Memory Cove" had been neatly painted in cursive, raspberry-red letters.

"My wife did that," Jeffords said, with discernible chagrin. "She likes makin' crafts n whatnot."

"It's nice," Dennis said, still feeling rather as though he were drifting through outer space. "Lovely, actually. How'd she come up with the name?"

"Dunno. I guess she's just the nostalgic type. It's what she's always called the whole cabin, actually. 'Memory Cove,' I mean. She says it's so peaceful here, somebody could live in their memories forever."

"They could," Dennis said. "I have no doubt of it."

Jeffords shot him a friendly but somewhat perplexed look, perhaps now realizing how deeply into his thoughts Dennis had receded. "Let's go take a closer look, if you like."

Dennis followed without saying a word, mesmerized all over again.

The spell broke, finally, as they were coming back up the path, returning to the house. The sun was directly overhead now, but the day remained cool. Dennis had yet to break a sweat.

"Mr. Jeffords," he said, "there's something I need to ask you."

"Go ahead." Jeffords did not sound alarmed, or even surprised. It was almost as if he had been anticipating the question since Dennis had arrived at his door all the way back in Odell.

"This house," he said. "At six hundred and fifty thousand dollars, it would be a steal. No, no, that's an understatement. Hell, at *that* price, it would be the Bargain of the Century."

Jeffords laughed, nodding. "Yes," he said, "I know that. The market value of this place is probably close to a million bucks. Or would be, had what happened not happened."

*Oh, Christ,* Dennis thought. *This is where he tells me that ten years ago somebody got slaughtered with an axe in the master bedroom and the murderer disposed of the body in the lake, and now, every year, on the anniversary of the brutal slaying, you can hear her screams echoing in the woods for miles.*

"My mother died here," he said. "Two and a half years ago. The place has stood vacant since. That kinda thing.. well, I guess it gives a lot of people the heeby-jeebies. First I brought the price down to eight-fifty, from nine hundred. I didn't get any bites, so I dropped it to seven-seventy-five. Still no takers. Then I tried seven hundred even. Nothing. The present offer is my *final* offer. I built the place back in 1981 for two hundred grand.

So, in today's money, at six-fifty, I'd wouldn't be doin' much better than breakin' even."

"You know, you're -" Dennis began, and then stopped cold, completing the sentence only in his mind: *You're not required by law to disclose that, even if she* was *murdered with an axe.* A jarring, alien feeling overcame him. It took him a moment to realize what it was: he had almost slipped back into his old self, his old mindset. He had almost resumed the role of a lawyer, and thus ceased to think and behave like a human being.

"What's that, Mr. Arbaugh?"

"Dennis," he said. "Please."

"Okay. And call me Sam."

"All I was going to say, Sam, is that you didn't have to tell me what you just did. Not by law, anyway. So why did you?"

Their pace slowed as they neared the house. At the top of the knoll the dirt path turned to concrete, more tulips bordering this segment. Jeffords lit a cigarette with a match he struck on the back of the pack. "Well," he said. "There's a lot of things the law don't make you do that you still ought to do, with all due respect to your profession."

"Of course."

"And one of them things is bein' honest."

"But when it would cost you..." Dennis trailed off, realizing how inane the comment would sound in light of what Jeffords had just said.

"Yeah, it's a shame. But that's how it is."

Dennis turned and cast one final glance at the pond, and at the little sign at the mouth of the dirt path. *Memory Cove*, he thought. *It's so peaceful here, you could live in your memories forever.*

"Dennis?"

He looked back at Jeffords and realized he had done it again. Only this time it didn't seem to matter much, and Jeffords seemed no more put out than he had last time. "Pardon?"

"I asked if you still wanted to rent the place."

"Yes," Dennis said. "Of course."

Jeffords smiled and dragged on his cigarette. "You're a true sport, buddy."

Dennis laughed. He had never felt so oddly flattered in his life. "Well, thank you, Sam. I appreciate that."

They resumed their leisurely stroll toward the front door,

almost under the deck now. A thought occurred to Dennis, and he debated briefly whether to broach it or simply ignore it. He decided the latter was probably safer, but the thought nagged at him until he finally gave it voice: "Mr. Jeffords, if you don't mind my asking... how did your mother die?"

Jeffords's expression, formerly serene, now grew somber, as if a shadow had fallen over his face. His stride faltered, and Dennis paused alongside him.

"Lung cancer," he said, regarding his cigarette with unmistakable distaste. "She went slowly, I'm afraid. I never saw anyone in so much pain as she was at the end."

*Holy fuck*, Dennis thought, and wondered if his own face had turned to chalk. A splash of vertigo struck him, but when he spoke he sounded composed: "You didn't want to put her in the hospital?"

"She wouldn't go," he said, staring vacantly at the tulips. He dropped his cigarette on the concrete, crushed it under his heel, picked up the butt, and deposited it into a small green bucket on the patio. Dennis saw a litter of old butts poking out of the sand like weeds. "She was stubborn that way. She wanted to die in her own bed. I moved her in here when my dad died back in '99." He swept his eyes across the grounds, the lake. "My, how she loved it out here! It was a paradise to her."

"It would be a paradise to anybody," Dennis said. His voice was soft, hoarse. He wanted to clear his throat but couldn't; he did not seem able to do anything but stand there, looking at Jeffords.

At last the old man broke the silence: "Let's go back to my place," he said. "I have some papers for you to sign."

"Sure."

They started toward the car, their scant noontime shadows drawn almost underneath them, and neither of them spoke again until the house was out of view.

## 18

When Dennis had first entertained the notion of holing up in a cabin in the mountains, he had envisioned something far humbler than the grandiose dwelling Sam Jeffords had shown him. He had, in fact, pictured something rather akin to the log cabin Jeffords himself inhabited. Perhaps by means of such a purchase he could renounce, symbolically, the lifestyle he had theretofore led, a lifestyle of extravagance and opulence and total disregard for those less privileged than himself. Perhaps that had been his subconscious aim, he reflected now: to perish in the very sort of modest surroundings he had so conscientiously avoided in earlier life.

And yet here he was, preparing to occupy yet another palace, to acquire still another castle for himself. He told himself it was all right, though, because he was spending only the twenty thousand dollars he had made on the sale of his car, and none of that was profit in the first place. Plus, renting elsewhere for more than a few weeks might have proved difficult (tourist retreats were apt to be booked up for months), and what could he have bought for less, except a total dump? He had hoped to die in modest surroundings, not undignified squalor.

He scanned the contract one last time, initialing all the places where Jeffords had stricken the words "sell" and "sale" and replaced them with "rent" and "rental," and, upon Dennis's recommendation, changed "Seller" to "Lessor" and "Buyer" to "Lessee." Then he signed on the line below the final clause, which Dennis had inserted by hand: "Lessee hereby agrees to pay Lessor the sum of TWENTY THOUSAND DOLLARS ($20,000.00) in exchange for Six (6) Months' occupancy of the House at 1 Mountain Run, provided both Lessee and Lessor comply with all the terms and conditions contained in this

Lease. Any dispute as to such compliance shall be resolved in accordance with Oregon law, by a duly appointed or elected judge sitting in this State. Lessee retains a Right of First Refusal at the expiration of said Six (6) Months, so that Lessee may renew this Lease for an additional six months at the same price ($20,000.00) notwithstanding any offer from another prospective renter. Said terms, constituting the Lease, shall comprise the entirety of the agreement between Lessor and Lessee."

"Now," Dennis said, placing the check from Ben on top of the lease, "you're satisfied if I simply endorse this check over to you?"

"I am," Jeffords said. "As long as, uh..." - he examined the name and address on the check - "... Price Motors is good for the money."

"It is," Dennis said with a laugh. He turned the check over, signed it, added "payable to Samuel Jeffords only" (blank endorsements had caused more nightmares for his clients than he could remember), and handed it to Jeffords.

"Thank you, sir."

"Thank *you*."

"Well," Jeffords said, setting the check aside, "I suppose

I ought to give you some kind of receipt, oughtn't I?"

Dennis nodded. "That... probably would be wise, yes."

Jeffords went to a roll-top desk on the other side of the kitchen, raised the tambour, and began rummaging through the heap of books and papers inside. "I believe I have a receipt book in here somewhere." Here he began to mutter to himself as he continued sifting: "It's real fancy... the receipts are in triplicate 'n' everything... ah, here it is."

He liberated the object of his hunt from beneath what appeared to be a gigantic encyclopedia and carried it to the table, where he proceeded to fill out the top copy. Then he handed a pink duplicate to Dennis. "I hope this suffices," he said.

"Sam," Dennis said, skimming the receipt, "your word alone is good enough for me." He looked at Jeffords. "But you understand the need for formalities, I'm sure."

"Of course."

Both men stood, reaching across the table to shake hands. "It's been a pleasure getting to know you, Sam."

"Likewise."

"So I can pick up the furniture today?"

"Yes, sir. It's all there in storage, at the address I gave

you. You'll want to rent a U-Haul, though, like I said. There's a couch, a bed, a kitchen table, a big old dresser, lots of little things."

"I'll probably enlist the help of some professional movers," Dennis said. "I don't think I could lift all that stuff by myself."

Jeffords frowned apologetically. "I'd offer to lend you a hand, but I have to be up in Portland by two o' clock to meet a potential buyer. I have some property in Klamath Falls I've been trying to get rid of for two years now, and I think this fella's gonna bite."

"I understand."

Jeffords's wife, Molly, now poked her head into the room. She was smiling rosily. "You boys finished up your business?"

Jeffords told her that they had indeed, and she offered to make them both a pitcher of iced tea.

"That's a kind offer, Mrs. Jeffords," Dennis said, "but I believe your husband has some further business in Portland, and as for me, I've got some furniture to retrieve."

Molly laughed. "Did you sell him all that old stuff we got in storage?" she asked her husband.

Jeffords blushed. “It’s quality furniture, Moll.”

“I ain’t sayin’ it’s not,” she retorted, her tone sharp but playful. “I’m just sayin’ it’s old, that’s all.”

“I’m sure it’ll suit me just fine,” Dennis said, hoping to stave off a fruitless debate, and spare Jeffords any unnecessary embarrassment.

“And if it doesn’t,” Jeffords assured him, “you just let me know and I’ll refund your money lickety-split.”

“It won’t be a problem, I’m sure. So long as the couch doesn’t collapse and the bed holds together, you’ll hear no complaints from me.”

“Oh, it’s sturdy,” Molly chimed in, “the lot of it. No worries about *that*.”

“All right, then.” Dennis extended his hand again, and Jeffords shook it. “I’ll be in touch, Sam.”

“Please do. Let me know how things work out for you down there. I think you’re gonna love it.”

“I already do,” Dennis said, and because he knew any further delay would land him on the porch with a pitcher of tea and, more than likely, a plate of lemon squares to boot, he seized the opportunity to make his exit.

Once outside, he paused for a moment on the porch,

looking up at the late-morning sky and the clouds rolling in from the west, the American flag flapping in the rising wind. He thought he could smell salt in the air but knew it was only his imagination, his longing to be near the ocean. He and Rachael and Sean had always gone to the cottage around this time of year. They went in early June, as soon as school let out, because that's when the weather was best and they had all felt the need to escape the city.

Now, standing here on the Jeffords's simple wooden porch, he could not smell salt but he could definitely smell something - he supposed it was smoke from a nearby brush fire, blown across the range by the gathering winds - and he could easily *imagine* it were salt, so acutely he could virtually taste it on his tongue, which now swept itself across his cracked lips, and he -

## 19

*He is standing on the wrap-around porch at the cottage in New Hampshire, leaning over the rail to watch the storm moving in, the first drops of rain just beginning to fall. He observes, with intense satisfaction, how crisp the air feels, how clean and fresh is its scent, and how invigorating the wind upon his face. He does not even mind (on the contrary, he rather savors) the cold, fat pellets of rain that the stronger gusts drive into his eyes. He has loved storms ever since he was a boy, wouldn't miss a chance to see one up close for anything, and this one promises to be good, what his father would have called a "real humdinger." The short intervals between the thunder and the increasingly violent blasts of wind, in fact, portend a storm on par with the biggest he has ever seen.*

*And then Rachael is behind him, standing in the doorway. She does not say anything at first but he senses her there, senses her eyes on his back, senses her tremendous upset. Later he will even think he already knew the source of it, that hurt, but mostly that will be just his conscience intruding on his memory, telling him that he* should *have known; for really he knows only that she* is *upset and that he wants desperately to avoid a noisy confrontation while Sean is sleeping, to watch the storm in peace and to deal with whatever he must deal with once it is over. But of course she isn't about to let him.*

*"Dennis," she says, but he does not turn around. She repeats his name: "Dennis."*

*"What is it, Rachael? I'm trying to watch -"*

*"Does she work for you?"*

*"Does* who *work for me?"*

*"The other woman you're fucking."*

*At this he feels no panic, nor even any great alarm. (And he should, he most certainly should, not only because she has found out what he's done, but because of the brashness of her accusation; to Rachael confrontations, even with one so familiar as her husband, are an intolerably bitter medicine.) Rather, he feels only a heavy sinking in his stomach, as if he had just swallowed a large stone. It is the kind of weary resignation that one feels when a moment he has long dreaded at last arrives and there is nothing he can do to fight it or to ease the unhappiness that it brings. He closes his eyes, wincing softly, and waits for her to say something more. When she does not he considers simply denying the charge, as per his custom, and realizes it would do no good: there is no hint whatsoever in her tone that she is bluffing. So, still without turning, he says simply, "How?"*

*"The bra in the bottom of your suitcase. Look at me, Dennis."*

*He turns and faces her. She is a mere silhouette, back-lit by the lamp in the foyer. But he knows she is scowling, and he can hear the tears in her voice. Soon enough she will be sobbing, and there will be nothing he can do but feel sorry for her, and feel sorry for himself, and detest himself anew. "What were you doing in my suitcase?"*

*"Did you stay with her for the week in March that I was visiting my mother?"*

*"No."*

Liar, *says her silence.*

*"Just for a few nights."*

*"Dennis."*

*"Four," he says, his tone a languid, doleful murmur. "Four nights, I think. Please tell me why you were looking in there."*

*"Why does it matter, Dennis? Jesus!"*

*"I just... I'd like to know. Please."*

*"I was looking for my book. I thought maybe you'd packed it. I wasn't snooping, and even if I had been -"*

*He does not mean to exasperate her but somehow cannot control his appetite for clarity:* "Jude the Obscure*?"*

*"Yes, yes,* Jude the Fucking Obscure*! Why the hell does it matter? What was her bra doing in there?"*

*He shakes his head. Thunder crashes and the house rattles ever so slightly. Lightning rips through the sky, briefly illuminating Rachael's face. It is drawn, livid, devastated. "I don't know. I used that suitcase to take some clothes over to her place. I guess I inadvertently put the bra in there when I packed up my stuff before I left. I never found it, evidently, and I didn't notice it when I was packing for our trip. Serves me right for being so oblivious, I suppose." He pauses here, turning slightly to admire the burgeoning storm, and then adds as an afterthought: "It's in the side pocket of your red bag, by the way."*

*"What is?"*

*He turns back to her. "Your book. I saw it last night when I was hunting around for the bottle of Tylenol."*

*She groans, horrified. "What's your point, Dennis? That if I'd just asked you where it was then I never would have found the bra?"*

*"No," he says hesitantly, his mouth gaping a bit. He is puzzled, for he meant no such thing. "I was just telling you that I saw it."*

*"Dennis!"*

*"What?"*

*She steps forward onto the porch now, and the bracket lights over the door cast a horrible, sickly glow upon her sneering lips. "Who cares about the goddam* book?*"*

*"Please," he says. "You'll wake Sean."*

*She raises her voice: "Who is she?"*

*"One of the paralegals at the office."*

*Nothing for a moment, then: "Does she know you're married?"*

*"Yes."*

*A longer silence this time. "Incredible."*

*There is of course only one thing he can say, and it is an absurd thing to say, but he must say it, and he does, and he means it sincerely: "I'm sorry."*

*It is then that she begins to sob and flees inside. He will not go after her because there is no point to it. He must leave her be for a while, he knows, and then he might be able to talk to her, might be able to calm her down some. Then, perhaps, he can offer her a more elaborate apology, and, if she would like, a more detailed explanation of his behavior (although there really isn't one, any more than there is a valid excuse for it). He might also furnish her with lengthy, impassioned assurances that he won't do it again, that the four-night tryst in March was the end of it, which is the truth. And perhaps she will sense that it is the truth and agree to stay married to him, and to shield their son, now almost sixteen, from the whole ugly mess. Meantime, he will let her alone to have her cry and watch the end of the storm.*

*When he turns around again and faces the darkness beyond the porch, something inside of him breaks and he, too, begins to cry. He cries for a long time, the lake barely visible through the whipping sheets of rain, his own sobs scarcely audible over the avalanche of thunder.*

# PART III:

# t r e a t m e n t

# (round 2)

## 20

His first night at Memory Cove was a long one.

First the movers were late showing up with the furniture because they had gotten hopelessly lost after leaving the interstate, most likely having detoured to the nearest bar. (It was a good thing he hadn't been waiting on them for his fridge, he'd thought sourly, else most of the groceries he'd picked up that afternoon would have long since spoiled or melted.) Then their efforts to assemble the bed frame were complicated by a rare blend of simple error, sheer incompetence, and moderate inebriation (partly Dennis's fault, as he had offered them beers despite smelling Scotch on their breath when they'd come in).

Not long after they'd finally left, around quarter of ten, Dennis tried cooking noodles on the electric stove and blew a fuse, darkening the entire house. Thus he was left to grope blindly along the basement walls for nearly fifteen minutes, toppling both a barbecue grill and what felt like a tricycle in his desperate search for the fuse box. (The handlebar on the latter item had done quite a number on his groin, incapacitating him for a long moment which he'd spent sprawled, in the pitch black, on the dank concrete floor.) For the grand finale, not five minutes after he'd climbed into bed, the washing machine in the downstairs laundry room inexplicably sprang to life and commenced to gyrate uncontrollably, ceasing only when Dennis yanked the plug from the wall socket. He blamed a faulty wire, as those who were neither superstitious nor mechanically inclined were forced to do.

Thereafter, he lay awake for a long time, tossing and turning, listening to the house settle and to the noises of the animals in the forest. That alien feeling which had gripped him as he lay sleepless in the motel room outside Portland now covered him again, a grainy quilt at once threadbare and suffocatingly warm. He wrestled with it, got tangled up in it, tried to kick it off but couldn't; it held him captive.

He started to cough and was off then on a jag worse than he had suffered all week. It went on for hours, it seemed, and he was forced to sit up and double himself over in order to abate it. He had just gotten it under control when he heard what he thought was the door to the Sunrise Room close itself.

He rose slowly, disoriented rather as if he had just woken from a deep sleep, his heart thudding in his ears. Beads of perspiration stood out on his brow, glistening in the moonlight that poured through the curtainless window.

Very gingerly, he brushed the bedsheets away and swung his legs around, planted his feet on the old, well-worn carpet. Then he crept out of the room, walking with his arms outstretched although there was nothing to bump into except for the walls. He opened his bedroom door and leaned out with his hand on the door jamb, looking first up and down the hallway and then across the open space to the deck-door. There was no movement anywhere, just the still shadows of the balusters reaching across the balcony like long, fallen vases.

While trying to sleep he had been able to hear seemingly every noise within a ten-mile radius, but now he heard only the soft fall of his footsteps on the carpet of the balcony. As he passed the deck-door he peeked out one of the octagonal windows at the deck. Nothing looked out of place and he moved on to the Sunrise Room.

The door was indeed closed, but he could not remember whether it had been that way when he'd arrived. Quite possibly it had been.

*Open it*, said a small voice in his mind. *Take a look inside.*

He hardly saw the point (obviously he had either mistaken some other noise for that of a door closing or else he had imagined the noise altogether), but supposed he had might as well humor the notion. What, after all, did he have to be frightened of?

*She died in here. Jeffords's mother died in this house, very possibly in this room.*

Yes, and so what? Did her sad old frail door-closing ghost now haunt it? Had it also caused the washing machine to malfunction? He laughed, was startled by the echo of his voice, and laughed again at his skittishness. He had not been to church since he was sixteen years old, had never witnessed a paranormal event in his life, never stepped over cracks in the sidewalk, and certainly didn't believe in spooks (least of all the rattling-chains-in-the-attic ilk). And if such entities *did* exist, then surely he had far more to fear than whatever ethereal creature might be lurking in his new abode, its unwelcome agitations aside: as sinners went he was no world champion but he definitely deserved a modest trophy.

*This is ridiculous, Dennis. Open the goddam door and go back to bed. You're a lawyer, for Christ's sake.*

Another fit of giggles burst forth from him. What did being a *lawyer* have to do with anything? He'd met hundreds throughout his practice who read comic books on their lunch breaks, all of them no doubt staunch believers in the supernatural.

He opened the door and peered inside.

Nothing. Absolutely nothing, save what was *supposed* to be there: a big window for watching the sun rise and an ancient rocking chair Jeffords had kept in the house for sentimental reasons, as it had belonged to his mother and he hadn't wanted to put it in storage with the other furniture. He had offered to remove it, if Dennis preferred, but Dennis had told him he'd be happy to keep it for as long as he stayed. It sat motionless in the corner of the room, bathing in serene moonlight.

He turned, walked out of the room, and shut the door behind him. He had gone maybe nine or ten paces when he heard a very quiet groan, or sigh, or cough - it was too soft for him to be sure which - drift past him, like a finger tickling his ear. A terrible chill ran up his spine and then spread throughout his body, the hair on the nape of his neck standing fully erect, as if jolted by a powerful current of electricity. For a moment all his limbs went stiff and numb; his heart did not seem to beat at all. Then it crashed against his chest and set off on a mad, terrific gallop.

He turned and saw nothing. He went back to the room,

put his hand on the knob, began to turn it... and then his hand stopped cold. He removed it from the doorknob and raised it to his eyes, examining his fingers as if they belonged to someone else.

He stepped back from the door very slowly. He stared at it for a moment before turning away and hurrying back to his room.

That night, his first at Memory Cove, he slept with the light on.

In the morning, of course, it all felt like a silly dream. By the time he finished shaving he had chalked the whole thing up to a case of first-night-in-a-new-place jitters, and before he gobbled down the last of the three eggs he'd cooked himself for breakfast he had forgotten the matter entirely. He was much more interested in how much his appetite had suddenly increased: the three eggs seemed hardly to put a dent in it. So he fixed himself some frozen waffles, added butter and syrup to them, and then polished off two big pieces of grapefruit. At last he was full, and retired to the deck to read a paperback novel he'd bought at a garage sale on his way back from the grocery store the day before: *Reckless Homicide*, by Ira Genberg.

The first twenty or so pages bored him. He dog-eared his place and put the book down on the armrest of the deck chair he was lounging in, then went over to the railing, leaning over to take the view in fully. As he swept his eyes back and forth across the lake, observing the birds flitting from tree to tree on the far bank (the creatures mere specks from this distance), he noticed something in the periphery of his vision. He looked closer at it and determined that it was a large glass bottle, perhaps once the container of expensive champagne. It was floating not thirty feet from the bank below him, drifting piecemeal to shore.

*Go look at it.* It was the voice from last night that had told him to open the door to the Sunrise Room. His own, yes, but queerly gruff. He didn't quite like the quality of it, or the tone; it sounded rude to him, somehow. Pushy. Nevertheless, some instinct within him, amorphous but keen, urged him to heed its command.

He went downstairs, out the front door, and down to the bank of the great lake.

After a few minutes of waiting he realized that the bottle might drift forever, and that if it ever *did* make it to shore, he would starve long before that happened. So he went in search of some tool to assist his effort, and, much to his delight, found a golf-ball retriever measuring nearly five meters long. That, at least, would get him halfway to the bottle. He combed the garage for some fisherman's waders but of course his luck did not extend that far; getting his legs wet was an inconvenience he would simply have to suffer.

He changed into a pair of Bermuda shorts (he had neglected to pack swim trunks) and carried the retriever down to the bank. He waded into the lake about fifteen feet. The water was pleasantly warm, as the day was bright and almost hot, and when he stopped it came nearly to his waist. After some delicate maneuvering, he managed to get the cup at the end of the retriever over the neck of the bottle and float it toward himself. It came loose a couple of times, and each time he had to carefully reposition the cup, but after a minute or two he had brought it close enough that he could get his hand around it. He lifted it from the water by its base, meaning to carry it back to the shore before inspecting it, then noticed the small card inside it.

He held the bottle up in the air, so that it was directly in the path of the sun, and turned it so that the tattered remnants of the label (Baron Albert, expensive indeed) faced away from him. He thought there was a word written on the card, but even in the sunlight the glass was too dark and grimy for him to make it out. So he took the bottle to shore, walked it over to one of the deck's stilts, and smashed it against the wood. It shattered into scores of jagged shards. The prize, about the size of a standard business card, was yellowed and curling at the edges. Dennis picked it up, being careful not to cut himself on the broken glass, and examined it. One side was blank, and on the other two words were scribbled in faded blue ink: *Marva Delonge*.

"Marva," he said, his voice but a hoarse, tiny whisper nearly lost on the wind.

He carried the card inside, not bothering to clean up the glass. He would get to that later, he told himself. For now he had more important things to worry about, chief among them figuring out who in the hell Marva Delonge was. The most rational answer was that, whoever she was, Dennis didn't know her. And why the hell should he? The card hadn't been intended for him, probably hadn't been intended for anyone.

*Then why did it float past my deck? And why would*

*somebody write someone's name on a card and stick it in a bottle, anyway?*

The possible explanations were of course endless: a lonely, drunken widower had meant it as a symbolic communiqué to his departed wife; young lovers on opposite sides of the lake had been playing the sort of silly game young lovers play; the card was mere refuse, the name jotted on it for a reason wholly unrelated to its voyage on the SS Baron Albert. Of course, Dennis didn't *like* these explanations, or any other; they demolished the mystery, which, *Reckless Homicide* being the total dud that it was, seemed for the moment the only available diversion.

He placed the card on the countertop in the kitchen and fished a beer out of the fridge, took it over to the counter and sat down on one of the tall vinyl stools he'd bought from Jeffords. He sipped his beer and turned the card over in his hands as he turned the name over in his mind: *Marva Delonge, Marva Delonge, Marva Delonge*. It sounded stranger each time he thought it, and whatever recollection he had hoped to spark only retreated further.

He put the card aside and continued to sip his beer, gazing out the bay window in the breakfast nook. After a moment a white-tailed deer ambled casually into the garden, nosing the plants and flowers. Dennis watched it, both he and the creature completely frozen, each transfixed by the sight of the other, until something startled it and it fled.

And then there was only the pond, with the blue holly bushes and dogwoods that crowned it, pale sunlight dappling the ripples which stood out on its surface.

Most people believed, Dennis was sure, that one who was unfaithful to one he claimed to love could not in fact love her, for true love precluded infidelity as true madness precluded sane thought. He himself, however, was not so sure: he had betrayed his wife repeatedly, with two different women, and yet now, as he thought of her, as he remembered the tenderest moments he had spent with her, all he and Rachael had gone through in their rearing of Sean (the long, anxiety-ridden nights at the hospital during his childhood bout of pneumonia; the constant worry of the three days he was missing after running away from home, Rachael never venturing more than ten feet from the phone just in case it rang and it was him - or, God forbid, a sheriff's deputy with Bad News; and all the good things, the school plays and the soccer games and the pretty girls he'd brought home, the birthday parties and family picnics and trips to the cottage), and the small kindnesses they had exchanged, the affectionate gestures, the late nights in bed, laughing at something silly on the radio or reminiscing about some good time after making passionate love... as he thought of these things now he was overcome with longing for her, for the past he had shared with her, and he broke much as he had broken on the porch of their cottage all those many years before.

He sobbed quietly, in the restrained way people do when they would be embarrassed to be seen in such a state. He cried for several minutes, relishing the catharsis it seemed to provide, soaking up the relief as a sponge soaks up a deep pool of liquid. In those moments, which objectively were short-lived but to him felt long and slow, as if an entire eon were transpiring inside them, he unloaded feelings he had kept buried for years in seemingly bottomless graves whose depths he sought now to plumb. And he did, reaching into them further by leagues than he ever had before, and carrying back up to the surface, where they seemed to dissolve, massive deposits of the corrosive stuff of which they were formed, the black soil in which they thrived. He considered dimly that he had never cried this way before even in front of Rachael, that he had never cried this way before at all.

And he knew, in his heart, in his soul, in the deepest, most abiding part of himself, that one could love someone purely and fully and yet nevertheless lie with another. One could do it, but only if he allowed himself to be perverted by his fears and insecurities, or fall prey to the lowest appetite of his ego, that terrible human need to feel desired far more than is actually deserved.

## 21

There was more strangeness on the second night, starting with his pillow.

It was on the floor when he went into the bedroom just after ten o' clock, meaning to turn in. He had no recollection at all of having put it there. Furthermore, the bed linen that he'd bought in town the day before was laid flat on the bed, rather than rumpled at the bottom as he'd left it - or, at least, *thought* he'd left it. The bed was not made, exactly, but all he needed to do *to* make it was to tuck in the sheet under the mattress and pull the edges of the quilt down. Had he begun to make the bed, tossing aside the pillow in the process, and then been distracted by something and forgotten to go back? No. No, surely he would remember that if it had happened.

*On the other hand,* he thought, *it's been an emotional evening. Maybe, along with all those nasty feelings, you also flushed out your memory banks. Who knows? It's not as if such forgetfulness were wholly out of character for you; you always used to say you'd lose your head if Rachael didn't keep it screwed on for you. And it's not like Casper took a shit in the middle of the bed, either. Now* that *would be cause for alarm.*

True enough. Still, it was odd, and he got into bed with a certain trepidation.

It was only when the washing machine whirred to life again, however, that his trepidation escalated into something closer to terror, for this time the phenomenon could not be blamed on a mere short circuit: he had never plugged the machine back in.

He lay there for a moment, just listening. Gooseflesh had broken out on his arms and legs, despite the warmth of the blanket spread over him. His heart thumped in his ears, slowly but heavily, the hairs on the back of his neck stiffening just as they had the night before.

What would he discover if he went down there? A mere poltergeist of sorts, or an actual specter hovering in mid-air? Both ideas were preposterous, of course, and he would accept neither, nor any other supernatural account of the noise still reverberating throughout the house. And yet, still, he could not quite bring himself to budge from the bed. He could not quite bring himself to confront what he knew in his rational mind could not be so.

*So go down there, then, if it can't be so. Investigate. Uncover the root of the problem, as it were. It's surely just electrical, right? A stray current or some such aberration?*

Yes. Of course it was. An aberration and nothing more.

Resolutely, he threw back the bedsheets and sprang to his feet. He was being ridiculous, behaving like a child, and there was no excuse for it. There were no goddam ghosts, no such thing as a goddam haunted house, and he wasn't about to let some silly little -

Out the corner of his eye he glimpsed a luminous white flash and turned quickly, catching only the tail of it, a tail which closely resembled that of a comet; and, indeed, it dissolved in precisely the same manner as a shooting star.

*You're seeing things, Dennis.*

*Bullshit I am.*

*You've been imagining all of this, in order to distract yourself from the shit you'd otherwise have to deal with. It's all in your head, all of it.*

*How about that washing machine? Is* that *in my head?*

No, clearly it wasn't, for it churned onward, magical miniature comet or none.

He crept out of his room almost on tip-toes, fumbling in the darkness for the handrail on the balcony. (He could not remember where on the wall the light-switch was for the ceiling lamps.) He found it and guided himself carefully toward the stairs, which he took slowly, his hand still tightly clenching the bannister, his heart thudding like a trip-hammer.

"Hello?" he called out stupidly. There was no answer but the washing machine itself, the whoosh of the drum rolling pointlessly and the clanging of metal against the wall: *thap thap thap thap.*

He went through the arched doorway, into the darkened living room, and through it to the main hallway, where he first lit up the chandelier and then stood and faced the laundry room door, as if preparing to break it down. Steeling himself, his heart hammering against his breast like a piston, he drew a deep breath and threw open the door, fully expecting (though he would later deny it steadfastly) to encounter something terrible.

When all he saw was the washing machine rocking slightly from side to side, he flipped on the light, crouched down next to it, and inspected the cord.

It was plugged securely into the socket.

*You're losing your mind.*

He unplugged the machine, stood up, and dusted himself off (although there was hardly any lint on him). He walked out of the room, flipping the switch on his way, and closed the door behind him. Then he turned off the chandelier and waited a moment. There was no movement, he saw no more weird white lights, and even the animals in the forest had for the time being fallen silent. The world was asleep, it seemed, but for Dennis Arbaugh.

"Son of a bitch," he said. "I'm the only fool still awake. And what am I doing? Hunting ghosts, for Christ's sake?"

His exasperation aside, it was a while before he found his own slumber, and he did not embrace it fully convinced that he was alone at Memory Cove.

*     *     *

Much to Dennis's surprise, *Reckless Homicide* was turning out to be a pretty decent read. The protagonist's brother, a commercial pilot named Charlie, had just taken down a flight with a hundred and twenty people on board, high as a kite on phenobarbital. He had abused the drug for a long time after the death of his daughter in a freak fire caused by dangerously flammable perfume, then sworn off it in an effort to re-establish credibility with his former employer. The protagonist, a corporate lawyer named Michael whose firm had represented his brother's airline in various lawsuits, had recently persuaded the company to give Charlie another chance, vouching for his sobriety. Charlie hadn't really needed the money, as Michael had won him a huge verdict in a suit against the perfume manufacturer. But the fellow loved to fly and thought it might help him get over the loss of his daughter. Dennis had an idea where all of this was going: the precedent Michael had set in the suit against the perfume manufacturer was going to come back to bite him in the ass when, in an all-too-ironic twist, the families of the deceased brought wrongful death suits against the airline.

Now a little more than a third of the way through it,

Dennis rested the book face-down on the edge of his patio recliner and stretched his arms high over his head, yawning. He had slept for almost nine hours, waking shortly before eight, but apparently had not slept very well. He was hungry, too, and craving something other than the few bare-bones meals he could prepare with the groceries he had bought. Perhaps he would drive into Dee or Odell, or even to Hood River, and get a bite to eat. He thought getting out of the house for a while might do him some good.

*Remember the Flynn Corp. suit?*

The voice came out of nowhere, and spoke in an ugly whisper. Of course he remembered the Flynn Corp. suit. But what the hell did it matter now?

*Remember what you did to those people? You were no Michael Ashmore, that's for sure.*

Yes, that was true: he had never facilitated mass killings as Michael Ashmore had done, the man's benign motives notwithstanding.

*You lied when you said that the product was safe. You stood there in that courtroom, looked those jurors in the eye, and told them that all of the laundry detergents manufactured by subsidiaries of Flynn Corp. were safe for children and household pets. And six months before that, in the depositions, you made a sixty-two-year old woman feel like a monster for even suggesting that five ounces of All Brite had fatally poisoned her granddaughter, and all but accused a twelve-year-old boy of fabricating the unsavory fate of his pet dachshund. But the All Brite* had *killed the girl, and the boy was telling the truth. Isn't that so, Dennis?*

Evidently he was cross-examining himself now, perhaps as penance for being such a rotten human being. He had only been doing his job, and yes, yes, doing his job had sometimes required the total annihilation of his humanity. He was acutely aware of this. It was precisely why he had quit his job, quit his old life altogether. It was precisely why he had moved out here: to get away from it all, to be done with it all, to put it all behind him. But apparently he had not run far enough.

*First you need to admit it to yourself. Out loud.*

"Fine," he said. "I admit it. I lied to that jury, lied to a lot of juries, and what I did to that child was downright abhorrent. I've never felt good about it. I've never felt good about *any* of it. For fuck's sake!"

*Now make amends. Find a way.*

He laughed softly to himself. What was this, a one-man

meeting of Corporate Lawyers Anonymous? How the hell was he supposed to make amends? The girl was dead. The dog was dead. It had all happened seven years ago.

And why was he thinking about these things in the first place? Where had all of this come from so suddenly? All he wanted to do was to forget about such things. Wasn't his impending death punishment enough? The big bad tobacco lawyer was dying of lung cancer. There could be no starker or more fitting justice; surely it made him square with the house.

*And that would certainly be convenient for you, wouldn't it? To just call it even and die alone out here in the woods, crossing your fingers that when the curtain falls the show's really over, hello everlasting darkness?*

"Goddammit," he barked, "why won't you leave me alone?"

He grabbed the book and flung it across the deck, considered going after it and chucking it into the lake, then decided he'd better not: he would wish for it once this surge of unhappy introspection had subsided. Besides, the book had been but an innocent catalyst; he had a pretty good idea that these thoughts would have surfaced eventually, anyhow. Still, one preferred to swallow vinegar in smaller measures - and on a fuller stomach.

He got up and went inside, dimly aware that he had barely coughed once since breakfast.

He carried through with his plan, driving all the way to Hood River for a late lunch. He ate at a mom-and-pop diner called Cindy's Steaks 'n' Such, where he enjoyed one of Cindy's signature country fried steaks with white gravy and a side of mashed potatoes. It was delicious and filling, and he left the place in much better spirits than he'd arrived.

On his return trip, since it was on the way, he decided to stop by Sam Jeffords's house and inquire into the matter of the Mysteriously Self-Starting Washing Machine. And maybe, while he was at it, he'd ask about one other thing, as well.

He knew right away that Jeffords was home because he saw the man's Jeep Wrangler parked in front of the house, alongside his wife's Chevy Corsica, and he hadn't made it up the first step of the porch before the front door opened.

Jeffords greeted him with true, expansive warmth: "Dennis! Good to see you! What brings you to these parts? Anything wrong at the cabin?"

He extended his hand and Dennis shook it. Jeffords was

dressed in work jeans and a flannel shirt; Dennis thought immediately of the man's lumberjack father. He smiled in a way that took ten years off his face.

"No, the house is great," Dennis replied. "I've just got a couple of questions for you."

"Sure thing. Come on in." He gestured for Dennis to step inside. "Molly was just fixin' to start supper. If you're hungry I could ask her if she wouldn't mind -"

"Oh, no, thank you." Dennis wiped his shoes on the mat and went in. "I just ate in Hood River, actually. Thank you, though. And I don't want to interrupt your meal, so I'll gladly come back later if it would be more convenient for you."

"Won't hear of it," Jeffords said, closing the door. "She whips up quite a feast, my Molly does, and I believe she's only just now thawin' the chicken, so I've got plenty of time. Don't you worry about it. Come in, come in."

"Well, thank you, Sam. I appreciate it."

"No problem, buddy. Let's go into the living room."

Dennis followed him into the living room, where Jeffords sat in a maroon leather recliner and Dennis took the couch with the patriotic pillows. Over Dennis's protests, Jeffords called to Molly that they had a guest, and within thirty seconds the woman had served them both iced tea in huge glasses, insisting that Dennis use the pop-out footrest in the sofa if his "dogs needed a nap" and urging him to reconsider her husband's offer of dinner. Theirs was the sort of hospitality, Dennis now decided, that if left unchecked might balloon into an outright psychosis.

"So the house is good?" Jeffords asked him.

"It's wonderful," Dennis said. "Couldn't have asked for a nicer place."

"But you had some questions for me?"

"Yes. Just a couple." He shifted on the couch, moved aside a pillow which wasn't really in his way. "The first is about the washing machine."

"It's not working?"

Dennis laughed a little. "Oh, no, it's definitely working. It's working overtime, you might say."

"How's that?"

"It springs to life in the middle of the night. It's happened twice now."

"Oh, dear."

"I know nothing about the things, so I simply unplugged it."

"Yeah, that'll work every time."

*Unless the place is haunted, of course,* Dennis thought, and in the daylight, in the company of so sane and sweet-natured a man, the idea merely amused him.

"You must be thinking the place is haunted," Jeffords said with an understated smile. The coincidence of the man's remark and his own thought sparked some consternation in Dennis, which he fought to squelch.

"Of course not," he said. "I just don't have the first clue about electrical issues, so..."

"Well," Jeffords said, "I've never had a problem with it before. But I can check it out first thing after supper, if you'd like."

"I'd be much obliged, Sam. If the thing only acted up in the daytime -"

"Has it been wakin' you up?"

"No, no. But it tends to happen not long after I've gotten into bed."

"Oh, dear," Jeffords said again. "I apologize for that, Dennis."

"No apology necessary."

Molly appeared again with more iced tea, which Dennis

politely refused. Molly asked him again if he couldn't stay for supper, and Dennis once again assured her that he'd already eaten and would have to take a rain check, as much as he appreciated the invitation. Placated for the moment, she returned to the kitchen to continue preparing the evening's meal. Jeffords watched her go with deep affection in his eyes. Dennis noted it with a pang of longing, and not-inconsiderable guilt.

"There was something else you wanted to know?" Jeffords asked him.

"I did." Dennis shifted again, thinking. For some reason he was having difficulty formulating the question. Jeffords sat and waited patiently for it. "Does the name Marva Delonge mean anything to you?"

*Yes, it was my mother's maiden name. Why do you ask? Have you seen her ghost?*

"Marva Delonge?"

"Yes."

Jeffords evinced no recognition whatsoever. "Can't say that it does," he said.

"You're sure? Marva Delonge?"

He shook his head. "Nope. Doesn't ring any bells at all."

"Hmm."

"*Should* it?"

Dennis shrugged. "No, I don't suppose so. It's just that I..." He tried to think how best to finish the sentence, then realized that, no matter how he finished it, it would sound utterly mad. He settled for this: "I found a business card in one of the drawers of the house, and that name was written on the back of it."

"Kitchen drawer?"

"Yeah."

Jeffords shook his head again. "I can't think who that would be. Maybe somebody my mother knew." He leaned out of his chair a little, a sudden intensity to his manner. "Do you mind if I ask why you want to know?"

"Sheer curiosity," Dennis replied. "I thought perhaps you'd like the card. I thought maybe it was the name of a client of yours."

"Oh," Jeffords said. "I see."

"But anyway- "

"I'm sorry I couldn't be of more help to you, Dennis."

"No, no, it's fine." He smiled and rose from the couch. "I appreciate your time, Sam."

Jeffords now stood as well, extending his hand again. "It's always good to see you, sir. And I'll come by the house around seven, if that's all right with you."

Dennis gave the man's outstretched hand a firm shake. He could smell the chicken that Molly was cooking and felt a twinge of hunger in spite of his full stomach. "That should be fine. Thank you again for tending to it so quickly."

"Well," Jeffords said with a smirk, "I *am* your landlord, right?"

Dennis laughed. "I suppose you are, yes."

"Then I'll only be doing my j -"

Dennis began to cough, at first lightly and then harder. He covered his mouth, struggled to get himself under control. His eyes started to water. He was afraid he might cough up blood and Jeffords would see.

"Are you all right, Dennis? Why don't you take a drink of your iced tea?"

He nodded and took Jeffords's advice, swigging what was left in the glass. It cooled and soothed his throat, and at last his coughs tapered off. "Excuse me," he rasped, wiping his eyes.

"You okay?"

"Yes, yes, I'm fine. Thank you."

"That was quite the fit," Jeffords said, still half-reaching for Dennis as though he might topple at any moment. "You sure you're okay?"

"Yes. I'm fine."

"Everybody okay in there?" Molly called from the kitchen.

"He's all right," Jeffords called back. "Just had a bit of a coughing fit, is all."

"Does he need more iced tea?"

"No, he's past it now."

"Oh," Dennis said, taking a long, deep breath. "One last thing: if I wanted to make a phone call, is there anywhere closer I could do it than Odell? I'll only be calling my wife every couple of days, so I don't want to pay for service at the house, and my cell doesn't work out there, I've discovered."

"Oh, gee, I'm sorry, I didn't even think to mention that when I was showing you around."

"It's okay."

"Now let's see here." Jeffords bit his bottom lip and closed one eye, thinking. "I believe there's a pay phone over at Cal's Cantina, about a mile and half from your house. That's west on Lost Lake Road until you come to a three-way junction, then hang a right. You can't miss it."

"Make a right at the junction. Got it."

They started for the door. "Your cell phone might work outside, you know. Have you tried it outside?"

"Yeah. Nothing."

Jeffords nodded. "Mine gets spotty reception even here in town."

*Mine's been lying at the bottom of a river in Washington for almost a week.* "Damned gadgets," he grumbled, shaking his head for extra effect. "I swear they're not worth the trouble, half the time."

"Couldn't have said it better myself."

Jeffords showed him out and once more he stood on the porch for a moment, this time looking up at a clear sky rather than a gray one, and this time without the heavy, biting sadness that had filled him a few days prior. This time he just felt full and sleepy and slightly short of breath.

When he got home he went straight to bed, coughing himself to sleep.

He dreamt that he was standing by the pond at the side

of the house, at nighttime, next to one of the benches, looking at his reflection on the water. The world around him was utterly still and utterly dark, save for the wan moonlight by which his reflection was cast. The reflection wavered almost indiscernibly in the lazy current, though he felt no breeze. The air was calm and remarkably cold, yet he did not shiver despite his meager dress.

The feeling inside him, as he stood and stared blankly at his image on the water, was sheer, unadulterated agony. The sensation was so *complete*, so incredibly whole and undiluted, as to paralyze his very being, mind and body both. It was dread bigger than a galaxy, despair deeper than the deepest cosmic sea, wild rambling sorrow, unholy remorse, bottomless regret, impossible dismay. It was an everlasting crucifixion of his soul.

Later, much later, when he could bring himself to recall it, he would think of it as the sort of feeling that might prelude the onset of irrevocable madness in one who had never so much as glimpsed the hardest truth of himself, and then had it revealed to him in a single, sweeping flash: whatever thing in himself he would most despise if seen with perfect clarity for what it was, whatever thing he would struggle most fiercely to hide from others out of shame. Homosexuals who committed suicide out of disgust with their own desires, or a parent who might have but somehow failed to rescue her child from death, perhaps knew in their final moments some semblance of such a feeling. But no conscious creature, he would decide, could withstand for even a moment the intensity of the particular emotion that had consumed him in his dream; such unimaginable horror, mercifully, was surely reserved for worlds unreal.

And the prospect that this newest vision should come to haunt him with anything like the regularity of the Mountain Dream would soon, in itself, prove a nightly wellspring of terror.

There was more to the dream, although the awful feeling did dissipate as it went on, replaced eventually by a more banal breed of fear.

First, the ghost of a woman he dimly recognized appeared on the opposite shore, drawing his eyes from his reflection as if by some magnetic pull. She wore on her body a simple house-dress of unremarkable appearance, and on her face a curiously dull, vaguely puzzled expression. She said nothing, did not move, and kept her arms folded across her middle in a V-shape, her head slightly bowed. While she did not exactly hover above the ground, nor did she stand on it; where there should have been feet there was only an indistinct nimbus of mist, creeping outward in long tendrils. Dennis raised a feeble hand and waved to her, his eyes those of a man under hypnosis, but she did not wave back.

Then, as she watched with seemingly total indifference, he bent at the waist and vomited one of his lungs into the pond, executing the act with the grace and delicacy of a veteran sommelier uncorking a bottle of wine. The lung was as black as charcoal, its contours sharply defined and edges tinged by a very faint reddish-orange glow, so as to contrast it with the darkness. It made a small, silent splash in the water, and then began slowly to float away, toward the opposite shore.

He righted himself discreetly and looked across the pond. The ghost of the woman had turned her face away, as if embarrassed by the mess he had made, as if wanting to shame him the way one might shame a vulgar child.

Jeffords woke him up, knocking on the door. He stirred gradually, by degrees, at first mistaking the noise for that of the washing machine rattling on its haunches, as his liberated lung tumbled around in the drum. Then he heard Jeffords call his name and groggily remembered his seven o' clock appointment with the man. He imagined himself warning Jeffords about the hideous organ that lay within the machine and grunted hoarse, uneasy laughter.

He coughed a bit, rose, and went downstairs to answer the door.

"Dennis," Jeffords said. "I thought maybe you'd forgot I was comin' and headed out for the evening." He stood in the dusty light under the deck, gripping a hefty red toolbox in his right hand.

"No, no. I didn't forget." He suppressed a cough and motioned for Jeffords to step inside. "I just, uh... fell asleep."

Jeffords chuckled and wiped his feet on the mat. "Oh, man, those late-afternoon naps will kill ya."

"No kidding. I was completely conked out."

Jeffords came in and Dennis closed the door behind him, led him to the laundry room. He flipped the light on and made a *have-at-it* gesture. "There she is," he said. "Been quiet as a mouse all day. But like I said, it only acts up late at night, from what I can tell."

Jeffords mused. "Hmm. How bizarre."

"Isn't it, though?"

"Sure is." He stepped into the room. "Well, all right, let me take a look." He went over to the machine and squatted before it, setting his toolbox on the floor.

"Thanks again, Sam. Can I get you a glass of water or anything? A beer?"

"No, I'm fine. Thank you, though."

"No problem. If you need anything, just holler, okay?"

"Ten-four."

Dennis left Jeffords to the obstreperous washer and went back upstairs to take a shower.

While showering he thought about his dream, recalled its details with surprising clarity (probably because Jeffords had woken him at the tail end of it, he supposed, and it was therefore still fresh in his memory). He thought in particular about the ghost of the woman, endeavored to place her face but could not. Was she someone Rachael knew, or had known? Had she been a friend of his mother's? A former client? Alas, the more feverishly he struggled to identify her, the faster his image of her face dissolved, and by the end of his shower he had gotten nowhere. He had now in his mind only the blurriest reproduction of her face, to which he kept adding random details in a vain attempt to reconstruct it.

He dried himself off and went back downstairs to check on Jeffords's progress.

"Did you trip a breaker recently?" Jeffords asked him, still hunched down on the floor. He had pulled the machine away from the wall and removed the back panel, resting it against the dryer. A flashlight lay in between his feet, shining a weak beam on the various exposed components. "From anywhere in the house?"

Dennis nodded. "Yes, from the kitchen. The day I moved in. I was trying to cook noodles and I guess I blew a fuse. The whole house went dark."

"Uh-oh."

Dennis saw the alarm in Jeffords's eyes and grew concerned. "Oh, Jesus, did I screw up all the wiring?"

"Well, no, because all your light fixtures and appliances are still workin', right?"

"I don't really know. I haven't used many of them yet."

"After you blew out the fuse in the kitchen, did you go down to the basement and reset the breaker?"

"Yes."

"And everything came back on?"

"Yes, from what I could tell. I know the lights did, and the stove."

Jeffords nodded and scratched his chin. "I'm worried you mighta had a ground fault and compromised the lower-level breakers."

"How's that, Sam?"

"It's something that happens when the black wire, the hot wire, touches the ground wire - that's bare copper - or the side of a metal outlet box, which is connected to the ground wire. It's basically a type of short circuit."

"Is it bad?"

Jeffords laughed and stood up, dusting his pantlegs. "Well, yeah, it tends to be. But I can't quite figure out why it'd be causin' the ruckus that it has been. With the washer 'n' all, I mean."

"Hmm."

"I suppose it mighta screwed up your whole circuit network and caused the laundry room circuit to generate too much current. But then the circuit oughtta've tripped itself to prevent an overload, and maybe a fire. I installed the fuses myself. When this has happened, have you always come down and unplugged the machine?"

"Yeah."

Jeffords nodded vigorously, a light clearly dawning in his head. "Well, see there now, that's prolly it. Prolly what's happenin' is, the circuit would trip itself when the current got too heavy and triggered an overload, except you're pullin' the plug and reducin' the current running through it. See?"

Dennis shrugged, smiling. "Electrics ain't my field, Sam, but yeah, I get the gist of what you're saying. The point is, it's nothing more than faulty wiring, right?"

"Looks that way, yeah."

Dennis nodded, considered. "Which means it isn't a ghost, after all."

Jeffords laughed. "Did you really think it was?"

Dennis shook his head and gave Jeffords a playfully dismissive wave. "Of course not," he said. "Don't be silly."

"Hey," Jeffords said, his eyes flashing with good-natured mockery, "there ain't no shame in believin' that stuff."

"Sure there is," Dennis retorted at once, a bit more sharply than he'd meant to. "It fosters ignorance, which in turn breeds superstition, and superstition is a dangerous thing."

Jeffords just looked at him, as if trying to decide whether he was joking or being serious. Realizing that the latter was more likely, he simply nodded and said, "I'm gonna go down to the basement and take a look at the breaker box, experiment with a couple things. I'll let you know if I find anything."

"All right."

He picked up his toolbox and brushed past Dennis, who simply stood there, flummoxed and vaguely bitter.

## 22

As he lay in bed that night, Dennis saw again and again in his mind's eye the woman by the lake, the silent ghost from his dream. He conjured her face as best he could, studied the various details he had filled in, rejected them all over again and replaced them with still others. Eventually the face seemed right to him as he had constructed it, and he held onto it as tightly as he could, and pondered it at length. He was still pondering it when he slipped into a half-doze, half-reverie from which he never fully awoke, but which sleep merely diffused. He descended then into a restless slumber rife with murky dreams, a shallow sleep poisoned by old and heavy sins he'd yet to purge.

## 23

*Across the long folding table between them are seated a woman, almost seventy, and a man, all of twenty-six. The woman is dying of lung cancer, and the man is her lawyer, some hick from Denny Creek who graduated from a third-rate law school less than a year ago.*

*She called him six weeks ago, Dennis will later discover, to find out whether she could get some money for her three children and five grandchildren before she died. James Baldwin, the lawyer from Denny Creek, was at that time already representing another plaintiff in a negligence suit against Stevens & Brent, for which, in light of his client's financial hardship and the defendant's deep pockets, he had negotiated a contingency fee. Shortly after his initial interview with Mrs. Dellong, his new client, a third person had called him, claiming to be the first client's barber, regarding a possible suit against the company. A few days after that, Mr. Baldwin had decided to put an ad in the paper, requesting that anyone with a potential claim against Stevens & Brent contact him immediately.*

*Within two weeks he had a dozen new clients, all of them eager to sue the tobacco giant. As the number grew and work on the case became increasingly time-consuming and complex, elbowing out the minor projects that were the staple of his practice (and therefore his livelihood), his modest resources now strained nearly to the breaking point, he persuaded the burgeoning pool of clients to scrap the contingency fee idea and instead each pay him a small hourly fee, just enough to defray the losses he was forced to sustain. As the case stands now, he has a total of thirty-three clients; it is at this juncture a mere "mass action," but by the end of the month, once the media has caught wind of it and scores of prospective clients have inundated his office with letters and telephone calls, he will have enlisted the aid of two Seattle attorneys, both far more experienced in class actions than he, and agreed to collaborate on a class-action venture in exchange for a hefty advance (really more of a referral fee, Dennis suspects, a device generally proscribed by attorney ethics). Mrs. Dellong will eventually become one of the class's four "lead plaintiffs," and hence a cardinal player in the newly reshaped litigation.*

*But for the moment Mr. Baldwin is all the dying woman can afford, the best legal representation her money can buy. He is all but completely impotent in his present capacity, poses not the slightest threat to men like Dennis Arbaugh and Mark Critchfield, with the full weight of the city's largest and most powerful law firm behind them. He probably realizes this, too, which only makes Dennis admire him all the more: he is a brave son of a bitch, maybe Dennis's bravest adversary yet. That his cause is unarguably just requires no stating. Unfortunately for his client, nothing could be more irrelevant to her likelihood of success.*

*"Mrs. Dellong," Dennis intones from his seat between Mark and the transcriptionist. "You understand what a deposition is, do you not?"*

*"Yes, sir, I do." She's a petite woman with low cheekbones and sunken eyes. Her skin is shriveled and waxen, lending her face an austere, almost haunted mien. She is dressed in a nondescript red blouse and a long satin pink dress, her white hair tied in a bun with exacting rigor. She speaks quietly, almost mumbling; twice so far the transcriptionist has had to ask her to raise her voice. The doctors told her she would be dead in six months, regardless of any treatment she sought.*

*"So then you realize," Dennis goes on, "that you're*

*under solemn oath right now? That you if fail to tell the truth you'll be subject to all the possible penalties of perjury? You know what perjury is, ma'am?"*

*"Uh huh."*

*The transcriptionist intervenes patiently: "Please say yes or no, Mrs. Dellong."*

*"Sorry," she says. Her head droops a bit, like that of a scolded child. "Yes, sir, I do."*

*Dennis leans forward, into the table, interlocking his fingers. Raising his own voice slightly he says, "So then did you receive such a letter or not?"*

*"Not that I recall," says Mrs. Dellong.*

*"You'd remember it if you'd read it, wouldn't you?"*

*"I'm going to object to that, Mr. Arbaugh," says Mr. Baldwin, the woman's attorney. "If she says she can't remember whether she got it, then that should be the end of it. Please, let's keep the badgering to a minimum."*

*Dennis and Mark exchange discreet glances, both incredulous but intrigued. Dennis's respect for the size of Mr. Baldwin's cahonies grows steadily. "Call me Dennis," he says to Mrs. Dellong's lawyer. "I insist."*

*"Mr. Arbaugh is fine, thank you."*

*Dennis nods. The man wants to play hardball. Dennis will gladly oblige him. "Look, this is a crucial question of fact, Jim. If I may call you Jim?"*

*Mr. Baldwin squirms uncomfortably in his chair. "I'd prefer that you addressed me by my surname, actually."*

*"All right, Jim, look here: we need to know whether your client received and read the letter that Stevens & Brent sent out four years ago, alerting their customers to a small increase in the nicotine and tar contained in their products. Because if she got that letter and never read it, then the culpability of our client in bringing about her current ailment is dramatically undercut. Likewise if she received the letter and* did *read it, but chose to continue her smoking, anyway. In either case, we're looking at a very different ball game than if Stevens & Brent had simply never informed consumers in the first place that they planned to augment the given ingredients."*

*"No," Mr. Baldwin says, "we're not. We're* not *looking at a different ball game in that case,* Dennis, *because Mrs. Dellong's physician has confirmed that her cancer almost certainly originated well after the increase but long before these alleged letters were sent out. So all this is really just a red herring, and you know it."*

*"Nonsense," Dennis says. "It's no such thing. The letter is a document that our client responsibly prepared and disseminated in order to keep their customers apprised of the risks of using their products. Mrs. Dellong and the others* assumed *those risks by continuing to smoke despite such timely and thorough disclosures." He motions for the transcriptionist to stop typing and lowers his voice: "And frankly,* Jim, *I don't give a rat's ass what her doctor says, because I can find a dozen other, more qualified doctors to say exactly the opposite if I need them to."*

*"Sure," Mr. Baldwin says, "and they'll be lying."*

*Dennis eyes him contemptuously. "I have a witness to depose, sir. If you don't mind?"*

*"Please," Mr. Baldwin says, raising his hand. "Continue."*

*Dennis holds the man's gaze for a moment, staring him down. He knows that Baldwin will avert his eyes first, and he does, giving Dennis a satisfaction as perverse as it is intense. He gives the transcriptionist a nod and she replaces her fingers on the keys of her Stenograph.*

*"Mrs. Dellong," he says, turning his eyes back to the woman. "I apologize for that ugly scene. Now, let me ask you*

*this: do you remember being contacted by telephone, sometime around August of 2003, by a representative of Stevens & Brent, or receiving an automated call with a message containing certain instructions?"*

*Mrs. Dellong shakes her head "I don't rightly remember that either, sir."*

*"But you may have been, right?"*

*"Well," she says, "yessir, I reckon so."*

*"And you may have told this person that you regularly purchased cigarettes manufactured by Stevens & Brent, correct?"*

*"Might have, yessir."*

*Dennis leans into the table a little further, bearing down on her with his eyes. "So then it's at least* possible, *is it not, that you got the letter and simply never opened it?"*

*She hesitates, looks helplessly at her lawyer. He simply nods, signaling that it is all right for her to tell the truth, that telling the truth is* all *he wants her to do. A flutter of guilt rises in Dennis's bosom and he crushes it like an irksome moth. "Yessir," she says finally. "I guess so."*

*"A little louder, please," Dennis says, gesturing upward with his finger. "So Ms. Stabenow here can hear you and record*

*your answer."*

*Hardly any louder than before, her hands shaking in her lap, her eyes tired, mournful circles in her face, she repeats herself: "I said yessir, I guess that's possible."*

*"Thank you," Dennis says, smiling a shark's smile: all teeth and bullshit. "Thank you very much, Mrs. Dellong."*

## 24

When Dennis had asked Jeffords about the availability of a pay phone, he'd had in mind only *one* call that he wanted to make. Now, upon waking, he realized there was another, perhaps more important one he needed to place: to Johanna, his secretary at the firm.

He worried he might be too late, that although only two full work-days had passed since his abrupt departure, McDiarmand might have already sent out a memo or something, advising all employees that Dennis Arbaugh was no longer a member of the firm and to ignore any requests by him for work-related documents. Dennis doubted this highly: Fred McDiarmand was an incredibly savvy and sophisticated man, but he wasn't a goddam psychic. How, then, could he possibly have deduced already a scheme which Dennis himself had just now hatched? Unless, of course, he had spoken to Rachael (a distinct possibility) and she had told him everything she knew (less likely). In which case simple prudence might have spurred him to issue such a notice, just as a strategic, self-defensive maneuver designed to guard against the range of retaliatory tactics, however improbable, that a disgruntled ex-partner might consider when flirting with the notion of sabotage. On the other hand, Johanna was *Dennis's* secretary, really more *his* employee than McDiarmand's, and though never explicitly tested, he suspected her professional loyalties were first to him and only secondly to the firm. If that were indeed the case (and Dennis wanted desperately to believe that it was), then it might not even matter whether McDiarmand had taken any preemptive measures; Dennis might get what he wanted regardless.

He got out of bed and went downstairs. Before making himself a breakfast of grapefruit and eggs, he inspected the washing machine. He didn't know what he was looking for (ectoplasm oozing out of the controls, perhaps?), but, whatever it was, he didn't see it. Nothing about the device was out of the ordinary, and he supposed now that nothing ever *had* been. He supposed now that the entire affair had been but a figment of his overheated imagination, fueled by a potent combination of unfamiliar surroundings and sheer solitude. Which suggested, by inference, that so had been the incident with the pillow on the floor, the weird white lights he had thought he'd seen, and the odd sensation he had experienced in the hallway after going to the door of the Sunrise Room - all of it, nothing more than wishful thinking.

He found himself bemused by how disappointed this made him feel, although in hindsight he realized how cogent an explanation it provided for his little outburst the evening prior, for why he had reacted so hostilely to Jeffords's jovial assurance that gremlins were not the cause of his washing-machine woes: he had wanted to believe they were because if gremlins existed, if ghosts existed, if the supernatural were real, then maybe he didn't have so much to fear in his encroaching demise; if a spook could be stirring up hijinks in his washing machine, then maybe anything was possible.

And if anything were possible, if such ostensibly fanciful creatures as ghosts and goblins were in fact not fanciful at all, then there might be a god, a *bona fide* deity, benevolent and omnipotent and infinitely complex, to forgive all his sins and spare him an eternity of oblivion.

Feeling smaller and sillier and more pathetic than he had

ever felt before, Dennis Arbaugh collapsed against the washing machine, the unextraordinary household appliance in which apparently he had sought some preposterous redemption, and then slumped to the floor, hugging himself.

An image of the child in the men's room at Prazzini's flashed through his mind and he closed his eyes, partly to focus on the image and try to console himself with it but mostly to hold back tears.

After breakfast he drove to Cal's Cantina, bought a loaf of bread and a six-pack of beer (asking the scruffy kid behind the counter to make all his change in quarters), put the goods on the passenger seat of his Bug, and then went to the phone booth to make his calls.

The line to Johanna's phone rang once, twice, three times. At the start of the fourth ring she picked up: "Dennis Arbaugh's office."

That was a good sign: not only was she clearly still employed by Stevens & Brent (and Dennis could only hope that once it became apparent he was really never coming back, the other partners would assign her to another attorney instead of just giving her the boot), but she was also still answering the phone as she always had, instead of perhaps simply informing the caller that he had reached McDiarmand, Arbaugh, & Critchfield - or, worse yet, that he'd reached the office of somebody else altogether.

"Johanna," he said. "It's Dennis."

There was a short, agonizing pause before she replied, "Sir? Is that really you?"

He laughed. It was good to hear her voice. "Johanna, you say that as if I'd been gone for months instead of a couple days."

"Well, nobody seems to know where you've been, sir. People keep asking me and I don't know what to tell them other than that I haven't seen you since last Thursday and that everything seemed fine then. We tried calling your cell phone - Mr. McDiarmand and Mr. Critchfield did, I mean - but they weren't able to get through. They also tried calling your wife but I don't think they ever got ahold of her, either. They thought maybe she was off looking for you. Was she?"

It was a thought Dennis hadn't even considered, and the moment he began to he got queasy. Trying to stay focused, he said, "No, no, nobody's looking for me. At least I can't imagine why anybody *would* be, because I'm not missing. I didn't run away. And I'll be back soon enough."

"Well, sir, where did you go? If I may ask?"

"Johanna, you don't have to call me 'sir.' Really, please."

"What should I call you then, sir?"

"Dennis is fine."

"Dennis. Okay." She sounded thoroughly uncomfortable so addressing him.

"But listen, Johanna, the point is, everything's fine. There's nothing to worry about. I just needed to take a couple days for myself. No TV, no cell phone, no computer, no work. Just some peace and quiet. So I skipped town and headed down to Oregon for a few days to relax. You know, back to nature and all that good stuff."

"You're camping, sir... Dennis?"

He laughed again. "Yeah, you could call it that."

"I see."

"But will you please tell everyone, especially Mark and Fred, that I'll be back by next week and that I'm still on top of the Stevens & Brent trial, so they have nothing to worry about?"

"Yes, sir. Pardon me. Yes, Dennis."

"And will you please also tell them that if they talk to

my wife and she seems upset, it's only because I left in kind of a hurry and didn't quite tell her where I was going, and to please reassure her that I'll be back in a few days? I've tried calling her myself but she hasn't answered for me, either."

"Okay, Dennis."

"Also, Johanna..." He paused, steeling himself. He had given considerable thought to how he wanted to phrase his request, all but rehearsing a spiel, but now decided to wing it. Spontaneity was always more convincing, right?

"Yes, Dennis?"

"I need for you to send me copies of a few things from the Stevens & Brent file."

"Which things?"

"The complaint, the answer, the deposition transcripts, and all correspondence, internal and external. That last's the most important. And overnight it, please. Use our Fed Ex account."

"Where should I send it to, sir?"

"Grab a pen and I'll give you the address of the cabin I'm renting for the week."

"Okay. Just a second." She took down the address. "Anything else, sir?"

"Yes. In order to avoid any confusion, use the name of the person who owns the cabin where I'm staying."

"What name is that, sir?"

"Ira Genberg. With an 'e.'"

"Okay."

"And make sure you return the originals to the office cabinet right away, just in case Mark needs them for anything. Have you got all that?"

"Yes, sir. Dennis."

"I appreciate it, Johanna. And I'll see you soon."

"Next Monday?"

"Somewhere around there, yes. And feel free to take this Friday off, if you like. Or Thursday. Whatever day suits you."

"Thank you, sir."

"Don't mention it. Good-bye, Johanna."

"Good-bye, Dennis."

He hung up, smiling at how smoothly the conversation had gone (he'd been expecting much worse), picked up the receiver again, and dropped another five quarters into the coin-slot.

This one was going to be a lot harder.

* * *

"Why would you do that, Rachael? That's absurd."

"Because I wanted to find you and bring you home."

He sighed. "What were you going to do, hon, search every motel along the border until you turned me up?"

"You told me the motel was in Vancouver. *Hon.*"

"I did?"

"Yes, you did. I guess it must've slipped out or something."

"I guess so. But anyway, that's beside the point."

"Well, what *is* the point, Dennis? That you've gone 'round the bend and run away from home and won't tell me where you are?"

"No, that isn't the point, either. And I haven't 'gone round the bend,' Rachael, thank you very much."

"Is it the other woman, Dennis? Is that it? You can tell me if it is. God knows I'm used to that by now."

"No, it isn't the other woman. And thanks for the dig."

"Then what is it? And don't tell me that you're dying. I don't want to hear that shit again."

"Well, I *am* dying, yes, but that's not the only reason I left."

"Then why did you leave? Goddammit, just tell me why you left! I deserve to know, Dennis!"

He felt sweat trickling down his neck, under his shirt collar. He felt his heart speed up a little. She was getting his dander up, like she always had, and he had to control it, had to fight it back. He closed his eyes, concentrated on being calm, just being calm."You're right. You *do* deserve to know. And if I could explain it in a way that made sense to you I would."

"I'm not incapable of understanding things like this, Dennis. Give me some credit. I've been married to you for twenty-six years."

"No, no, I didn't mean it like that."

"Didn't mean it like what?"

"That it wouldn't make sense to you in particular. I don't think it would make sense to anyone. It barely even makes sense to *me*. And I imagine that if I tried to articulate it, it would make even *less* sense to me. So I'd rather not, if it's all the same to you."

"Well it's *not*. It's *not* all the same to me, Dennis. I'm your *wife*, for God's sake! How do you think it makes me feel to know there's something so important to you that you left me over it and you can't even begin to tell me what it is?"

"Oh, goddammit," he said. Now he was openly angry, and let himself be so. There was no point any longer in trying to contain it. "You just aren't going to be happy until I give you *some* sort of explanation, are you? Even if I have to make one up."

"No, I won't. And if you make one up I'll know it. And that -"

"Will just piss you off even more. Got it."

"Right. Exactly. So give it your best shot, Dennis. I'm all ears."

He sighed again, pulled at his collar. He heard a fly buzzing around but couldn't see it. He swatted in the air blindly, then opened the door to the booth, hoping it would take the cue.

"I left because I had to, Rachael, okay? There's no other reason, no other way to say it."

"That's not telling me anything, Dennis. *Why* did you have to?"

Now he wanted to growl. He closed his eyes again, took a deep breath, and spoke slowly: "Because I knew that as long as I was there, I'd never confront the things I needed to confront, never deal with all the stuff I've tried for so long to ignore, never see all the things I've failed to see. Never get over all the... all the crap, okay? The crap that ruins more lives than all the drinking and cheating and gambling and lying in the world. Never find a real, meaningful, lasting peace of mind. I've got demons, baby, big fucking demons, and they weren't going anywhere so long as I could continue to hide in my comfortable little rich-lawyer's existence. They may not go anywhere even now that I'm away from it all. But I'm going to try, dammit. I'm sure as hell at least going to try. Can you understand that?"

"You won't humor me with specifics, I take it?"

"No," he said. "Specifics are neither possible nor necessary. Trust me."

She gave a derisive little laugh. "'Trust me,' he says."

"Yes, that's right. Trust me. I know you have no reason to, but just do it anyway, please? Take this one on faith."

Long pause, then: "When are you coming home?"

"I don't know. Maybe never."

"Dennis, please."

"I'll see you again, I'm sure. But I don't want to die up there. I want to die down here, where I belong."

"No, Dennis, no! You *don't* belong there! Wherever the hell you are, that is *not* where you belong! You belong at home, with me, and you're not dying so stop fucking *saying* that!" She burst into tears.

"Rachael."

More sobbing.

"Rachael? Sweetheart?"

"Don't *call* me that, you piece of shit!"

"Rachael, calm down."

"No!" she bellowed. "I *won't* calm down! I *won't*! How dare you do this to me? How dare you put me through this, this... this *torture*? What a horribly selfish man you are, Dennis Arbaugh! How can you be so selfish and cruel? How -"

"Rachael, calm the hell down and listen to me, please."

At last she got herself under control. "What?" she rasped.

"I need you to do something for me."

"Oh, oh, don't even- "

"Rachael, goddammit, Jesus Christ, *shut the fuck up and listen to me for one second, would you*?"

He heard one last muffled sob and then total silence.

"Fred McDiarmand and Mark Critchfield have been trying to call you to find out where I am and what the hell I'm doing. They'll no doubt try to call you again. You haven't spoken to them yet, have you?"

"No," she said faintly. "I only got home this morning."

"Okay. Well, when they *do* call again, and they will, I want you to tell them that everything's fine and that I'll be back at the office no later than next Monday, all right? Just tell them I'm taking some personal days, that I'm on a retreat of sorts. This is very important. It's very important that they not think any different. Okay? Have you got that?"

Another long pause, then: "Oh, so you don't want to upset your fucking lawyer buddies but you don't mind upsetting me? Killing me, even? Because you *do* know you're killing me, don't you?"

"Rachael." He squeezed his eyes shut tighter. "They're not my lawyer buddies - Fred McDiarmand can go straight to hell for all I care, and Mark Critchfield is no better than I was - and, far more importantly, this has nothing to do with whom I wish to upset or not upset. I don't want to upset anybody. I just want to do the right thing for once. And if you cooperate with me on this, you'll be helping me do that. You'll be helping me to do the right thing. Will you believe me about this? Please? Rachael?"

"Whatever," she said. She spoke with all the vigor of

one who has just attempted suicide and now must endure a lecture on how foolish a thing it was to do.

"Rachael, come on. Just tell me you'll do this for me. I'll explain it all later. You'll be glad you did, I promise you."

"Okay, Dennis." She sighed. It was a small, hollow, defeated sound, awful and eviscerated and barely audible in the earpiece. It broke his heart.

"Thank you, Rachael. I really appreciate it."

"Uh huh."

He began to speak, hesitated, closed his eyes still tighter and plowed forward. "I love you," he said. "I do love you. I mean that."

"I have to go, Dennis." She was crying again.

"Okay."

"Bye."

She hung up before he could say good-bye. He stood holding the receiver to his ear for a moment, listening to the line disconnect and then sound its stupid, unceasing hum.

He went to his Bug and drove home.

## 25

He had the Mountain Dream that night, for the first time

since arriving at Memory Cove. All the details were the same, except that, in this version, the pond at the side of his Oregon retreat appeared to lie at the bottom of the slope. And on the surface of the pond, much as it had in his earlier dream, a single black lung - presumably his own, and badly deformed, pulsating with the disease that grew inside it - floated aimlessly in the calmer winds of the valley.

After a long moment, the face of the ghostly old woman in the house-dress emerged from the depths of the pond and took shape in the pale arc of moonlight that fell across its surface. For a while she just stared up at him, as the lung bobbed gently around her nose - and then she opened her mouth wide and swallowed it, gobbled it down as a child would a rare holiday treat. Watching in horror as she did so, he nearly lost his footing on the snowy slab of rock and tumbled, righting himself only at the last second.

Dennis did not wake from this dream but only stirred, groaning softly as he scrambled in his mind to escape the whole wretched affair.

The documents arrived the next day, as promised. They were, Dennis noted with some gratitude, the first piece of mail he had received at the Lost Lake house - rather surprising, he'd thought, in an age when, thanks to blindly inhumane bureaucracy, folks five years' deceased were routinely invited to enter contests, take trips to Tahiti, and enjoy the upcoming sale at Macy's.

He found the package sitting on his doorstep a little after noon, when he went outside to drink a beer on the thin strip of beach he called his own. He was relieved to see that Johanna had addressed the package as he'd requested, to one Ira Genberg, and relieved that it had nevertheless made it to the house without incident. He had been worried the name might somehow delay delivery, perhaps on account of some persnickety postal worker, but had thought it too risky to have her use his real name if she was going to mail the package from the office (obviously, asking her to mail it from a post office would have raised eyebrows even higher).

He put the thick blue-and-white envelope under his left arm and held his beer in his right hand and carried both items to a spot on the beach just a few feet from the water. There he sat, cracked open his beer, took a sip, savored the bitter taste of the hops, and then tore open the envelope with his fingers.

He reached inside and removed the treasure.

* * *

He immediately tossed aside the complaint and answer, which he had asked Johanna to include merely as a diversion, so as not to draw particular attention to the *real* objects of his interest: the deposition transcripts and a certain internal memo. He delved first into the former, scanning the names of the deponents at the top of each. He came at last, upon reaching the eleventh transcript, to the name he'd been expecting, and hoping desperately, to find: Martha Dellong.

He glanced up at the lake, his jaw hanging slightly open, eyes outwardly vacant but in fact concealing a frenzy of thought. His mind whirled madly, rapidly, juxtaposing the deponent's name with the one scribbled on the card he'd found in the bottle, fuzzy images of the woman in his dream and the woman in the deposition room meanwhile each battling for clarity: *Martha Dellong, Marva Delonge. Martha Dellong, Marva Delonge.*

So had he been wrong, after all, to conclude there was no mystical or otherwise extraordinary force at work in the events of the last few days? Should he ascribe this latest, stunning turn to mere coincidence, as he had ascribed the bizarre behavior of the washing machine to a simple malfunction, and dismissed the bedroom incident and strange white lights as but curious hallucinations? Of course he did not, could not, know.

And since for the moment it seemed to make no difference, he turned, with an almost rabid concentration and purposefulness, to the transcript of the deposition he and Mark Critchfield had conducted with Mrs. Dellong, knowing already what he had to do, what he *would* do, but somehow needing first to relive the awful occurrence, as though it were as necessary to his penance as his death itself.

While reading, his thoughts occurred, as one's thoughts perhaps always do, on two separate and distinct levels. On the first, the conscious level, they were fully absorbed by the deposition itself and the harsh memories it awoke in him. On the second, wholly subconscious level, they consisted completely of inchoate notions, dim but harrowing recognitions, building piecemeal, of certain facts, certain axioms of human existence. They amassed themselves into a kind of fiery, flourishing cluster, as if in his bosom, overflowing eventually into whatever tenebrous domicile one's dimmest, most incipient thoughts could inhabit.

He thought of the way most childhood pains were simply and easily cured, while adult pains could seldom be erased at all, but only diminished or buried. He thought of how easily a whole lifetime could expire before it had been examined, even once, with unflinching honesty. He thought of how the most significant moments of a person's life were rarely recognized as such until much later, when their extinction could only be mourned and the moments themselves merely remembered. He thought, too, of how the crime most frequently prosecuted on earth was not murder or theft or arson, but simple naiveté, a kindness which had no awareness of itself or the grinning evil with which it might be met; and, conversely, of how the crime perhaps least frequently punished was that evil itself, the gross and perfectly self-aware exploitation of another's essential innocence, the brutal raping of the good will extended instinctually to the rapist. Indeed, this crime occurred so regularly, wove itself so seamlessly into the fabric of society's daily life, as to be hardly even noticed. Oftentimes, in fact - perhaps more often than not - it was widely praised as exhibiting strong survival skills, as a shrewdness to be valued and refined, rather than condemned for the atrocity that it was.

None of these things he thought consciously; of none of

them would he be remotely cognizant, intellectually, in the wake of their unlighted eruption in his breast. But he would carry them as primitive, unarticulated knowledge forever thereafter, and the knowledge would afford him, eventually, a solace otherwise unobtainable, and he would find a way to embrace it even while believing it undeserved.

Buried among the documents Johanna had sent him, which consisted of nearly three hundred pages, was the item most crucial to his plan - the jackpot, as it were. It was a memorandum dated February 24, 2006, authored by none other than Fred McDiarmand himself, circulated among the partners at the firm. (Whether or not the associates had seen it, or somehow caught wind of its underlying import, he did not know; but he strongly suspected that McDiarmand had at some point briefed them on the matter more informally, and by means of a much more limited, sugarcoated disclosure.)

The memo had been issued, in a rather covert fashion, shortly before the first deposition in the Stevens & Brent case had been conducted. McDiarmand had opted for hand delivery by one of his paralegals, rather than the usual method of having his secretary simply distribute copies to the partners' office mailboxes, or, where available, their own secretaries. Dennis scanned it now, delighted to find it every bit as candid as his recollection had suggested:

FROM: Fred McDiarmand
TO: Partners
RE: S&B case
DATE: February 24, 2006

Partners:

As many of you are aware, the class-action lawsuit filed last year against our client, Stevens & Brent, has increasingly become the focus in the last few weeks (as the trial has drawn closer) of widespread media attention. It is therefore particularly important, now more than ever, that we protect our client's interests with the utmost vigilance, as required by our professional duties of confidentiality and zealous advocacy.

Thus, to the extent that some interaction with members of the press may prove unavoidable, I would exhort all of you to keep these duties in mind when dealing with them. Specifically, I would ask you to keep your comments to a bare minimum, express unfamiliarity with the case where appropriate, and stress the importance of respecting the parties' privacy and the need to allow the judicial process to resolve the dispute responsibly and efficiently, without distracting, premature, and unhelpful commentary by observers on the sidelines.

Most or all of you have undoubtedly heard or read of recent reports that S&B undertook a massive effort four years ago to personally inform as many of their customers as possible of an increase in certain ingredients contained in their products (namely, nicotine and tar), by first identifying these customers through a weeks-long series of phone calls - both automated and live - and then disseminating letters to them. Inasmuch as the proper weight to be accorded the customers' knowledge of dangers associated with the products will likely prove a pivotal issue in the later stages of this litigation, it is **utterly imperative** that S&B's above-described endeavor to ensure such knowledge be given maximal credibility.

Regretfully, however, a rumor has emerged within certain circles of this firm that, in cooperation with S&B, those involved in the litigation (perhaps justifiably, with the best and most defensible of intentions) essentially concocted the entire enterprise out of whole cloth, that in reality, no such letters were ever mailed. Needless to say, this is a gross exaggeration. The fact of the matter is that S&B attempted in good faith to reach a large segment of its market, and indeed succeeded in reaching some portion of it, with letters to the given effect. Due to various practical and financial obstacles, unfortunately, the effort was cut short earlier than desired and, much to the dismay of our client, far fewer customers were contacted than it would have liked.

Nevertheless, the undertaking was not

a pure fabrication, it is not merely a tactical or strategic maneuver on our part, and any suggestion to the contrary should be dismissed as a baseless insult both to the integrity of this firm and to our profession. Furthermore, it is our duty as S&B's legal representatives to underscore its attempt at full disclosure as forcefully and fervently as is permitted under the Rules of Professional Conduct.

Any implication, however, that this firm or any of its members have engaged, or intend to engage, in any manner of dishonest behavior in the course of representing S&B, is both completely groundless and wholly contrary to the very spirit, as much as the letter, of the ethical code by which attorneys are bound, and which the members of McDiarmand, Arbaugh, & Critchfield have always taken special pride in faithfully observing. It is also wholly contrary, of course, to the express policies of this firm. Again, to cast aspersions on that honor is decidedly counterproductive, not only to the business interests of this particular client and to the morale of the partners directly representing S&B, but to the confidence of our clients generally in our adherence to lawful, morally sound practices and the morale of our entire membership. Accordingly, I would strongly encourage those who might have contributed to the perpetuation of this rumor to cease and desist **at once** in any activities tending to foster it.

I have tentatively scheduled a conference, which all employees will be expected to attend, for one week from today (March 3rd) to discuss the status of this matter if need be. It is greatly hoped that no such need will arise and that the meeting will be unnecessary. In the meantime, I should caution you once again to exercise extreme discretion in managing unavoidable inquiries or requests for comment from the press on the subject of S&B, and to strictly avoid gratuitous contact with the media in all related matters.

Sincerely,

Fred McDiarmand

Senior Partner

Dennis could not help but smirk as he read the last paragraph, recalling how (shockingly enough) "no such need" had in fact arisen, and then dwelled for a moment on McDiarmand's signature, on how indisputably genuine it was, albeit Xeroxed.

He carried the memo and the rest of the documents into the house, where he placed them on the kitchen table, and then drove into town, wanting to buy some lunch and, if he could find one, a cheap typewriter.

He was unable to locate a manual typewriter at the thrift shop in Odell, the town's sole outlet for such items, but was able to find a well-used IBM Selectric at an antique store in Hood River called Second Time Around (he and the store's elderly proprietor shared a hearty chuckle that a device which to them still seemed perfectly modern should now be considered "antique"). He had wanted a manual typewriter because he had fond memories of the clunky Royal he'd owned as a kid, when he'd enjoyed writing short stories and the occasional playlet, and could not resist the nostalgia he'd felt at the thought of owning one again, the inefficiency of the machines themselves and his limited use for one notwithstanding. Second Time Around did have an Underwood for sale, but it was a later model, the ribbon in it was completely worn out, and he could not afford its price in cash, the only form of payment the store accepted. In fact, his purchase of the IBM Selectric, reasonably priced though it was, nearly wiped his wallet clean, and he made a mental note to stop at an ATM before he headed home. He had already learned the hard way that Cal's Cantina and most of the shops in Odell likewise operated on a cash-or-check-only basis (out-of-town checks excepted). It was one of the hazards, he supposed, of residing in such a remote location, the sort of place he'd once heard Sean refer to as "BFE." (He had only the vaguest idea what this acronym stood for, and, if forced to guess, would likely have said "Barely Fucking on Earth.")

After buying the typewriter, he ate another late lunch at

Cindy's Steaks 'n' Such, in fact exactly the same meal he'd ordered two days ago: country fried steak with white gravy and a side of mashed potatoes. He also had the same waitress, a pretty girl from Norwich, England who had gone to school in Portland that spring as part of a student exchange program run by King's College in London, and had decided to spend the summer working and traveling before returning home. At one point he caught himself almost flirting with her... no, not almost: he was smiling and telling jokes and, each time she walked away, ogling her backside. Then he thought of Sarah - Sarah, who was probably waiting on a lecherous customer of her own at that very moment, a brand-new Dennis Arbaugh to complicate her perfectly quiet, uncomplicated life and ultimately break her heart - and promptly cut it out. The moment he finished his meal he called for his check, wished the young waitress a happy summer and safe return trip, left her an ample tip, and quickly departed as discreetly as he had come.

There would be no more broken hearts on *his* account.

After lunch Dennis made a brief stop at the Hood River Drug Emporium, where he purchased a ream of computer paper (not exactly the long-grain mimeo he'd used as a kid, but it would do) and one pack of Winston full-flavored cigarettes, the brand he had smoked for over thirty years. He paid the clerk with the last piece of cash in his wallet, a crumpled ten-dollar bill, and left the store whistling a tune.

He did not remove the cigarettes from the bag until much later, and until then forgot he had even bought them.

As soon as he got home he carried the IBM Selectric upstairs and plonked it on the little desk in the corner of his bedroom, under a window with a much smaller version of the same spectacular view afforded one standing on the deck. Then he inserted a sheet of paper from the ream he'd bought at the drugstore, fed it through the platen, and punched out the following letter in all of twenty-two minutes:

Dear Mr. Baldwin:

Enclosed you will find a memorandum written by Fred McDiarmand, senior partner at McDiarmand, Arbaugh, & Critch-field, and circulated among the partners at that firm - <u>my</u> firm, until last week.

In it, he details a rumor which developed at the firm, not long before the scheduling conference was held in the case, that Stevens & Brent fabricated its principal factual defense to the class action suit brought against it in late 2004. That defense being, of course, that it warned hundreds of thousands of customers, via letters, of the .2 mg increase of tar and .5 mg increase of nicotine administered to its products beginning September 12, 2000 - and that, therefore, they did not breach their duty of fair and honest advertising; hence weren't negligent in the manufacture or sale of their cigarettes; and, ergo, are not liable for damages to those whose deaths their products vastly accelerated, or simply made unbearably slow and painful, or both.

This rumor was absolutely true. No letters - not a single one - of the type described were ever mailed by Stevens & Brent at any time. Approximately 750 phone calls were indeed placed to potential customers, but due to the cost of the automated service used and the sheer infeasibility of the project itself, the effort was abandoned shortly thereafter (on the heels of an equally ill-conceived attempt to reduce expenses by hiring several dozen people to place live calls). But, I repeat, <u>not a single letter was ever mailed to a single customer.</u>

In March of '05, shortly after the class was certified, Robert Thorne, Vice President of Stevens & Brent, approached Fred McDiarmand about the possibility of "hyping" the company's efforts to personally apprise at least the bulk of their customers of the tar/nicotine bump. Mr. McDiarmand was initially reluctant to cooperate, for fear that the scheme inevitably would be exposed, but shortly found himself persuaded. At first he agreed only to maintain that a few thousand letters had been mailed (and of course whip up a convincing sample). Then it was 10,000. Then 25,000. Eventually he simply caved to S&B's insistence that the campaign be represented as a rousing success, i.e., as having reached fully 83.5% of its market base, or roughly 525,000 regular customers. The ruse was irrevocably effected when, around the third week of April 2005, S&B presented its bald-faced lie to the press. And for almost a year afterwards, nobody doubted the story - at least not publicly.

Then, sometime around the

end of January or beginning of February of '06, a disgruntled partner originally assigned to the case got drunk and spilled his guts to an associate (or so the legend goes, anyway). The man's name was Leonard Freemont. He was ferreted out by an uncompromising investigation - spearheaded, naturally, by Mr. McDiarmand himself - followed by a series of equally ruthless interrogations of the chief suspects thus identified, whereupon he was summarily fired. The firm's sole but apparently sufficient guarantee of his future silence was a threat to have him disbarred for failing to report what he'd known for more than nine months. Coupled, of course, with a sizable severance package.

As you will see, Mr. McDiarmand himself, in the enclosed memo, teeters precariously on the brink of conceding that the rumor was true, before promptly denying all allegations of improper conduct by the firm and demanding blind allegiance from his servants. This was not a careless oversight or naive expression of trust on his part. On the contrary, it was a shrewdly calculated attempt, I am sure, to make all those who read it (and failed to immediately report its underlying sentiment to the proper officials) automatically complicit in the misconduct. In any event, whether by design or mere good fortune, Mr. McDiarmand accomplished his goal of preventing a leak to anyone outside the firm and keeping the illegal scheme under wraps.

Obviously, it is highly unlikely that, if you took the case to trial, the memo would be admissible as evidence against S&B. In addition to the obvious hearsay problems, S&B's lawyers would undoubtedly invoke the attorney work-product doctrine. And, of course, any attempt to call Freemont as a witness, even if he agreed, would inevitably be met with an objection that his testimony violated the attorney-client privilege, despite his no longer representing the company. Arguably, because the illegal activity at issue here would fall within the crime-fraud exception to the A-C privilege, a decent case could be made for letting the document in. However, that still leaves the hearsay and WPD issues, and I do not offhand see any way around <u>them</u>. This is unfortunate, because a public exposure of both the firm's and its client's corrupt dealings would, to my mind, effect a most poetic justice, and doubtless go a long way toward destroying both entities' financial viability. It is hard to imagine how either could ever recover from so visible and dramatic a shaming. Alas, perhaps such emotionally satisfying denouements are possible only in John Grisham novels.

Not all is hopeless, however. Several options remain. The first is simply to use the memo as leverage in negotiating a favorable settlement for your clients. The mere threat of media exposure would likely net you at least half the expected damages. On the other hand, there's always the option of actually *going* to the press. That would virtually guarantee a total breakdown in settlement negotiations, of course, followed by a protracted change of venue and potentially endless search for impartial jurors. On the upside, both S&B and the firm would get exactly what they deserve, and in all likelihood they'd eventually cave and give you most anything you asked for, anyway. Perhaps there are alternatives I haven't thought of, and I leave it to you and your co-counsel to determine which of them is most promising.

No doubt you're wondering what prompted me to write this letter and surrender the memo. Am I the mythical corporate lawyer who, late in his career, suffers a crisis of conscience (or, more hopefully, enjoys an epiphany), renounces the Dark Side, embraces the Light, and forever thereafter lives a life of Purity and Goodness? The answer is both yes and no. Yes, I was a corporate lawyer for a long time, and yes, I've since given up the trade. But I was motivated by far more than just moral qualms; I wanted out as much for selfish reasons as for utopian ones. I was tired of the grind, tired of seeing the same (mostly unhappy) faces every day, tired of being a slave to the clock and the calendar. I was a well-paid cog, but a cog nonetheless.

And then, quite suddenly, I came to want a life wholly my own, in which destructive and dishonest aims would play no part. I wanted to wake up each day without the aid of an alarm clock, fully rested, and without the vague remorse of a chronic if mild emotional hangover; and I wanted, upon waking, to face something other than the dull horror of yet another day at the paper mill.

I call it that because, in a sense ("from a cosmic perspective," one might say), all the firm accomplished on a daily basis - indeed, all any firm has ever accomplished on such a basis - was to produce and assemble vast numbers of what were, for the most part, individually meaningless documents. When combined, of course, those documents often became lethal. At a bare minimum, they furthered ethically dubious causes and afforded tangible relief to no one particularly worthy of it.

All of which is to say, quite simply: I had had enough. But as for the life of Purity and Goodness, that remains to be seen. I've only been at it for a very short time, and this is my first clearly virtuous act since calling it quits. I would like to believe that I am doing it solely because it is virtuous, but I know that, once again, my motives are rather muddled. The inherent virtue of the act appeals to me plenty, but what appeals to me even more is the vastly lighter conscience I hope to procure from it. Fortunately, I have decided that why people do the right thing, if it matters at all, matters far less than that they do the right thing.

In closing, sir, I have but one request, and that is that you forever keep the source of the memo strictly confidential. I have no desire to take the credit for whatever comes of it, nor any wish that my earthly legacy be that of the corrupt-lawyer-turned-unexpected-savior. Far more importantly, I do not want my family subjected to the onslaught of media attention that would inevitably ensue such a revelation. Please respect this wish at all costs.

My former colleagues will of course suspect my

involvement. I would suggest you allay their suspicions by telling them that an anonymous S&B exec with a serious axe to grind leaked the memo to you. They may well buy such a tale. I know for a fact that Fred McDiarmand forwarded a copy of it to Thorne, and let's face it: nobody likes to think they're credulous or careless enough to have been duped twice by enemies masquerading as allies.

Finally, Mr. Baldwin, I owe both you and your clients a profound apology. Throughout the entire course of the S&B litigation, I was a smug, bullying, uncooperative prick. Never was this more evident, perhaps, than on the day of Mrs. Dellong's deposition. I behaved as inhumanely as a dog-catcher who uses a club instead of a collar, projected my every ugly feeling onto her and rendered her in my mind a caricature, the greedy plaint-iff with at best a semi-legitimate grievance, in order to feel okay about it. If she has since passed, as I suspect she has, please extend my condolences to her family. If she has not, then please extend my sincerest apologies to her.

Warmest Regards,
Dennis Arbaugh

Writing came easily, he discovered, when you knew exactly what you wanted to say.

He would mail the letter and the memo first thing the next morning, but for now he simply added the last page to the small stack and laid it beside the typewriter. Then he stood, very deliberately, and went to the plastic shopping bag he'd dropped on the bed on his way in. He reached inside it and removed the pack of Winstons.

Moving now with an unmistakable aplomb, he carried the cigarettes out to the deck and walked all the way to the rail.

He broke the seal on the pack, tore out the foil sleeve, tapped the pack against his palm, and drew a cigarette from the middle, as he had always done. He fixed it between his lips, savoring the familiarity of the butt, which time seemed not to have eroded at all; he recognized the feel of it as he recognized his own face.

He dipped his hand into the right pocket of jeans. There was a pack of matches from the antique store in there. He brought it out and lit one of the matches, pinching the head between the cover and the strike-pad. He relished the brief flash of fire, the crackle of the flame as it flared to life and the soft hiss as it contracted.

He touched the flame to the end of the cigarette, drew in deeply, coughed out most of the smoke immediately, and released the rest as slowly as he could. His eyes watered and his mind purred with an old comfort he had sorely missed. He inhaled more shallowly on the second drag, coughing less this time. On the third drag he did not cough at all. He smoked the cigarette clear down to the filter, his head swimming agreeably all the while.

When he was finished, he placed the butt in an empty beer bottle, which he threw away in the trash bin in the upstairs bathroom. He washed his hands and face, brushed his teeth, combed his hair. His gait still possessed of an almost eerie assuredness, he descended the stairs, went out the front door, and walked to the pond, the pack of cigarettes pressing gently against his thigh.

At the bank of the pond, he took the cigarettes from his pocket, squatted, opened the lid, and squeezed the pack at its middle to create as big an opening as he could. Then he scooped a handful of pebbles into it, pressed the lid down firmly, and stood up.

*Here's to you, Martha*, he thought, and tossed the pack of cigarettes into the center of the pond. It bobbed, floated for just a moment, then capsized and quickly sank.

He turned, putting the mid-afternoon sun behind him, and walked back to the house.

# PART IV:

# t r e a t m e n t

# (round 3)

## 26

He read several more books that summer, most of them classics. He checked them out of the public library in Odell by the half-dozen. Many of them were books he had seen Rachael read throughout their marriage. At some point he even read *Jude the Obscure*, finding it difficult in some parts - for all the opaque jargon of the law, ingesting reams of it daily did little to facilitate one's comprehension of prose, in fact likely hindered it, and he was startled more than once by his inefficiency as a reader of old novels - and riveting in others. In a few places he found the characters and the action rather uncomfortably familiar, identifying with Jude's loneliness and futile search for happiness in stability. He pitied the hapless hero, resented Arabella's promiscuity and Sue's ultimate cowardice, deplored the moral intolerance of their society and the cruel fates in which it trapped them. It was by far his favorite of all the books he read that summer.

On Tuesdays and Thursdays he ate lunch at Cindy's, often chatting (but never quite flirting) with Nicola, the pretty waitress from England, until she left for Denver the third week of June. After that he occasionally made polite conversation with Cindy, the restaurant's owner, but kept his interactions with the waitstaff to a minimum, concerned he might come to be seen as an old lecher. The other days of the week he took all his meals at the house, preparing them with groceries he bought mostly at Cal's Cantina.

One Friday night he drove to Hood River and played Bingo in the basement of a Catholic church, winning the last game and taking home a prize of two hundred and sixteen dollars. Buoyed by his good luck, he stopped at a Radio Shack and purchased a 19" color TV. Even with rabbit ears two feet high, most of the stations were pure snow, but he turned it on for *The NewsHour with Jim Lehrer*, David Letterman, and, on those rare occasions he was awake in time to catch the tail-end of it, *Good Morning America*. After a while he barely even noticed the static anymore.

Toward the end of June he invested in a radio so he could get drunk and listen to Mariner games (one of his favorite recreations in college, when he had been unable to afford a television for his dorm room). He spent most of his time, however, simply lying in the patio recliner on the deck, watching the birds and reading his books. He had never found a more relaxing or enjoyable pastime.

A few days after he'd mailed the letter and memo to

James Baldwin, he realized he'd been subconsciously monitoring the washing machine and the house generally for any signs of a supernatural presence. None had appeared. He'd scolded himself for being silly, reminded himself of the powers of self-suggestion, consigned his early suspicions to the waste bin of his mind all over again. But he had kept half an eye open all the same, looking for anything that might vindicate his initial credulity. Nothing ever had, and in time he came to accept that he was completely alone at Memory Cove.

At first the solitude bothered him a little, but eventually he grew comfortable with it, and then rather grateful for it. Eventually he nearly forgot what it was like to live alongside other human beings, to compete with them constantly for space, attention, and favor. He wondered that he should have done it for so long in the first place.

One night in early July, Jim Lehrer announced on his program that Stevens & Brent had settled the class-action lawsuit against it for three-and-a-half billion dollars. Neither defense counsel nor plaintiffs' counsel had released a statement explaining how, exactly, they had reached the figure. However, James Baldwin, chief counsel for the plaintiffs, *had* issued a brief statement to the effect that his clients were extremely pleased with the settlement and were glad to have the litigation behind them.

Interestingly, he noted that Martha Dellong, the woman from Denny Creek who had initiated the suit, had passed away shortly before the settlement had been reached. "I visited her in the hospital the day before she died," Baldwin had informed the press, "and told her that the helpful assistance of a Good Samaritan had saved the day, and that her family would never again struggle to make ends meet. I think she heard me and understood. I think I saw her smile a little." Baldwin had declined to identify the Good Samaritan in question.

Dennis cried when he heard the news, but not like he had on the day he'd seen the deer in the garden. He would never cry like that again.

As he had known it would, his health deteriorated steadily over time. By mid-July he weighed all of a hundred and forty-two pounds, despite standing just over six feet tall. His ribs had begun to protrude. His face had grown pallid and drawn. In mirrors his body looked wispy, wraithlike, frightfully insubstantial, as if he were barely there at all. His cough worsened, the phlegm he expelled containing more and more blood. He suffered dizzy spells, slept for inordinately long stretches, ate less and less. Worst of all, his headaches had gradually evolved into a breed akin to migraines, sometimes disabling him for entire days during which he'd pop two or three Excedrin, shut himself in a dark room, and drape a damp washcloth across his forehead. The relief this afforded him was minor, but it was the best he could manage without getting a prescription from a doctor, the very thought of which made him shudder.

By the end of July he was too embarrassed to be seen in public for extended periods, and soon quit eating at Cindy's altogether. One day Sam Jeffords knocked on his door, probably just to pay him a friendly visit, and he hid in the kitchen, pretending not to be home. Soon the only trips he made were to Cal's for groceries, and he always made sure to wear baggy clothes so as not to draw attention to himself. The proprietor, at least, never asked any awkward questions or cast any nosy glances in his direction (not, anyway, so as to be caught). Dennis was enormously grateful for this.

One day, after shopping there, he noticed a headline on a newspaper in a box outside the store. It said: "Bands Gearing Up for Local Charity Gig Next Month." He popped a quarter in the slot and took a copy from the rack, drove home with it on the front seat, stole periodic glances at the headline. He remembered reading back in May, shortly before his move, about some music festival to be held in Corvallis over the summer. He couldn't recall any details, except that the event was supposed to benefit cancer research. He'd been grimly amused by that, he remembered, although the memory seemed impossibly ancient now.

When he got home he carried his groceries inside, put them away, and then sat down at the table with the newspaper. He read the article he had bought it for, and then a few others, but his mind kept drifting back to the concert.

He should go, he decided. As a last hurrah for himself. A final farewell to his own existence. One last blowout before the grim reaper carried him off to the Great Beyond.

He could get a ticket just by calling a one-eight-hundred number, the paper said. The event was nearly sold out, though, so he would have to hurry.

*Call. Do it. Why the hell not? What else are you going to do, sit here and rot?*

He glanced at the counter. There was a stack of books sitting on it that he hadn't even cracked open. He thought of the television in the bedroom, the jacuzzi in the back deck that he'd used only once. He thought of the deck and the pond, and the forest behind the house. These things were all he had now. By his own choice, he was utterly alone. He had spoken to Rachael but twice in eight weeks. During the last call she had threatened to divorce him if he didn't come home soon. He believed her. She'd still refused to accept that he was dying, despite his description of his physical condition. She said he probably just wasn't eating well because he'd never learned to feed himself properly. Denial, he supposed, ran deep. She'd also told him that, not long before the settlement was announced in the Stevens & Brent case, Fred McDiarmand had called to tell her that he was fired and would be physically barred from the building if he attempted to come back. He had laughed. She thought him mad, and he supposed she wasn't entirely wrong.

He went to a drawer, got a pencil and a pad of paper, and wrote down the number in the newspaper. Then he tore off the sheet, folded it into quarters, and stuck it in his back pocket.

He grabbed his keys and drove his bug back to Cal's.

## 27

*There is a storm brewing outside, not like the one in*

*New Hampshire, not quite as ferocious, but neither one to be sneezed at, even by Seattle standards. It seems fitting, somehow. Appropriate for the occasion. It is an awful occasion, as dark and turbulent and unhappy as the clouds gathering over the coast, and his stomach is in knots. His stomach is doing somersaults. He has been chewing on Tums for twenty minutes, to no avail. He wonders if it would have been as hard to tell Rachael, had she not come across the bra in the suitcase. (What, in that case, might have compelled him to tell her he isn't sure; he has begun to wonder whether he still possesses anything which might pass for a conscience.) No, certainly not. Surely, telling your son that you were unfaithful to his own mother is as agonizing as confessions come, as the betrayal of such an innocent seems somehow infinitely worse.*

*But isn't Rachael an innocent herself? What has she done to merit his infidelity - or, for that matter, any of the various cruelties to which he routinely subjects her? How does she deserve to be so frequently ignored in conversation, or rebuffed in bed? To be regarded increasingly as but an insignificant pest, a mere nuisance to be scolded or, where easier, simply appeased? To be made the object of petty ridicule, skewered for his own childish and bitter amusement?*

*Nothing and nohow, of course. He understands this intellectually. So why can't he translate it into action? Why does the understanding itself get him precisely nowhere? He must blame her subconsciously, at least a little bit, for what he has done, for driving him away. Only, she has done* nothing *to drive him away, and he knows it. On the contrary, she has tried at every turn to draw him closer, perhaps sensing the distance growing between them (and the danger that such distance can pose).*

*Deep in his revery, he scarcely notices when Sean walks into the room and sits down on the bed beside him.*

*"Dad?"*

*He jerks a bit, refocuses, turns to his son. "Sean," he says, and places a cool, damp hand on his son's cheek. His skin is ruddy and warm to the touch. The boy himself, just turned sixteen, is tall, broad-shouldered, noticeably fit; he has been playing soccer for nearly four years now, and has recently begun to lift weights daily in the garage, no doubt to impress his newly acquired girlfriend. In his face, especially his eyes and nose, he favors his mother, growing handsomer by the day. Dennis is afraid that Sean may withdraw from his hand - they have spoken to each other less and less in recent months, and*

*Dennis, as a result, has found it nearly impossible to show the boy physical affection of any kind - but he does not. He allows the gesture with no outward reluctance. "Mom said you wanted to talk to me."*

*Dennis nods. "Yes, son, I do."*

*"Why in here?" Sean asks, briefly surveying his parents' bedroom.*

*Dennis shrugs. It is a question he was not expecting. "Because your mother's in the kitchen," he says. Somehow the answer seems to make perfect sense, at least to him.*

*"Oh." Sean blinks, shifts a bit on the bed. "Okay. So what's up?"*

*"Well -"*

*"Is this about how much you and Mom have been fighting lately?"*

*This question, too, catches Dennis off guard. He ponders it for a moment. "I'm sorry you've had to hear all that, son. That... bickering."*

*Sean's face grows incredulous. "Bickering? Dad, she threw a shoe at you. One of her high-heeled ones. It almost broke the patio door."*

*"Yes, well. Grown-ups do that sometimes, Sean."*

*"None of my friends' parents do that."*

*Dennis feels himself growing irritated; this is not how things were supposed to go. Things are deviating from The Plan, and The Plan was a good one.* Script, you mean, *mutters a voice in his head.* The script you wrote right here in your mind, the one full of sappy, bullshit sentiments like you serve up to juries, and frothy appeals for forgiveness like you've been using all your life, never meaning a word of them, never changing a thing. Is that The Plan you mean, Dennis?

*"Maybe not, son," he says, maintaining an even tone. "Or maybe your friends just don't see them do it, or don't tell you about it. In any event, I apologize for what you've had to witness. Sincerely."*

*Sean nods. "Fine. Is that it? Can I go now?"*

*"No, son."*

*"Why? What more do you want to say?"*

*Dennis runs his tongue over his lips, wishing for water. He clears his throat, being mindful to navigate this terrain with supreme care. He recalculates, recalibrates, gently fine-tuning the words racing through his brain. "The fights you mentioned," he says slowly. "Do you know what they've been about?"*

*"No."*

*"No idea at all?"*

*"Dad?"*

*"Yes, son?"*

*"Are we playing Twenty Questions?"*

*Dennis chuckles despite himself, mostly, he supposes, on account of his nerves. "No, son. We're not."*

*"Then what is it that you want to tell me? Just say."*

*"Well, son, I'm afraid it's a rather difficult thing to say."*

*Now Sean shrugs, as if imitating his father. "The longer you take to say it, the harder it'll be."*

*"True enough." Now his throat is a veritable desert, and a lump has formed in it the size of a camel's toe.*

*Sean looks at him, more with exasperation than anticipation.*

*When at last Dennis finally utters the words, they sound to his ears as if he were speaking them in a dream: "A few months ago I met a woman."*

*His son, youthful cheeks full of color, gorgeous brown eyes full of life, simply goes on looking at him, his face awash in disbelief.*

*"I met another woman, Sean. A woman I work with.*

*Well, who works for me. I suppose I shouldn't really say I* met *her, because I already knew her. I just... you know, began seeing her. Romantically."*

*Sean blinks again, and now the rage begins to surface in his eyes. His lips start to quiver almost imperceptibly. He clenches his jaw. "Fucking her, you mean?"*

*Dennis now recoils a bit himself. An overwhelming urge to smack the boy, to heave the back of his hand across his face, seizes and then promptly leaves him, replaced only by an all-consuming remorse. Whether it is for the violent urge or the terrible deed which has brought him and his son together here, in the bedroom he has shared with Rachael for some thirteen years, does not occur to him. It simply is, and owns him completely.*

*"Son," he rasps, barely able to find his voice. "Please don't talk like that."*

*"Why not?" Sean's voice is trembling, as are the hands he's fumbling in his lap, as if searching for something to grasp onto, something solid that will support him. "That's what you did, isn't it? Fucked her?"*

*"Sean!" It is more a growl than a discernible word.*

*"How many times?"*

*"None of your -"*

*"It is* too *my business, dammit! She's my mother! You're my father! How many times, Dad? Two? Three? Ten?"*

*Dennis lowers his head in shame, speaks in little more than a whisper. "I don't remember."*

*"That many times, huh?"*

*"Sean. Please."*

*He shakes his head, his disbelief now transforming into disgust. Thunder rumbles crossly overhead, and the first real burst of rain sprays against the window. "Over and over," he says quietly, almost absently. Then his voice gains strength. "You betrayed Mom, over and over again, with some lady who runs your work errands for you. Is that what you're telling me, Dad?"*

*"She doesn't.." He looks up now, tears streaming from his eyes. He hates himself anew. He hates Rachael, too, for making him do this, for putting him through this awful thing, on pain of divorce. He wishes he already* were *divorced from her, and off somewhere, drunk and alone with his thoughts, or in bed with Kristina, and the peace of mind of knowing he won't be forced to make inane chit-chat afterwards, to discuss some boring fucking book or Sean's latest report card. He despises*

*himself for thinking these things, supposes he deserves something like death as punishment for them, recognizes them for the wildly crass and selfish thoughts that they are; yet he cannot wholly deny them, cannot quite banish them entirely, is forced to feel them writhe and struggle deep inside himself, slimy, vile, loathsome creatures thrashing stupidly upon the floor of a great morass. His stomach seems to turn inside out, and he wants to howl. "She doesn't run errands for me, Sean. She's a paralegal. That means -"*

*"I know what it means."*

*"Okay."*

*"I don't give a damn what it means."*

*"I understand."*

*"And I don't ever want to talk to you or look at you ever again."*

*Dennis begins to sob. His heart has never weighed so heavily in his chest. "Oh... son."*

*He reaches out again, but this time Sean* does *withdraw from his hand. This time he shrinks from his father's touch as if Dennis's fingers were aflame. And he is crying, too, though trying hard to conceal his tears. He has turned his face away, is furiously working his jaw. He wants to run one of the sleeves of his hooded sweatshirt across his eyes, Dennis can sense it, but either he hasn't the strength to raise an arm or else is unaware that he* is *crying. Or, perhaps, is simply too ashamed to acknowledge it. His voice wavers slightly when he speaks. "I can't believe you'd do something like this, Dad."*

*"Me either, son. I don't know what else to say. I'm ashamed of myself, completely and thoroughly ashamed."*

*"You should be."*

*"Well, I am."*

*"How long has Mom known?"*

*"Couple of weeks now."*

*"Why doesn't she just divorce you? You deserve it."*

*He shakes his head, very slowly. Thunder rumbles again. The rain is picking up fast. He gives no thought to what he says next, for it is that rare and precious jewel which requires none: the plain, unpainted truth. "I don't know, son. Maybe she will." He pauses, collects himself. "Look at me, Sean."*

*"I can't."*

*He fights back the tears welling up in his eyes all over again. "Please, Sean."*

*"Just say whatever it is you want to say, Dad."*

*He tightens his grip on his knees, closes his eyes. A terrible headache is beginning at his temples. "Is that what you'd want to have happen, son? For your mother and me to get a divorce?"*

*There is a long silence, throughout which Dennis keeps his eyes shut. Somehow the darkness comforts him. And then: "I want Mom to do whatever she wants to do."*

*Dennis feels a sigh of relief emerging from deep within his breast. But then, before it can quite escape his lips, Sean adds, "But I don't think I could ever really respect her if she decided to stay with you. And I'll never be able to respect* you *again, no matter what she does."*

*Now he looks at his father, directly in the eye, tears glistening on his cheeks rather beautifully in the weak glow of the bedside lamp. What he says next he does not say in a spiteful or even an indignant tone, but rather as if he were amazed at the statement himself, astonished by the reach and depth of its import. "Dad, I don't know if I'll even be able to* love *you anymore."*

*At this Dennis weeps violently, his whole body collapsing on itself. Inwardly he pleads with Sean to put his arms around him, to take back what he said and tell him that his forgiveness might be slow coming but will come eventually, will come someday, someday when things are better and his father has proven himself worthy of it, has won back his mother's love and trust and begun to act like a real father again. Eventually, someday.*

*But Sean says nothing, nothing at all, and when Dennis finally turns to look at him he is gone, the spot on the bed where he'd sat as empty as any such promise of forgiveness too likely would have been.*

## 29

He had closed his eyes for a moment, playing out the scene in his mind, seeing it as clearly as if it were projected onto an actual screen, transported by the images and the feelings they conjured up back to the very moment in time when it had taken place. When he opened his eyes, there was a deer in the center of the road.

He jammed the Bug's brake to the mat with both feet but could not halt the car in time. It fish-tailed immediately, wildly, the passenger side slamming into the animal at a ferocious speed. The impact was devastating, crushing the door inward by almost a full foot and shattering the window into a thousand shards. These exploded onto the passenger seat, the dashboard, and Dennis's lap, glinting marvelously in the sunlight. The wing mirror snapped off briskly, fell under the car, and was flattened by one of the wheels. Dennis caught only the briefest glimpse of the antler that smashed through the glass before it was torn loose from the creature's skull and catapulted into the woods.

After several sweeping, hectic oscillations the Bug finally came to rest about fifty feet from the point of impact, its tires spewing dirt and dust in giant clouds that completely enveloped the car. As Dennis sat bent over the wheel, panting furiously while his heart hammered in his ears, the dust slowly settled on the hood and windshield. With a shaky hand he flipped the wipers on, sprayed some fluid, and watched them cut away swaths of dust until eventually he could see the outside world again. This was good, because in his rattled state he had begun to feel the first twinges of claustrophobic panic, struck by the terrible idea that his car had somehow been rendered a metallic, dust-encased tomb.

*But now there are angel wings,* he thought dazedly, disjointedly, gawking through the clear spaces in the muck. *I made transparent angel wings and now I can see.*

He fumbled with the door-handle for a moment, his hand still trembling a little, craving fresh air as if he really *were* suffocating. The door swung outward and sunlight flooded in. He took a deep breath, savored the influx of a cool breeze. He got out, his legs a bit unsteady at first, and grasped the top of the door for support until they firmed up.

He turned and looked over his shoulder, bracing himself for a grotesque sight. Instead he saw only the deep grooves in the dirt that the Bug's tires had made as it had careened back and forth, rubber no longer spinning upon but rather digging into the earth. Puzzled, he walked the short distance back to the point of impact, searching the road in vain for the fallen deer. It occurred to him, finally, that a collision so severe was certain to have propelled the animal quite a ways. He walked then over to the ditch at the side of the road and looked into it.

There the unlucky beast lay, just as horribly mangled as he had feared it would be. One of its back legs was bent at a hideous angle, the portion below the knee jutting up toward its sunken belly. Its left eye had popped out, lost somewhere in the thicket that crowded the ditch, doomed now, like the carcass itself, either to slowly decompose or to be ravaged by whatever critters might come upon it. A large patch of its fur had been stripped from its body, most likely by the wing mirror. One of its hooves appeared to be missing entirely. Where its right antler had been there was now but a gaping hole in its skull, the defunct matter within peering out blindly at him. The animal had been torn asunder, its tattered remains scattered throughout this lonely, forgotten ditch and the woods beyond. Somehow worst of all, flies had already begun to collect around it, hovering over and crawling upon the deer's flesh with their stupid and sickening buzz. Dennis couldn't stand the thought of such profanity.

He walked back to the Bug, dolefully noting the damage but too intent on the task at hand to care much about it, and took the blanket he had placed on the backseat to protect the upholstery. He carried it back to the ditch, knelt before the deer (the swarm of flies was thicker now and his stomach did a somersault he scarcely noticed), and began to spread the blanket over the animal's body.

Then he noticed something: the deer's tail was white. He rose a little on his haunches, releasing a small breath of surprise. He cocked his head to one side and studied the creature's face for a moment (or what was left of it). The notion that one could recognize a wild animal he had seen only once, and not terribly recently, was patently absurd. Nevertheless, Dennis was somehow certain, absolutely *positive*, that this was the same deer he had seen through the bay window in his kitchen nook some two months before. He just knew it, as infallibly and immediately as he knew his birthplace.

He leaned in closer, now wholly oblivious of the gore and the flies and the encroaching stench, and lightly ran his finger along the animal's slender snout. Though the creature was surely lifeless, its chest as still as the rest of it, at least this extremity continued to radiate a terrific warmth.

"Hey," he whispered. "Sorry, guy."

He pulled back, tears on his cheeks, and waved the flies away. Then he covered the deer with the blanket and stood up. He gathered some rocks and twigs from the ditch and placed them on top of the blanket, then shoveled as much dirt as he could with his hands over the rocks and twigs. Scavengers would still get to the meat underneath eventually, he supposed, but at least this crude grave would hold them off for a while. And hopefully keep some of the damned flies away.

He climbed out of the ditch and dusted himself off. Casting his gaze upward for a moment, he saw nothing but endless blue. Clouds, he had discovered, were often unwelcome in northern Oregon's summer skies.

"Sorry," he repeated, stealing one last look at the shape beneath the blanket, and went back to his car. Incredibly, it started on the first try.

## 30

The concert grounds were vast, consisting of perhaps four square miles of open field near the campus of Oregon State University. The grass, cut to less than an inch, was a lush, sprawling carpet upon which some eighty-four thousand souls sat, lay, and strolled, most drinking beer and smoking cigarettes. A few, largely the college-aged long-hairs clad in their tie-dyed Grateful Dead tees and ripped jeans, smoked a more potent substance.

Dennis initially found the throng stifling and unwelcome, but eventually settled into it, blending rather smoothly despite his age and gaunt appearance. Nobody, at least, paid him much mind, and the few people with whom he spoke were exceedingly affable. One of them, passing him on the mulch-covered path which led from the parking lot to the grounds themselves, even gave him a high-five and happily blatted, "Hey, bro! You feelin' good?" It was a form of greeting

Dennis found strangely flattering. He replied that he was feeling very good indeed and thanked the gentleman for asking.

For the three hours since he'd arrived, he had been asking himself over and over what he was doing here, what he really hoped to accomplish. Certainly he liked the bands slated to appear (particularly Tom Petty), and that, he supposed, should be reason enough. But that was not why he had actually come, he realized now; he had come, rather, to do something as corny and rare and essential to salvation as find himself, or continue finding himself. He had come to make further peace with his past, pour more soil onto the grave in which he'd buried it, and inveigle his demons into a deeper rest.

One last blowout before the grim reaper came calling, was how he'd originally characterized it in his own mind. And sure, superficially it was exactly that. But under the surface it was something far more, he knew, or ought to be... and *had* to be, if he was to justify the expense of so much time and energy when both had become for him such precious commodities. The nagging question remained, however: how in blazing Hades was he going to do anything so lofty and profound as Find Himself while in the midst of a hundred thousand stoners, vagabonds, frat boys, and hippies (some of them aging as rapidly as himself, by the looks of it)?

He hadn't a clue. But he would try. And for the moment, he decided, he would put such awkward metaphysical questions aside and simply enjoy himself.

The Eagles were up first, opening the show with a decidedly lively rendition of "Tequila Sunrise." Dennis, almost within spitting range of the stage, marveled at the sight of Glenn Frey. He looked quite good for a man of nearly sixty, but juxtaposed against the backdrop of Dennis's memory of him from television and the Eagles concert he'd gone to in college, this latter-day version of the star might have been a million-year-old fossil. When Frey turned the mic over to Don Henley to belt out "Desperado," Dennis saw that the same was true of him. And of Joe Walsh and Timmy Schmit, as well. The whole band, he realized quite suddenly, was a living, breathing anachronism: they no more belonged on the stage here tonight than a sword belonged at the side of a modern-day soldier.

Dennis had never felt older or more awkward in his life. A wave of terrible, pungent sadness struck him hard, squarely in his gut. Yet he kept dancing, nonetheless. He kept dancing and singing along with the band and the rest of the crowd, because the weather was fine and the moment felt right and he would never have the chance again. He kept dancing because he knew that tears would get him nowhere, and nostalgia, however cruel, was never better starved than fed..

Then came the Stones. It was dusk now, and the air had turned cool. Dennis liked that; it felt good on his face, reminded him of springtime in childhood, of baseball and pretty girls in short skirts and the vague excitement of youth. Mick Jagger, never one to be outdone, found himself in rare form, blasting out "Start Me Up" as if for the first time, his scratchy, unpolished, electrifying voice saturating the darkening sky like a bucket of intensely vivid paint. Keith Richards, the walking relic, was doddering on his feet but rock-steady on guitar, tearing up "Midnight Rambler" with flawless precision.

Dennis sang, cheered, grooved with the music, his breast spilling over with feelings miraculously reawakened, his mind brimming with fond memories he had feared forever lost. He was a kid again, and could embrace again all the stupid, lovely sentiments age had slowly extinguished, revel again in all the intellectual and emotional frailties he had been conditioned, over time, to abandon or conceal. He could be heedless and reckless and unaccountable to everyone, even himself, just for a short while. And he was. And it healed his heart, repaired his spirit, rebuilt his soul - all those magnificent, intangible feats contemporary society decried as frivolous, empty, banal, the stuff of silly self-help books written for middle-aged housewives in despair.

Maybe it was a testament to the incredible power of music. Maybe it was just being around so many young, idealistic people, as yet uncorrupted by the world they sought so bravely and foolishly to change, gathered for a purpose so laudable and benign, in a charming place so much warmer and brighter than that he'd inhabited for too long. Or maybe he really had accomplished the task he'd set out to and had Found Himself, at least for the moment, at least until another dawn broke and the world once again challenged the equanimity he'd grasped. But, whatever the reason - and this was all that mattered to him now, all that he cared to mind - when he went to sleep that night, in a sleeping bag in a small tent he'd erected with his own hands at the edge of the concert grounds, his last thoughts were good ones, having nothing to do with cancer or death or his own moral turpitude. When he went to sleep he liked the person he was, just then, at that moment, in that place.

The feeling was quite new to him, and he could not help but wonder how often others felt it, too.

He awoke not long after sunrise, hazily aware that he was soaked with sweat. The temperature in the tent must have been well over ninety degrees. His eyes were gummy and scratchy, his throat sore, his mind still bleary with sleep. He clumsily unzipped the sleeping bag, threw back the top half, and sat up, wiping perspiration from his brow. He needed water, and fast.

Falling to his hands and knees, he unzipped the door-flap at the front of the tent, crawled out, and stood up, looked around. The concert grounds were lifeless and still, a desolate landscape littered with thousands of nylon tents. He could have almost supposed them the bizarre geological formations of some queer, alien planet, the beer bottles and candy wrappers and cigarette butts the unsightly wreckage of its defunct civilization. And yet, despite the rubbish, in the dim morning light the scene was actually quite tranquil. Dennis savored it, knowing how short-lived it would be.

There were water faucets placed at roughly equal distances around the grounds, perhaps ten of them in all. Dennis now set out for the nearest of them, yawning and smacking his lips, his stomach growling as his appetite awakened with a fury (he had eaten almost nothing the day before). It was hot this morning, but compared to the stuffiness of the tent the open air was a most welcome relief. He breathed deeply of it, the music from the evening prior now flooding his head. He smiled.

When he got to the faucet he stuck his whole head underneath it, cranked it on, and guzzled the ice-cold water that issued forth. His thirst finally quenched, he wheeled the faucet in the other direction and righted himself.

His mind had just turned back to breakfast (and how he might get it) when, a short distance away, he saw his son strolling toward a port-a-potty, himself yawning and stretching, shoulders slightly stooped in the way Dennis had always walked, head down.

Though he had not seen him in almost seven years, he recognized him immediately; his mind doubted but his eyes did not. It was Sean, no question. He walked into the port-a-potty and closed the door behind him. Dennis watched, utterly transfixed, all of his thoughts at once replaced by a void of total, paralyzing shock.

Completely unaware of his own movements, he managed somehow to unglue his feet from the grass where he stood and started toward the port-a-potty, his eyes unblinking, his jaw agape.

*That's my son*, he thought. It was the first coherent, conscious thought to penetrate his mind in well over a minute. The numbness began now slowly to wear off. His heart, seemingly frozen till now, slammed against his chest with an abrupt, violent jolt. The blood was returning to his brain in a great, dizzying rush. *That's my son who just went into that port-a-potty.*

All of a sudden he, too, felt nature's call - and, numb with shock as he was, nearly answered it unwittingly.

*My son just went into that port-a-potty. My son Sean. He's in there now. He's in the port-a-potty. Right now. My son. My son Sean.*

And then the door opened. He stepped out, gave Dennis a friendly nod as one would give a stranger in passing, and walked right by him. Dennis simply stood where he was, facing the port-a-potty, frozen in place.

Then he felt a hand fall on his shoulder. He turned around, very slowly, and saw sudden, total recognition in Sean's eyes. For a moment they simply looked at each other in disbelief, as if seeing a ghost. And in a way, Dennis supposed, for Sean that was almost true.

"Dad?" he said. His voice was a whisper, the word dying almost instantly in the vast open air.

Dennis collapsed in his arms.

## 31

They found some shade under one of the few trees on the grounds and sat in it, facing each other, legs crossed in front of them Indian-style. They did not speak at first, had barely spoken on the way over here; Dennis, in fact, still felt on the verge of fainting. His stomach kept growling, the heat bore down on him, and he could not shake the conviction that the young man seated before him was in fact a mere hallucination, induced, perhaps, by the ravages of his cancer. Yet momentarily this supposed hallucination spoke, and spoke clearly, in a way that drcam-figures did not.

"Dad," his son asked him, "what in the hell are you doing here?"

"I don't know," he replied.

"You look so *thin*," his son said.

"Yes," he replied.

"I spoke to Mom."

"Oh?"

"She said you've gone crazy."

Swooning again, he replied, "Well, you know your mother... always exaggerating."

He told Sean that he felt woozy and needed some food. So his son helped him to his feet and led the way to his tent, where he said he had some yogurt bars and other things he could snack on, just to tide him over until the concession stands opened and began serving "real food." Dennis, despite his hunger and shock, managed a weak laugh at the notion that funnel cakes and corn dogs should constitute substantial fare. Such, he supposed, was standard folklore among twenty-somethings. And how old *was* Sean now? He found himself confronted with a most distressing mental block, such basic and familiar knowledge wholly blotted out.

Then it dawned on him in a flash: *Twenty-five. Of course. He turned twenty-five last month. He's four weeks after me. Or is it five? Maybe it's five. Something like that. But he's definitely twenty-five because I... I remember the storm, the storm that came out of nowhere, at our cottage, on the night that Rachael found the bra, the red bra... I remember the wind, and* Jude the Obscure*... don't wake Sean, I told her. I don't want to wake our boy.*

"Dad?" Sean's voice, jerking him out of his reverie. "Are you all right?"

He looked at his son, a grown man now, handsome and clear-eyed and exquisitely fit, full of the life Dennis had long ago surrendered. "Yes," he said. His voice was small and croaky, his forehead slick with sweat. "I'm all right."

"Still dizzy?"

"A bit."

"We're almost there now. Just another fifty yards or so."

"Okay. I'll be fine."

The other concert-goers were beginning to stir and emerge from their nylon abodes. They passed several grungy, hungover-looking hippie sorts in dusty khaki shorts and muddy t-shirts with sweat stains in the armpits, nonc of thcm making eye contact with either Dennis or Sean.

"Mom told me you think you're sick," Sean said quietly. "Like sick-sick."

"I am."

"With what?"

"Cancer."

Sean looked at him. "Dad."

"It's true, son."

They came now to his tent, and Sean told him to wait a moment while he went inside and retrieved the snacks. He emerged a moment later with a handful of yogurt bars and trail mix. Dennis thanked him and gobbled down two of the bars in about thirty seconds.

"Want another?" Sean asked him.

"No, thanks," Dennis said. Already he could feel strength returning to his meager body. "I'm fine for now."

"Let's sit."

They sat, Indian-style again, in front of Sean's tent. There was a little blue charcoal grill on the dirt before them, the bowl filled with burnt coals and ashes. The smell was still strong. More faintly, underneath it, was that of the hotdogs and hamburgers which had been cooked on it the night before.

"You're here with friends?" Dennis asked.

"Yes," Sean said, seeming to hesitate a little. "Two of the guys I work with in L.A."

"L.A.? That's where you're living now? I thought you

were in Santa Barbara."

"Not since I graduated in May, Dad. I just got my MPA from UCSB, remember?"

Dennis nodded vigorously. "Yes, yes, of course. I remember your mother telling me that not long before I... before I left. I was so proud of you, Sean."

His son simply nodded.

"And now you're working where? For some non-profit organization, right?"

"Yes, a citizen action group. It's called 'GLACAH': 'Greater Los Angeles Citizens for Affordable Housing.' We do advocacy work on behalf of the homeless. Lots of joint projects with HUD and Volunteers of America."

"How wonderful," Dennis said. He meant it. "Such noble, benevolent work."

"Yeah, I love it. Couldn't be happier."

"I'm so glad to hear that, Sean."

"Thanks." He nodded, appeared to mull something over. "Dad?"

"Yes?"

"I'm also here with my fiancée." He pointed to the tent. "She's still asleep."

Dennis reeled. “You’re... getting married?”

“Yes. The wedding’s tentatively scheduled for October.”

*I won’t make it that long*, Dennis thought.

“Dad?”

“Does your mom know about this?”

“No, I haven’t told her yet. This only happened last week. I proposed to her at Venice Beach. To my fiancée, I mean. The concert’s sort of an engagement gift.”

“She’s met her, though, right? Your mother has?”

“Twice, yes.”

“So then it’s the same girl you’ve been seeing since last fall?”

“Yes.”

“Wow. Okay. What’s her name again? Susan, isn’t it?”

“Sarah.” He smiled. “She’s so beautiful, Dad.”

“Sarah?”

“Yeah.”

“Wow.” A tear spilled down his cheek. The irony was almost too much to bear. And his joy, and his sorrow. “I’m so happy for you, son.”

“Thanks, Dad.”

He threw his arms around his boy and sobbed on his

shoulder. "So, so happy."

The morning wore on. Sean told him all about Sarah and how brilliant she was, how they'd met at a UCSB campus fundraiser for some progressive group or another and hit it off immediately. How they'd dated for nine months before Sean had finally popped the question. And then all about his work for GLACAH, and Sarah's job at Legal Aid. She was a lawyer, Sean joked, but not to worry: she was one of the good ones. Dennis had laughed, taking no umbrage at the remark.

He kept waiting for the conversation to turn back to him, and what on earth he was doing at such an event by himself, and his illness and alleged madness and abrupt retreat into the wilderness. He kept waiting for the conversation to turn sour, for Sean to renounce all he had done lately, scold him for abandoning his mother, and shun him all over again. He kept waiting for the axe to fall, to be alone again, unpitied and unloved. It never happened. The closest Sean came to doing any of that was when he asked how long it had been since Dennis had last seen Rachael and whether they planned to divorce. Dennis had answered the questions as honestly as he could, saying he did not intend to seek a divorce but couldn't speak for

Sean's mother.

"She said you haven't seen a doctor and just decided on your own that you're dying," Sean said. His face suggested he was as doubtful about the matter as his mother was.

"I saw a doctor," Dennis replied. "Two months ago. He told me all I needed to know."

"Which was what?"

"That I wasn't coughing up blood and getting terrible headaches and constipation from bronchitis or pneumonia or the flu. He scheduled a biopsy. He knew I had cancer, Sean. He just didn't want to say so until he was a hundred percent sure. But I didn't need any further confirmation. I was a hundred percent sure already."

"But *how*, Dad? That's irrational. You're not a fucking psychic, pardon my French."

Dennis chuckled. "Son, look at me. I may not be psychic, but I *am* a goddam skeleton. I've lost nearly seventy pounds in the last eight months, thirty in the last eight weeks alone. And it's sure as hell not from dieting."

"Yes," Sean said. "I saw. I just didn't want to say anything."

"You didn't have to. I saw it in your eyes. You knew

right then I was dying. You just didn't want to believe it. Neither did I."

"So you *have* been eating?"

"As much as I've wanted to and been able to."

"Well, would you at least *consider* going to a doctor, if I went with you?"

"What's the point?"

"Dad, come on. Be reasonable here."

"I *am* being reasonable."

"No, you're not. A reasonable person who sincerely believed himself to be dying of cancer would seek confirmation from a medical professional before calling the undertaker. Isn't that what the law is all about? What a reasonably prudent person would do?"

"Supposedly," Dennis said.

"And wouldn't a reasonably prudent person in your shoes do just what I've said he would?"

"I suppose."

Sean nodded, as if to say, *All right, then, what are we arguing about here?*

"Son," Dennis said, "I'd rather not discuss it further, if it's all the same to you."

Sean shrugged. "Whatever, Dad."

"I'd like to meet your fiancée, though."

"You want me to wake her?"

He shook his head. "No, let her sleep. She'll be awake soon enough. Can we maybe get some lunch, though? I'm still hungry."

"Sure."

"Somewhere off the grounds, I mean."

"Yeah, no problem."

"Shall I drive?"

"I don't mind."

They stood. "Hey, Dad, listen," Sean began.

Dennis looked at him, wanting to cry again. "You don't need to say it, son."

"I wanted to call you," he said.

"Really, son, it isn't necessary. I deserved what you did to me. I don't even deserve to be here with you now."

"I wanted to reconcile," he said.

"Sean."

"I never hated you, Dad."

Now Dennis *did* begin to cry. This time, for the first time all day, it was Sean who put his arms around his father.

"I'm not going anywhere," he said. "Don't you worry."

Dennis's knees gave out. A wild sob, almost a howl, escaped his lips. He collapsed again against his son, who this time not only caught him but embraced him, in the way that one does not out of duty but out of sincere and heartfelt love.

## 32

They took breakfast at a diner called Café Corvallis (bypassing a burger-and-wings joint, slightly closer, which went by the rather unfortunate moniker The Flying Pig), about three miles from the concert grounds. Dennis had a western omelet, of which he ate roughly one-third, and Sean a huge plate of buttermilk pancakes with bacon and eggs on the side, of which he consumed the entirety in about half the time it took Dennis to choke down the first few bites of his omelet.

Sean watched him carefully as he ate, no doubt observing what a struggle it was for him. And the more closely he watched, the more intensely he scrutinized the affair, the harder Dennis found it to chew, and to swallow. Especially to swallow. His mouth always seemed terribly dry anymore.

"I'm worried about you, Dad," Sean said, raising a napkin to wipe his mouth.

"Son."

"I know how absurd that must sound, what with our having been apart for so long."

"No, it doesn't sound absurd. I never -"

"You must think I couldn't give a damn whether you live or die, but I do. I *do* care. I always have, Dad. Not a day's gone by that I haven't though about you, and there's been dozens of days I nearly asked Mom to put you on the phone. God knows *she's* tried before... to get me to talk to you, I mean. And I wanted to, I really did. But the more time that passed, the harder it became, you know what I mean?"

"Sure, Sean. Sure I do." He poked his omelet with his fork, watched it crumble around the prongs, broke off a small chunk of it and pushed it to the side of his plate. He thought if he tried to eat even one more bite, he'd throw up everything he'd managed to get down. Instead, he drank thirstily from his glass of water.

"And I was furious with you, Dad. For what you did to Mom and me. I still am. I won't lie about it."

"Really, Sean, we don't have to talk about this."

"But I want to."

Dennis nodded. "Then let's. Let's."

The waitress came by and asked if there was anything else they'd be needing. They both shook their heads and thanked her.

"So polite," Dennis said, savoring the sight of his son, astonished anew. "So well-mannered you are, Sean. And well-spoken!"

"Must've gotten it from Mom, huh?" he said with a wink.

Dennis laughed, then coughed, slumping over the table a bit. "Must... must have, yes."

"Are you all right?" There was alarm in Sean's voice, heartrending and acute.

"Yes," Dennis said. He summoned a smile. "Of course I am."

"Are you going to finish your omelet?"

Dennis glanced down at it, forgotten and quickly cooling. "I don't think I can."

"Are you full?"

He nodded again, a sudden fatigue stealing over him. "Yes."

"Wanna get back to the concert?"

"What I want," Dennis said, "is to meet your fiancée."

Sean called for their check. "Done," he said, "and done."

"What does *that* mean?"

He laughed. "It means that won't be a problem."

"Ah." Dennis fidgeted in his chair. "So do you still want to talk about... you know?"

"Nah," Sean said, casting his eyes downward. "Not right now. Maybe later."

The waitress brought their check, which Sean paid over his father's noisy protest. There was faint thunder as they left the restaurant, and the rain started up not long after. By the time they made it back to the concert grounds it was torrential, an almighty summer downpour of the sort children relish. They relished it, too, racing each other back to Sean's tent for as long as Dennis could keep pace, which was no more than thirty or forty yards.

Then they simply walked, side by side, Dennis occasionally turning his face up into the rain because he loved the way it felt on his skin, against his eyelids, the startling coldness of each drop, washing away again and again all awareness of his plight, teeming with all the manifold mysteries of life.

*  *  *

Sean's Sarah was even more beautiful than Dennis's, and Dennis's, by all accounts, had been one truly comely creature. She stood about five-foot-six, with a shapely figure that drew attention to itself without boasting of its own appeal. Her hair was flaxen and long, tumbling freely over her shoulders and down her back in fairy-tale ringlets of gold, her bangs as straight as a schoolgirl's. Fair-skinned, narrow-shouldered, her eyes chips of ice buried in a round, glowing face, she was a woman no man could miss even in a crowded room. Had he seen her thirty years earlier, Dennis might have fallen instantly in love with her himself. As he soon discovered, she was also graced with, in fact radiated, a rare natural magnetism, a soothing and almost maternal warmth to which men and women alike no doubt helplessly gravitated. His son had done well.

She came out of the tent about a minute after Sean had gone into it, plainly nervous. She greeted Dennis with a timorous, dainty handshake. "It's a pleasure to meet you, sir."

"And you," he said, enfolding her small, soft hand within his own. "But please, call me Dennis."

"How about 'Mr. Arbaugh'?" she asked with a bashful

smile.

"Really," he said, "'Dennis' will be fine."

"Sean's told me a lot about you."

"Not too much, I hope."

"Only good things," she assured him.

"I doubt that, somehow, but I appreciate the gesture." He gave her the biggest, heartiest smile he could muster, to let her know it was all right, that he knew the score and the past was behind them and there was no cause for discomfort.

"Well," she said, still nervous nonetheless, "it's great to finally meet you."

"And you," he said. "You know, I only learned of your wedding plans not two hours ago."

She laughed. "Quite a surprise, huh?"

"The loveliest I could possibly imagine."

"Well."

Sean came out of the tent now, perhaps having wanted to give the two of them a minute alone. "How's it going out here?"

"Your father's charming me," she said, blushing.

"Well," Sean said, "I'd expect no less." He turned to his father, beaming proudly. "And what do *you* think of *her*, Dad?"

"Completely unacceptable," Dennis said. He flashed

Sarah a grin to reassure her that he was only joking.

"Rats." Sean made an *aw-shucks* gesture and laughed.

Dennis drew his hands up to his chest, held them there for a moment, and then gestured fondly at Sarah. There were tears in his eyes. "Honestly, though, son... I couldn't have dreamt up a finer woman, by the looks of her. And she seems every bit the angel she could pass for, the beauty that she is. I'm delighted for the both of you."

Sean's laughter dwindled, was replaced with an expression of pure and total gratitude. "Dad," he said, "you've no idea how much it means to me to hear you say that."

Dennis was all at once overcome by a powerful bout of dizziness, his legs giving out from under him and spilling him to the ground.

He spent that night, the final night of the concert, resting in his tent while Sean and Sarah watched the last three bands perform (Steve Miller, The Doobie Brothers, and Dave Matthews). They'd both objected, insisting that at least one of them stay back and keep an eye on him, but he'd eventually persuaded them that he'd be all right on his own. They'd promised to check in on him every so often, in shifts, lest anything should happen. They kept their word, Sean coming by first and Sarah second, between each of the sets. Sean found his father nodding off; Sarah found him fast asleep. He did not wake until early next morning, just before dawn.

He stepped out of his tent on unsteady legs. His stomach was painfully empty, gave a nasty growl full of primitive need. He wove his way through the assembly of tents, trying to follow the most direct line to the nearest water fountain. He smacked his lips, trying to work some saliva into his mouth. It was parched, arid, his lips themselves chapped and blistered, his throat raw. He winced when he swallowed. He felt rested but woozy. The dark was disorienting, the moonlight scant. Eventually he stumbled upon the fountain, a chrome job jutting up from a slab of cement and operated by way of an old-fashioned pedal. Dennis jammed it down with his foot, pressing it all the way to the cement, and lowered his mouth expectantly to the faucet. The water was spectacularly cold and thirst-quenching. He sighed inwardly with relief, almost orgasmic in its intensity: *Ahhhhhhh.*

He turned, raised his head, and regarded the pre-dawn sky, dim red-purple light finally creeping into the western horizon. It was a magnificent sight, an incipient sunrise blooming first delicate violet petals, then blazing orange leaves beneath a crown of sparkling white jewels, dazzling even as they faded into nothingness. Dennis observed it with rapt, giddy awe. He half-sat, half-melted into the ground, wide-eyed and jaw gaping. He was staring, he knew, into the face of the only God there was or had ever been, the only deity anyone might ever need. All truth and knowledge, all solutions and answers, all the mercy and benevolence and righteousness and salvation one could ever seek lay spread before his eyes like some heavenly banquet. He feasted upon it, and forgot all about his physical hunger. He submerged himself in it, and, with his eyes closed, prayed silently that it might cleanse his insides and kill the thing that ailed him, heal the foul and corrupted tissue that sought to steal his breath.

"For Sean," he whispered. "Please, do it for Sean. And his new wife... his new wife-to-be." He hesitated, squeezed his eyes shut tighter. "And for Rachael."

He opened his eyes then, and simply sat there, on the grass moist with dew, completely still, legs splayed before him, hands folded in his lap. The grounds were his alone; no soul stirred but him. And, save for the occasional distant birdsong, perfect silence prevailed.

Once the sun had fully risen he went back to his tent and, though hardly tired, fell fast asleep.

## 33

*She reaches for him and he tells her again that he's married, not to deter her but so that he won't be accused later of deceit.*

*"For how long?" the woman asks him.*

*"Many years," he says. "Twenty-five."*

*"That's a long time."*

*"Yes, it is."*

*There is a pause, a pause he expected, and he knows what question is coming next: "Do you love her?"*

*He hesitates, not because he is unsure of the answer - of course he loves Rachael; she is the mother of his only child - but because he knows if he tells the truth she won't sleep with him. And that's what he means to do, right? That's why he brought her here, isn't it? Of course it is. A married man doesn't bring a woman (married or not) to a hotel room except to sleep with her.* So you're going to lie to her, *he thinks*, deny your love for your own wife, betray her in word as well as deed, for sex. For sex. For fucking *sex*. There is nothing lower; there is no one lower. This is what you've become, then. This is all you are: everything your father was, and everything you swore you'd never be. No better. Not one iota better. Just regular, run-of-the-mill human scum. There've been millions before just like you, and there'll be millions more. Won't there, Dennis?

*"Dennis?"*

*"I don't know," he says. "But I know I want to be here with you right now." He cringes and hopes she didn't notice.*

*"Do you mean that?"*

*"Absolutely."*

*"Good."*

*She reaches for him again, takes him in her hand, and he knows then that it's over, that he's crossed the line, there's no turning back, no redeeming himself. It's too late for that, and besides, the little willpower he had to begin with, the modicum of self-control, just evaporated in her hand. It's going to happen. It's inevitable. He's going to betray his wife all over again.*

*"Sarah," he says, closing his eyes, clenching his teeth. But he can only think the second word:* Stop. *He cannot bring himself to actually utter it.*

*"Dennis," she says, consumed with passion now, with*

*an animal lust to rival his own. "Oh, Dennis."*

*"Sarah."*

*"Shhhh," she says.*

*When he opens his eyes, he sees that the woman lying next to him on the bed is not Sarah Reynolds, the waitress from Kirkland who had once dreamt of owning her own restaurant, but Mary Ferguson, his high-school girlfriend. And they are not lying on a bed at all, but on a blanket in a field, under the stars, late at night, with the sound of crickets and cicadas and bullfrogs all around them. And he is not the pursuer but the pursued; and he knows no arousal, no excitement, adolescent or otherwise. He knows only embarrassment and guilt, a vague but powerful sense of shame, a horribly dirty feeling that he knows can't simply be washed off or scrubbed away. For it is deeper than that; it is all the way down inside him, in his very marrow, where water and soap can't reach.*

*This time he actually manages to say the word aloud: "Stop." But it is too soft to be heard, a mere useless whisper, and he knows in his heart he doesn't mean it, anyway.*

## 34

"Sarah? Is he all right?"

"He's fine," said a female voice. For a moment he thought it was Sarah, his lover. Then it occurred to him that it might be his mother, twenty years in the grave, back to rebuke him for the sins of his later life. "Just sleeping."

"You sure?"

"Yeah. His eyes are closed."

The door-flap was pulled open again, dousing him with another blast of bright, hot sunshine. He squinted against it, still half-caught in his dream. A gravelly, muffled groan escaped his lips.

"Dad?" Sean's voice. "Are you okay?"

He tried to say yes and simply groaned again.

"Dad?"

"Fine," he croaked.

"Did Sarah wake you up?"

"No."

"Sorry," Sean said, ignoring Dennis's answer. "She had to get some sunscreen out of her bag. It's gonna be a scorcher today."

"Uh huh."

"Do you want to go back to sleep?"

He sat up a little now, still dazed but gradually coming

around. “No,” he said.

“No? You want to get up?”

Dennis swallowed thickly and fixed his eyes on his son’s. “I want,” he said, “to go home.”

# PART V:

## cure

## 35

He awoke to find a bar of dusty sunlight cast across his chest, and remembered the concert, the tent. He could not have guessed the time within five hours. He knew it was August, almost September, that his name was Dennis Arbaugh and his son Sean was somewhere in the house, a lake house near Mt. Hood, but that was all. That, and that he was dying, now quickly, of a still-undiagnosed yet certain cancer.

He rolled laboriously onto his side, drew a long and difficult breath. He coughed. He had managed to get his eyes half-open, but now they sank closed again. His eyelids were terribly heavy things. His whole body ached, and he wished only for sleep to reclaim him. At least until Sean came with his soup, as he did most every afternoon.

*But* is *it afternoon? It might be morning. When did you fall asleep?*

He tried hard to remember but could not. He did not especially care, either. Between his pain and fatigue and rambling disquiet, he did not especially care about anything.

Except Sean.

He lay awake for a bit, losing himself in his thoughts.

Most of them were cloudy, like a jar of water to which sediment had been freshly added, like the turbid shores of the lake outside. And all of them were tinged with sorrow, an alga clinging to the glass: a swollen yearning, a glum nostalgia fueled not only by a fondness for things and people past, but also - even more so - the necessity of letting go even his memories of them, memories now faded almost completely into oblivion, reduced increasingly to flakes of rust. But, more than any nostalgia, simple sadness, and a profound, childlike rage at the prospect of losing Sean again, so soon after he'd found him - and of losing himself, newly rediscovered and so fleetingly reanimated.

Naturally this rage was rather dulled by his debility, but only outwardly. Inwardly it led a clear and powerful existence, affixed to his breast like frost to tundra. Had he had the strength, he would have bellowed night and day just to drown out the voice of that rage, to silence its own screams.

But he did *not* have the strength. He did *not* have the kind of energy necessary to do such things. Anymore, even on a good day, he barely had enough to speak.

He drifted a while longer before slumber returned.

*    *    *

When he awoke again, the light in the room had changed. It was a little dimmer now, and fell across his bed at a different, sharper angle. It felt like late afternoon, early evening. He lay in a puddle of sweat.

Sean sat on a chair beside his bed, his face pale and concerned. Such was his usual countenance these days, but today, Dennis thought, there was something different about it, something more to it. His pallor was a bit deeper, yes, but that wasn't all... the anxiety in his eyes was greater, too, more intense.

"Sean?" His voice was muffled by the phlegm in his throat, thick with the sleep that was still receding.

"Hey, Dad. How're you feeling?"

"I'm fine." He sat up a little, as much as he could. He saw that Sean was fiddling with his hands in his lap, a nervous habit Dennis remembered from his childhood. Steam rose from an orange ceramic bowl on the bedside table: his afternoon soup. "What's wrong, son?"

"Molly Jeffords came by the house a little while ago."

"Oh?"

Sean nodded, softened his voice. "She said... she said

her husband died a couple nights ago, of a heart attack."

At first Dennis simply looked at him, uncomprehending. He blinked, struggled to clear his mind and make sense of Sean's words. "Wait, who? Sam?"

"Yes, Dad," Sean said patiently. He knew that his father was having one of his bad days, and was beginning to regret even sharing this news. He should have waited, he decided. But it was too late now. "Sam Jeffords died. Two nights ago."

"Of what?"

"A heart attack."

"Sam's dead?"

"Yes. I'm sorry."

"Sam the landlord?"

"Yes, Dad."

"Jesus," Dennis muttered. "Seems like the popular thing to do these days."

"Dad!" Sean frowned, checked the anger in his voice. "What a terrible thing to say. You shouldn't say things like that."

"I'm sorry," Dennis said. "I shouldn't make light of it, I know."

"You're not *dying*, Dad. You're just sick. You need to

see a doctor."

Dennis lay back down, propping up the pillow under his head. "I liked Sam."

"Will you?"

"He was a good man. He was good to do what he did for me, giving me this house and all. He didn't have to do that"

"Dad."

Dennis fixed him with a stern, irritated glare. "No more talk of doctors, Sean. I've told you before, the issue isn't open for discussion."

"But you're being *unreasonable*."

"Good," Dennis said. "It's about time. I spent my whole life being reasonable, behaving safely and logically. The time has come, at last, for a little insanity."

Sean sat quietly for a moment with his head down, battling an assortment of uniformly unpleasant emotions. Then he lifted his head and handed the bowl to his father. "Do you want your soup?"

"What kind is it?"

"Chicken noodle."

"Ah," Dennis said, reaching for the bowl with unsteady hands. "My favorite."

*  *  *

"Sean!" he called from his bed. "Have you seen my book? My paperback?"

"Which book, Dad?" His voice echoed off the walls of the stairwell and drifted feebly into the bedroom.

"You know," Dennis called back, not nearly loudly enough, "the one I've been reading the last few days."

"I can't hear you, Dad! Hold on, I'll come up."

A moment later Sean appeared in the doorway. "Which book, Dad?"

"*Treasure Island.*"

A strangely skeptical look came over his face. "You're reading *Treasure Island*?"

"Yes. Have you seen it lying around?"

"No. Are you sure you're really reading it?"

"Don't talk to me like I'm some imbecile, son."

He sighed. "I'm not. I wasn't. It's just... you're known to make a mistake or two from time to time, is all."

"Well, I'm not making one *this* time." He looked around his bed, as if it might suddenly manifest there. "I just had it last night."

"Did you take it with you to the bathroom, maybe?"

He shook his head, shrugged his meager shoulders. "I don't know."

"Let me go look."

"Thanks, son."

Sean started out of the room, then Dennis called him back. "Yeah?"

Dennis just looked at him for a moment, overcome with an impossibly sudden and abysmal shame. "I'm sorry," he said. "For being so damned snippy. I really appreciate all you're doing for me, son."

Sean smiled. "Don't worry about it, Dad."

A minute later he returned with Dennis's battered, dog-eared copy of *Treasure Island*, on extended loan from the Hood River County Library. "I read this as a kid," he said, handing it to his father.

"So did I."

"So then why're you reading it again?"

"It's a classic," Dennis observed matter-of-factly, as if it were the most obvious truth in the world. "Plus," he added, a wisp of a smile creasing his lips, "I don't remember a damned thing about it."

"Neither do I," Sean said, and they both laughed.

*    *    *

A week passed, and then another. Dennis's condition seemed for a time to improve, his spirits to rebound. One day he even forewent his afternoon nap to watch a baseball game with Sean. For those few brief hours, he almost let himself believe that his prayer had been answered, the one he'd offered up to the heavens at the concert grounds, just before the break of that magnificent dawn.

But then he took a rather abrupt nosedive, finding himself bedridden for the next three days, scarcely half-lucid for even one of them. His headaches became intolerable; he was vomiting up more blood than ever; there was now always at least a trace of blood in his stool, and typically far more than a trace. Oftentimes the toilet paper was soaked through with that dark-red harbinger of doom.

On the last of these three days, he heard Sean calling for an ambulance on his cell phone. Dennis dragged himself out of bed, groaning at the pain this caused his joints, and stumbled downstairs. Sean heard him coming and ran for the bathroom. Dennis grabbed a vase off a shelf and chucked it over his head. It smashed against a wall and fell to the floor in big, misshapen shards that looked like shark's teeth. Clutching the recliner for support, woozy with fatigue and choler, he roared at Sean to hang up the phone, to quit meddling in his affairs, to mind his own business and let him alone, just let him alone to die. But Sean refused to hang up, giving the dispatcher the address for the house over Dennis's voluble protests. Dennis knew that an ambulance (and perhaps a patrol car) would arrive shortly, do-gooder paramedics and nosy police officers with medical kits and clipboards and all sorts of officious, cumbersome questions. He wanted no part of it, and so, once Sean had turned his attention back to the dispatcher, he slunk out of the house and into the woods.

He crested a hill and, completely out of breath, panting and sweating profusely, collapsed on all fours in a bed of pine needles and stones. His palms slid across slick patches of moss and he fell face-first onto the forest floor, gashing his left knee, displacing a few pine cones and a crumpled beer can (Labatt Blue, the paint was faded but he could still read it) as he went down. One of them stabbed him in the side and he let out a yowl dampened by the dirt and the rocks in which he now lay prostrated, his pajamas ripped and muddied, bones aching and skin bleeding. It occurred to him that he must look like the world's silliest UFO abductee, his captors having dumped him in the woods before taking off in their spaceship, laughing hysterically all the way back to Planet Polyp. He nearly laughed a little himself, then raised his head and saw it.

There, tucked away in the woods, like an oasis in the desert, was a tiny cottage, not entirely unlike the one he owned in New Hampshire. Only smaller, much smaller, and far older. And, by the looks of it, long abandoned.

*I'll find a little cabin tucked away in the mountains down there and hole up for a spell,* he heard himself telling Ben the Used Car Salesman. *Just enjoy the peace and quiet and maybe do a little writing.*

His jaw gaping, still wheezing a little, he hoisted himself to his hands and knees and began crawling toward the structure, part of him convinced that it was indeed a mirage.

It was then that he heard Sean calling for him from the back porch, followed shortly by the first distant wail of approaching sirens.

## 36

*Everything goes gray, color sucked from the world as if by some cosmic vacuum, and then black. And then, finally, there is a brilliant burst of white, exploding around him like a star. It is not light, exactly, at least not the ordinary kind familiar to denizens of the material world. It is something far brighter, far bigger, far richer and more enveloping, strangely akin to milk in its appearance and to honey in its texture. It warms him and enfolds him, sweeps him up in a great surging wave on whose crest he rides freely, heedlessly into a tremendous pool of stunning, vibrant colors, restored to the world tenfold. These colors presently coalesce into a series of images, unfolding around him as if on a panoramic screen.*

*He does not for a moment suppose himself dead, transported into some fantastic supernatural realm, a comic-book hereafter; he knows better. He knows he is alive, though not well. He knows that he is not seeing his life flash before his eyes at the instigation of some heavenly creator. He is not even altogether certain that he is seeing his life flash before his eyes. He does not seem, in fact, to be engaged in recollection at all. On the contrary, he feels as though, far from merely remembering them, he is instead actually* reliving *all the events portrayed to him, leaping from scene to scene apparently as he must, as is somehow prescribed.*

*He is a child in Cedar Falls, wandering around in the family barn, wanting to pet the horses but too scared to because his father forbade it, said they might turn vicious on him on account horses are temperamental like that. He doesn't know what "temperamental" means, not yet, but he knows he is afraid of his father and ought to mind him, that he shouldn't even be in the barn in the first place. There's a lot of ways for a little kid to get hurt in a barn, his dad said, dangerous tools and rusty nails and plenty of places to fall from, high-up beams and lofts and things like that. So stay out, his dad had told him. Just keep clear. One day, when Dennis is just twelve years old, his dad will catch him drinking a bottle of beer in that barn and whip him so hard with his belt that his ass will be red and raw for weeks afterwards. That will be his last visit to the barn.*

*And then he's a teenager in Puyallup, chasing the cheerleaders around the field after a football game, grinning as their skirts flap, trying unsuccessfully to score a hand job under the bleachers. What he scores instead is a slap across the face, a slap which leaves a mark rather reminiscent of the one his father put on his ass with a belt four years earlier. This one he doesn't mind so much, though, because at least it'll give him some fodder when he meets up with his buddies later on at the pizza joint or the drive-in. Tonight he'd prefer the drive-in, because there's a new Dennis Hopper out that he's been dying to see.* Easy Rider, *he thinks it's called. He's not worried about getting drafted and sent over to the jungle because everyone says the war will be well over by the time he turns eighteen, that Nixon has a plan to get us out. And besides, he's already made up his mind to go to college, mostly to piss off his dad, who thinks he should take over the family farm. But his dad, he's decided (with a certain rebellious glee), can go straight to hell.*

*And now he's three years old and sitting on his mother's lap. She's wearing a long, cotton house-dress with a polka-dot print, black dots on white fabric. He curls his chubby fingers around them, giggling as he tries to peel them off. His mother laughs too, stroking his hair as she bounces him up and down, up and down. The sensation is exhilarating, addictive, much like he'll find racing cars on back roads when he turns sixteen, and chasing girls around the football field, trying to make Mary Ferguson on that blanket out by the lake, trying to conquer the world with sheer bravado.*

*Similar, yes, but without the underlying guilt and fear, shame and uncertainty, those ugly emotions that always find a way to intrude somehow on an otherwise perfectly lovely experience, or simply lie dormant and wait, wait to defile a moment, a feeling, still finer. They are emotions which will dog him throughout his adult life, but he will never really confront them. And he will realize, toward the end, that hardly anybody does, because when you try to they usually win, and if they don't they aren't killed but only resurface later, and must be contended with all over again, pacified with some newer trick. They are perhaps invincible, at least for so long as they matter; and once they cease to matter so does everything else, and there is no time left to enjoy their absence. It is a conundrum, he will conclude, which admits of no solution, which for the human species is the ultimate challenge, the hardest test: holding onto happiness in the face of its imminent demise, and despite all the suffering that preceded it; silencing the doubts and the worries long enough to construct some meaningful repose, some substantial contentment.*

*He is a college student, and then a law student. He is with one girl, and then another. He meets Rachael, in the weird way that he does, on the day that he might well have died, had events occurred just slightly differently. He will forever be grateful that they didn't, and that he lived, because his first couple of years with her, while certainly not his most carefree, were undoubtedly the best of his life. Their love for each other;*

*their passion for their careers and the things they could do in the world, the good they could bring to it with their energy and intelligence, their youth and their drive; the birth of their son; the humble beginnings of their life together... no one in all the recorded history of the ages had been happier, and no one reasonably could have asked for a more charmed existence. It was his - fleetingly, yes, but it was his, and it could never be undone, and he will cherish his memory of it for as long as he can, right up till the end, when it, too, will fall prey to the indiscriminate appetite of his cancer, and be blotted out, erased, devoured.*

*He is sitting now on a beach, contemplating of all things life's fragility. It is unclear to him how old he is, or where he might be. He does not offhand remember. It might be Maine, or California. Judging by the landscape and the weather it is somewhere out east, and by his appearance, his clothes and his haircut and the lines in his face, he is perhaps twenty-nine or thirty. Sean has just been born, is a mere toddler, scampering about somewhere, probably getting in his mother's way. When he watches her watching him, sees the unbridled, the unsurpassable love for him in her eyes, truly a manner of love which only a mother can fully know, his heart wants to burst, so full does it become with his own love, his own simple and incomparable affection for the child. And then he wonders that he ever found her, ever made love to her as he did the night that he met her, in his bed, with thunder rolling away outside, retreating, receding, making room for them. He wonders that she fell in love with him, and bore his child,* their *child, whom they regard as a miracle because parents cannot help but so regard their children, and as beautiful, and as their greatest blessing. It does not matter that there are millions of children almost identical to him in size and shape and age and ability. It does not matter that he means nothing to nearly anyone but them. For he is theirs, they made him, he is the fruit of their love for each other, and simply by being he binds them ever closer.*

*He is with Kristina, the girl from work, and then Sarah. Neither is Rachael, his wife, yet he knows them both as if they were. He knows them carnally. He knows them as he shouldn't. In so doing he betrays not only Rachael but Sean, his entire family, himself. He lies down with them as the Bible instructs him not to, as every human code of ethics proscribes, as his own conscience warns against. He is with Kristina in a shopping mall, four days before Christmas, buying her clothes and jewelry, taking her to a movie, buying her dinner. He is with Sarah at her restaurant, and then in a motel. He is lying beside her, struggling to resist her, failing, falling short. He is with her on a plane to Maui, taking her along on a business trip when he could've taken Rachael instead. Mark knows. Fred McDiarmand knows. The whole firm knows, but says nothing. They are complicit, accomplices to the deceit. They are long past the point in life where such things trouble or offend them, too smugly defiant of their own deficiencies to find such things unseemly.*

*He is on the beach again, then holding Sean in his arms, soothing him to sleep as he paces back and forth in front of a window, in a room with gray berber carpet. It is the living room at their old house in Beacon Hill, the split-level with the oak fence in the front yard. He's just made partner at his law firm, the youngest associate ever to do so. They'll be moving soon, to a bigger place farther away from the city. Mercer Island, maybe, and why not? They'll have enough money now. They'll have all the money they could have ever hoped for. Rachael can't wait; she's always wanted a home with a view of the ocean. Dennis will happily provide it for her.*

*He's on the beach, contemplating of all things life's*

*fragility, and strangeness, the unexpected turns it takes that catapult people in entirely new directions, often without their realizing it. The delicacy and volatility and randomness of the thing, that's what he's thinking about, as he sits there on the sand, watching the tide come in. His first affair is still two or three years in the future, but he finds himself wondering how it happened, how he ever let himself be drawn into something so depraved, not once but twice. He is frowning severely, his lips turned so far downward they are nearly parallel with his chin (reminding him, jarringly, that none of this is real, because in real life such an expression would be impossible), as if trying to solve some difficult equation.*

*He realizes that ultimately there is no satisfactory answer to be had, that to blame anything other than his own weakness of will would be irresponsible and dishonest. But still, he suspects there is something more to it by way of explanation, some solution to the riddle that, while perhaps insufficient to exonerate him, might at least illuminate his motives and insure against such unfortunate lapses in the future.*

*Something breaks his concentration and he looks down. Without thinking about it, he reaches a hand out and scoops up some of the sand, studies it for a moment, and then lets it run through his fingers like the sand in an hourglass. Before it was day but now it is night, and the grains twinkle in the moonlight as they rush toward the cracks between his splayed fingers, spilling back to the earth with a soft whooshing sound.* Like finely cut diamonds sliding down velvet, *he thinks, and, while the thought makes no literal sense, it seems to capture the sound beautifully.*

*He smiles faintly. He looks up.*

*Standing before him, in the tide, his translucent legs vanishing into wet sand (*can ghosts have feet, and can they bury them?*), is Sam Jeffords. He is wearing the same outfit that he wore on the day Dennis met him: blue denim bib overalls over a plaid shirt, exactly as Dennis had pictured him over the phone. He remembers thinking the getup decidedly ill-suited for summertime weather, but charming nonetheless. And that the only thing he needed to complete the persona was a hayseed sticking out the corner of his mouth. But he didn't have one then, and he doesn't have one now.*

*His kind, mild eyes seem to glow. He steps closer, and smiles.*

*"Sam?" Dennis is surprised by the loudness of his voice, the crispness of it. It sounds as strong and healthy as*

*ever, impervious to the wind. "What are you doing here?"*

*Sam does not reply, only kneels before him, glances over his shoulder at the ocean.*

*"I was sorry to hear about... you know."*

*The old man turns back, and now his whole face seems aglow. His eyes have grown solemn but somehow retained their softness. His voice is every bit as tender and unthreatening: "It's so peaceful here," he says, "somebody could live in their memories forever."*

*Awestruck, Dennis leans, peers around him, and sees in the distance, bobbing on the waves, the tiny silhouette of a sailboat against a great white moon. It's the one, he knows, that he used to sail on with Sean, at the lake in New Hampshire.*

*"Go to your boy," Jeffords says, standing up. He brushes sand off his overalls. "And your wife."*

*"I don't have a wife."*

*"They need you."*

*"I have a son."*

*"And you need them."*

*"She left me."*

*"I wish I still had mine."*

*"I was a lawyer in Seattle."*

*"Molly's alone now."*

*"I've been alone my whole life."*

*"I don't know how she'll cope."*

*"I just found my boy."*

*"Go to them," Jeffords says again. "They need you."*

*"I was a lawyer and I lived only for myself."*

*"Every man has his cross."*

*"I gave up religion."*

*"They're waiting." He turns back to the ocean. Somehow Dennis knows he's crying. "Somebody's always waiting for somebody else, I guess."*

*"My life, our lives... they're so small."*

*"Son," Jeffords says - and now he's Dennis's father, the old man with silver hair who never laughed and never slept past five and drove a brick-red Chevrolet pick-up truck and whipped him with a belt so hard his skin broke apart - "the whole* universe *is small."*

## 37

As he got closer to it, he realized that the cottage was really more akin to a cabin, even a shack, bearing only the most superficial resemblance to his home in New Hampshire. As he reached the lilliputian front porch, in fact (on his feet now, but doddering more than walking), the sirens growing louder behind him, he began to think he really *had* been hallucinating a bit: the structure was fit to be condemned, and likely would be, were it situated closer to civilization.

The walls were constructed of flimsy pine logs of which termites apparently made a regular meal; some on the front of the dwelling sported craters the size of golf balls. The roof was a traditional slate job, narrow and steep (*like the one in the fairy tale,* Dennis thought rather wildly, *the gingerbread house that the witch lived in*), several of its shingles either hanging askew or missing completely. A tree branch lay near its apex, twisted and gnarled. Somebody a while back (around 900 B.C., by the looks of it) had gotten an idea to paint the thing white. Most of the paint had by now flaked away, exposing largely rotten wood underneath. That which remained was dirty and dull, left unaided to battle the elements. Moss clung to the bottommost logs, and in patches along the walls. It had been many years, Dennis concluded, since anything other than termites had lived here.

He was sure the door to the place would be locked, but it wasn't.

*  *  *

The inside, shockingly, appeared perfectly habitable, as if the family who owned the abode had simply vanished the day before. There was a wood furnace, a wood stove much like the one in Dennis's kitchen, a big green Coleman ice chest, a card table in the middle of the room (an electric lantern serving as its centerpiece), a couple of lawn chairs, a decrepit sofa against one of the walls, and a sink in the sliver of kitchenette, under the cabin's only window. (The pipes, of course, were exposed.) Finally, against another of the walls, across the room from the couch, was a fold-out canvas cot - slender, but just wide enough for an adult of average size. Oddly, it was unfolded and covered with a sheet, a blanket and pillow on top. The linen, moreover, looked to be spotlessly clean, maybe never before slept on.

*Sam did this,* Dennis thought. *He put it here for me, maybe even built the goddam* cabin *for me.*

A crazy idea, to be sure, but then, wasn't he dressed in pajamas and possibly on the lam, hiding out in here at least from paramedics if not the police? This was the proper juncture, then, for crazy ideas. And the sirens, indeed, drew closer all the while.

He went to the cot, bent down, and took a whiff of the

blanket with his nose about six inches above it. No mildew. No mustiness. No odors whatsoever. He did the same thing with the sheet and the pillowcase and got the same result. Mystified, he moved his nose closer, took another, longer whiff. Same thing again.

Tired as he was, he marveled at his good fortune. And, after briefly assessing his other options (sitting on the couch, which by comparison looked decidedly unappealing, or simply standing there), he decided he'd might as well exploit it. He lay down on the cot, without getting under the blanket, and hesitantly rested his head on the pillow. After a moment his hesitation dissipated, and he let his head sink deeper into the cushion. A moment later he instinctively wrapped himself in the blanket. The cot itself turned out to be surprisingly comfortable.

He closed his eyes, and within less than a minute he fell asleep, precisely as the sirens fell silent.

Sean woke him up, with a gentle shake of his shoulder. "Dad?"

He stirred slowly. "Son?"

"What on earth *is* this place?"

"Sean?"

"Yes, Dad, it's me." Sean took one of the lawn chairs and pulled it up to the cot. "Have you been in here this whole time?"

"Yes."

"I was worried sick about you. I thought maybe you'd died in the woods."

"No." Dennis rubbed his eyes, smiled pallidly at his son. "Nope, still kickin'."

"Did you know about this place before?"

"No."

Sean looked around, his face awash in bewilderment and concern, then returned his eyes to his father. "Are you okay?"

Dennis sat up a little, his mind clearing now, remembering where he was and what had been happening just before he fell asleep. "Are they out there?"

"Who?"

"The sirens," he said.

"Oh. No, they're gone now."

"You're sure?"

"Positive, Dad."

But Dennis was skeptical. He sat up fully and turned to peer out a window that wasn't there. "If you're lying to me,

Sean..."

"I'm not lying. I wouldn't lie to you."

"What did you tell them?"

"That you were sick and very upset, and must've left in your car."

"Didn't they see my Bug?"

"I told them it was mine."

Dennis yawned and smacked his lips. "I'm starving," he said.

"You want something to eat?"

"Yes. Bacon. Lots of bacon."

Sean laughed, as if surprised into it. In the little room the sound reverberated crisply, a bit eerily. "I think we can manage that."

Dennis looked at his boy, a strangely earnest gaze carved upon his features. "But I want to eat it in here."

Sean's own face grew baffled. "Dad, why?"

"I just want to. I like it out here."

"All right." He wasn't quite able to mask the worry in his voice, that worry that said, *Dad, I think you might finally be losing it for good.* Dennis had heard it several times over the past month or so. But he hadn't lost it yet, and hoped to stave off that eventuality awhile longer. He had a few things he wanted to discuss with his son first, a few things he wanted to iron out.

"You'll bring it to me, then?"

Sean nodded. "Yeah, sure. Just bacon, you say? No eggs or toast?"

"No," Dennis said. "Just bacon. A whole plateful of it." He'd been craving bacon since last night, the first food he'd actually desired in weeks. His appetite these days was virtually nonexistent.

"Got it. Something to drink?"

Dennis smiled feebly. "Remember that George Carlin joke about the unfortunately named airport restaurant?"

"Huh?"

"What was it called? Ah, that's right... The Terminal Snack Bar." He chortled, closing his eyes as he lay back down.

"What about it, Dad?"

He almost said it aloud: *I feel like I'm ordering from it.* Then he thought better of it, decided it wasn't worth the risk of upsetting his son. His son, who still refused to accept the fact of his father's imminent death... or pretended to, for Dennis's sake. "Never mind," he said. "A tall glass of milk would be nice."

"Coming right up." Dennis was reminded of the day he'd met Sarah at the restaurant where she worked, in Kirkland. As Sean rose from the chair he pushed the thought away, turned his mind back to the things he wanted to tell his son.

"Oh, and Dad?"

"Yeah?"

"Sarah's decided to fly in tonight. Is that okay?"

"Of course. You know I love her company."

"So do I," Sean said, and was gone.

He returned twenty minutes later, with a huge, heaping plate of bacon and a glass filled to the brim with ice-cold milk. *Manna from heaven,* Dennis thought, and indeed it was: he wolfed it down in about three minutes, polishing off the milk at two draughts. Sean was clearly encouraged to see his appetite so abundantly restored. Dennis, meanwhile, paid it little mind, well aware of the thing's fickle nature, that it would likely wane again tomorrow, its momentary resurgence a meaningless aberration.

"It's good to see you eating so well," Sean remarked, as if to confirm the quiet celebration in his eyes.

"I was hungry," Dennis agreed. "Ravenous."

"Maybe it's a sign you're turning the corner, on the

mend."

"Sure." Dennis nodded to show he really meant it. "Sure, maybe it is."

Sean was sitting in the lawn chair again. "I'm sorry I called for an ambulance. I was just worried about you."

"It's all right. I'm sorry I threw that vase at you."

Sean laughed. "I thought we might end up on *Cops*."

"Oh, Lord. One can hardly imagine a more embarrassing fate."

"I cleaned them up, by the way. The pieces."

"Thank you. I made sure to aim high, I swear."

Sean laughed again. "It's okay."

"I just wanted to get you off the phone."

"The paramedics were a little pissed."

Dennis burped and handed Sean his plate. "Excuse me. Were they?"

"Yeah, a little." He put the plate on the table. "Well, I mean, they drove all the way out here from Odell."

"Sure, that's understandable. But what could you do? I was gone." He made a lazy swooshing gesture in the air, gave a shrill little whistle through his teeth. "Outta there."

"That's what I told them."

"They didn't think it was a prank or something, did they? I don't want you to get in trouble."

"No," Sean said. "It's fine. They knew it was for real."

"I tell you, if they'd gotten their mitts on me, hauled me off to some hospital..." Dennis trailed off, affected a little shudder.

"Since when are you so phobic about doctors, Dad?"

"Since the last one told me without telling me that I was dying."

Sean looked incredulous. "Ravini?"

"Yeah."

"What did he say, exactly? You've never actually told me."

"I've never told you," Dennis said, "because, as I *have* told you, it doesn't matter."

"It matters to me."

"Well, it shouldn't."

Sean sighed. "I don't know why you feel the need to be so goddam *difficult* about all this, Dad. Do you think this is easy for me? Being here all the time, looking after you, suffering through your morbid monologues on your slowly approaching death? Because it isn't. It *isn't* easy. It's hard as hell, as a matter of fact, and I'd really appreciate it if for once you could actually try to *understand* that!"

"Sean -"

"No, Dad, listen to me!" He was turning red in the face now. "I've taken a month off work, which was *not* easy to do, to come here and care for you around the clock! I think the least you could do is not act so goddam... *blase* about the whole thing!"

"You're right," Dennis said. "I'm sorry."

"My ass you are."

"I am. Sincerely. But you mistake acceptance for indifference, son."

"Oh, please," Sean said, sneering, and waved his hand dismissively."Don't give me that wise-old-man, I'm-above-all-the-drama, let-me-help-you-achieve-enlightenment bullshit. I'm sick of it."

"It's not bullshit. And I never claimed to have... found enlightenment." He was growing short of breath. "Far from it. But I... I did accept a long time ago... that I've got limited time."

"We've *all* got limited time, Dad."

"Mine's particularly... limited."

Sean's face was still painted with the same sneer of contempt. "He says, on the basis of one fabricated diagnosis by a general practitioner."

"Jesus Christ," Dennis said. His tone was an odd blend of exasperation and disbelief, imploring assent (or at least acquiescence). He'd been propping himself up on one elbow and now let himself fall back down, onto the pillow. Sweat had broken out on his forehead. What little color he'd had in his cheeks to begin with now drained away. His palms were clammy.

"Dad?"

"How much more evidence do you need... than what you've seen with your own eyes?"

"Are you all right? You sound winded."

"I am."

"Then rest," Sean said. "I didn't mean to fight with you in the first place."

"I'm not tired. I just... need to catch my breath."

Sean shook his head, lowered it, as if disappointed in his child. "Why did you have to smoke for all those years, Dad?"

Dennis, despite his shriveled and burdened lungs, managed a chuckle. The sound was raspy and thin, the hiss of a snake, a *bona fide* death-rattle. "What, you didn't hear?"

"Hear what?" Sean asked.

"Nicotine, it turns out, is highly addictive."

The day waned, yielded to evening. They remained in the cabin, at Dennis's request. He had not found a place so tranquil, nor felt quite so at peace, since he had first toured the grounds of Memory Cove. He had not told Sean of its effect on him, that first exposure to the place, nor the strange events he had witnessed (or *thought* he'd witnessed) after moving in. The last thing he needed was for his son to think him nuttier than he already did.

"When does Sarah's flight land?" he asked.

"Any minute now. She ought to be here in a couple of hours."

"It's been awhile this time."

"A week," Sean said. "That's all. She works, Dad. And to tell you the truth..." He trailed off, averted his eyes. "Never mind."

Dennis sat up a little. "No, what? To tell me the truth, what?"

Sean sighed, looked at him again. "She's not entirely

comfortable with the... financial arrangement."

"What do you mean? With me paying for her flights and rental cars?"

"All of it," Sean said. "I mean, she's enormously grateful, we both are, but neither one of us was raised to accept charity like this. We're talking thousands of dollars here."

"I can afford it," Dennis replied. "You can't. And it's for my benefit as much as hers, anyhow. I want her here. I want you both here."

Sean's gaze suddenly hardened. "But not Mom?"

Dennis felt his pulse quicken. He clenched his jaw, relaxed it. "Son."

"I'm just saying."

"I know what you're saying. We've been through this. I don't want to take that journey again. Not right now."

"When, then?"

"Some other time."

Sean hesitated, as if debating whether to take the shot. He did: "But Dad, your time is limited. Remember?"

Dennis only looked at him, refusing to reveal how much the barb had stung.

"I'm sorry," Sean said.

“Never mind it. Let it go.”

“We really are grateful, Dad.”

“I can tell.”

Sean threw his hands up in frustration. “Jesus, Dad! I apologized, didn’t I?”

“Yes,” Dennis said. “You did. Now forget about it.”

Sean leaned in closer, as if about to relay confidential information. “She comes as often as she can, even if she *does* feel a little weird about taking your money. And I tell her you’re fine with it, she *knows* you’re fine with it. But you know how she is... things like this just aren’t easy for her. This is a highly unusual, difficult situation for anyone, and she’s doing her best. We’re both doing our best. But honestly, Dad, she comes as often as she can.”

“I know,” Dennis said. “I know she does.” He sipped from his cup of water, acquired from the cabin’s sink. He found it every bit as drinkable as the water from any tap in the house. “Believe me, I’m impressed by how often she *does* make it. I admire her dedication to you.”

Sean nodded. “We’re very much in love. I like to believe I’d do the same for her if the situation were reversed.”

“I’m sure you would. You’ve always been generous,

Sean, always. With your things, your time. Biggest heart in anyone I ever met."

He looked fondly at his boy, his own heart swelling with affection, and with that old, stubborn mourning. He had accepted the imminence of his own death, perhaps, but apparently not the separation from his son that it entailed, this one undoubtedly far longer than the last. Or his unresolved guilt over having mucked up things between them so badly. The latter, fortunately, he did not *have* to accept; the latter could be amended, at least, if not erased.

Sean smiled. "Feeling guilty about our little dustup earlier, by any chance?"

"No," Dennis said, with a playful obstinance. "Why should I? I was in the right, as usual."

Sean's smile widened. "No wonder Mom got so fed up with you." He saw the look on his father's face and his smile withered instantly. "I'm sorry. I didn't mean it like that."

"How did you mean it, then?"

"Just... you know, what Mom used to call it. 'Playing Lawyer at Home,' wasn't it? She used to say that in arguments you had an unfair occupational advantage." He laughed, and Dennis relaxed.

"I hope Sarah doesn't do the same to you."

"Oh, she does. Once in a while. I sometimes joke that the only thing worse than needing a lawyer must be living with one."

"Or being one," Dennis mused.

"Sarah likes being one."

"But she isn't," he said. "She's a humanitarian whose instrument of charity happens to be the law."

"Wow," Sean said. "Not bad. She ought to get that printed on her business cards."

Now Dennis smiled. "I want the credit if she does."

"Isn't your legacy secure enough already?"

"Sure," he scoffed. "But it's not one I want. It's not one *any* decent person would want."

"Why's that, Dad?"

"Who'd want to be remembered," he asked, "as a champion of the rich and powerful?"

"Is that how you saw yourself?"

"No," he said. "I saw myself as a lawyer, a working stiff like any other. Just one who happened to make a lot more money than most."

"But that's what you now consider yourself to have

been?"

He pondered the question for a moment, then nodded slowly. "I think I'd have to. All I did, really, was give a voice to those who already had one. Those who spoke with a bullhorn, in fact. How redundant!"

"I suppose."

"Those kind of people don't need any help, Sean, much less that of the caliber they can afford. They can do just fine on their own - better than fine, actually, with the breadth of monetary and political resources they command. They don't even need the *legal* assistance, really. They've gleaned enough knowledge of the law from their own frequent interactions with it, being the privileged breed that they are - business moguls and property owners and the like - to navigate the matrix of American legal rights and duties more competently than the av-av... average attorney."

He stammered, his thoughts becoming tangled and confused, his mind cloudy and all at once exceedingly tired. He had not meant to prattle on like this. But when he looked up at his son, he saw, not the expression of boredom or pity (*listen to the old man rant, you can almost hear his marbles rolling around in that dusty attic of his*) he'd completely expected, but one of genuine absorption, fascination even. Heartened by this, he marshaled his mental reserves and picked up where he'd left off: "In any... any event, my point is, the object of the law should not be to protect the wealthy and the well-entrenched. It should be to empower those... who have little or nothing in the first place. That's something Sarah has probably understood since her first day of law school, because that's... that's just the way she's built. Putting her own material comfort first likely never even occurred to her. But it took me... almost thirty years to figure it out."

"At least you *did* figure it out, though."

Dennis smiled, his face ashen but slowly regaining color. He drew in breath slowly, as deeply as he could, and let it out, then repeated the exercise twice more. "I'm glad," he said, "you met someone who didn't *need* to figure it out. That's the kind of person... you want... to spend the rest of your life with."

His son smiled back at him, with terrific warmth and gratitude. "That means a lot to me, Dad. It really does."

"It shouldn't," Dennis said. "But I'm glad it does." He gave a quiet laugh. "I'm glad to know my opinion still counts for *something*."

Sean scoffed. "Easy on the self-pity now, Pops." His

face grew serious again. "So when did you decide all this? Reach all these... startling conclusions?"

Dennis smiled. "I had a lot of time this summer," he said, "for introspection."

"And you never..." Sean struggled to find the right words. "You never had any qualms about what you did, while you were actually *doing* it?"

"Sure I had qualms," Dennis said. He'd turned his eyes up to the ceiling, and now turned them back to his son. "Especially early on. But I just did what most everyone else does who spends a good deal of time depriving others of what's rightfully theirs, or otherwise facilitating the gradual erosion of human decency: I ignored them. And eventually, after I'd ignored them long enough, they went away. I just woke up one morning and noticed they weren't there anymore. I couldn't even quite remember the last time I'd consciously acknowledged them. I was just grateful they were gone."

Sean's eyes narrowed dubiously. "Grateful? Why?"

Dennis laughed. "Well, because they were an enormous inconvenience, obviously."

"Oh." Sean pursed his lips, ruminating.

"See, the thing is, son..." Dennis paused, choosing his

words carefully. "The thing is, most people don't ignore their consciences because they're... because they're sociopaths, or morally corrupt. At least not at the outset. No... no, in the beginning, they ignore their consciences out of necessity, or what... what *seems* like necessity. If they let their principles get in the way, they ask themselves... if they... if they do *that*, how are they going to survive? Survival, alas, all too frequently seems to require... a total disregard for moral dictates."

"But it doesn't?"

Dennis shook his head, just once, back and forth. "No," he said. "Survival doesn't require it. Only surviving... as comfortably and as wastefully as we've grown accustomed to, and somehow now... feel entitled to."

Sean mused. "So if your qualms eventually just went away, what brought them back? What re-awoke them in you?"

Dennis said, "A most serendipitous convergence of two events. Well, two that I was consciously aware of. Subconsciously, there might have been a million things going on that helped spur it along. But it was quite sudden, definitely quite sudden. I can even pinpoint the exact time and place, give or take ten minutes."

"Really?"

He nodded. “Yes. May twenty-second, just after one o’ clock, in the men’s restroom of Prazzini’s Restaurante.”

Sean’s eyes widened comically. “You’re joking.”

“I’m not.”

“Prazzini’s downtown? On Puget?”

“Yes.”

“In the *bathroom*?”

“Yes.”

Sean shook his head, as if to deny comprehension. “What were the two events?”

“Huh?”

“You said there were two events that led to your... epiphany, I guess you could call it?”

“That’s as good a word as any, I suppose.”

Sean nodded, urging him to continue. “So what were they?”

“Well,” Dennis said, “one was what you earlier referred to as the ‘fabricated diagnosis’ of my cancer.”

Sean didn’t acknowledge the swipe. “And the other?”

Dennis hesitated, looked at him. “You’ve heard of Stevens & Brent, haven’t you?”

*   *   *

When dusk arrived, Sean suggested they move the party back to the house. "I don't know how well Sarah would like it out here," he said. "She's no princess, but she does enjoy her home comforts. Especially after a long trip."

"That's fine. I wouldn't mind getting back into my own bed, anyhow." He looked down at the cot. "This thing gets a tad uncomfortable after a while."

"I'm surprised it's comfortable at all. You're positive the sheets are clean? We don't need you getting sick from germs."

Dennis gave a small, rueful laugh. "I wouldn't worry too much about that, son. Nothin' they could do to me that ain't gonna happen already, know what I mean? But yes, somehow they're clean."

"Who could've put them there?"

"I don't know."

"Your landlord, maybe? Or his wife?"

"That's about the only thing I can figure out."

"Well, he owns the house," Sean said. "Only makes sense he'd own this place, too."

Dennis nodded, lifting himself from the cot. His back groaned amply in protest. "I wonder why he never mentioned it, though."

"Well, why would he, really? I don't think it comes with the house."

"Then why was the front door unlocked?"

"Because whoever was in here last," Sean said, "forgot to lock it on the way out."

"Or purposely neglected to do so."

Sean looked at him. "And why would somebody want to leave it unlocked, Dad? So the animals would have a place to keep dry during a rainstorm?"

Dennis shrugged. "Maybe so I'd have a place to hide when you called the authorities."

Sean laughed and shook his head. "The authorities? That's rich, Dad. Now gimme a break and get the hell up."

He got to his feet carefully, leery of taking a spill like the one he'd taken the week before, and followed his son back to the house, back to Memory Cove.

## 38

Sarah, forever thoughtful, brought a tuna casserole with her. She'd wrapped it in tinfoil, popped it into a translucent blue Ziploc bag, and slipped the little sucker into her carry-on. She wasn't sure if it was allowed, she said, but if it wasn't, security hadn't hassled her about it. Dennis was profoundly touched by the gesture, and thanked her profusely.

His sensitivity to small kindnesses, it seemed, had grown incredibly acute of late, a lifetime of stifled, pent-up gratitude finally spilling out. In truth, he realized, it had far more to do with her, the fact that *Sarah* had done it, than with the act itself; she could have brought him a fresh turd in a Tupperware bowl and his reaction would have scarcely differed. Time had only amplified his fondness for the girl, and he thought of her already as his daughter-in-law. Nonetheless, he politely declined when she offered him a wedge of the casserole. Still full from the bacon, he asked Sean to save it for him in the fridge, promising to eat it later. Sean dutifully obliged.

Now, sitting up in his bed, Dennis regarded her warmly, his whole face aglow. She made him feel almost healthy again, almost as alive as when he had first set out on his trek to the wilderness, some reasonable seclusion from the bustle of modern life. She sat on the same armless wooden chair that Sean normally sat on to feed him, or, more typically these last few weeks, simply to keep him company. Sean stood behind her, his hands gripping the back of the chair; whenever the two of them visited him in his bedroom Dennis always told him to bring in the rocker from the Sunrise Room, but Sean always told him he didn't mind standing, that it was good for his bones, and Dennis did not demur. Laziness, he sometimes thought, had been one of his own many downfalls, one which his son fortunately had not inherited

When Dennis spoke his voice was gruff but strong. "How are you, sweetheart?"

"I'm good," she said, beaming beatifically. Beatifically to Dennis, anyway. "How are you? You look well."

"It's you," he said. He was grinning himself. Pretty girls, of course, had been another of his downfalls. "You're magical."

"Please," she said. "I get enough flattery from Sean. I don't need more from you."

"He'd *better* appreciate you. Few men are so lucky."

"Most of the time he does," she said, smirking puckishly now.

"Hey!" Sean protested.

"I'm kidding," she said, craning her neck to see him. "Chill."

"The way kids talk," Dennis said. "I don't get it."

"'Simmer down,' old man," Sean offered.

"I'm simmered."

Sean laughed. "No, I was explaining what 'chill' means."

"I know what it means. I was kidding."

"Fuckin' with us, you mean?"

Dennis shot him a mock look of disapproval. "Watch your tongue, boy!"

Sarah giggled in her delightfully girlish way. Sean, meanwhile, flexed his arms and leaned over the chair. "Hey, I'm a grown-up now. I can talk however I want."

"Not in *my* house, you can't."

"You don't own it."

"Well, maybe I'll buy it."

"When?"

"Tomorrow."

"I'll believe it when I see it."

"Me too," Dennis said, and they all laughed. He looked back at Sarah, at her lovely pale blue eyes. "How's work, darlin'? You hangin' in there?"

"It's rough," she said. "At the moment."

"Why's that?"

"Funding cuts. We've had to turn down four worthy clients this week alone. The money just isn't there right now to hire all the attorneys we need to satisfy the demand. Plus, for the third year in a row, they've added all sorts of new restrictions on the types of cases we can handle."

"What kind of funding cuts?"

"Big ones," she said. "The state legislature just passed its budget for the new fiscal year, and Legal Aid's usual apportionment was cut in half."

"Why? Angry taxpayers?"

"'Higher priorities,' is the official line, I believe."

"Like what?"

She shrugged. "Schools and prisons? I don't know. The usual stuff, I guess. Public support for free legal services has been on the decline for decades now. There's no real awareness of the problems confronting the kinds of people we help, so there's not much sympathy for them among the folks in government."

"Or the collective heart," Dennis suggested, "has simply cooled."

She wrinkled her nose, considering. "You think?"

He nodded. "I do." After a moment's thought he added,

"Never overestimate the capacity of the masses to give a shit about anything that doesn't directly concern them."

"Seems a little cynical."

He chuckled. "Trust me, darling, I speak from personal experience."

"With people who don't give a shit about other people's problems, you mean?"

"No," he said, and looked at Sean. "As such a person myself."

Later that night, after they'd retired to their room (not the Sunrise Room but the other guest bedroom, what Dennis sometimes thought of as the "Sunset Room," although the view its windows afforded was largely obstructed by trees), he overheard Sean and Sarah arguing.

It did not *begin* as an argument, of course, but merely as a *discussion.* The difference between conversations and discussions, Dennis had discovered, was that conversations seldom led to arguments, whereas discussions almost invariably did. Sometimes, in fact, they *sped* toward arguments, leaving dust in their wake. He had seen it happen with bickering parties to legal disputes (usually, and nearly always fortunately for the firm, culminating in litigation), had *had* it happen with clients and opposing attorneys, had experienced it countless times with Rachael. Sean's and Sarah's little tiff built up slowly, until eventually it devolved into a simple, muted screaming match.

"He seems well," he heard Sarah say. He'd been on his way to their room just to say good night and make sure they didn't need anything (typically the situation was reversed, and he was thankful to have enough energy to return the favor). He was perhaps five feet from the door when her words drifted out and halted him in mid-stride, just loud enough to be audible from where he stood. Unable to resist his curiosity, he now resumed his approach, not quite tip-toeing but walking with measured, quiet footsteps. He stopped when he was about a foot from the door, turned sideways, and very gently pressed his ear against it.

"My dad?" Sean asked (rather stupidly, Dennis thought).

"No," Sarah said with good-natured sarcasm, "your accountant." Dennis imagined she was smiling, and smiled a little himself. Her voice was like butter to him, smooth and luxuriant and pleasantly sedative. Thank God, he sometimes thought, her soul was intact; she could have saved corporations billions of dollars pleading their cases to juries.

"Very funny," Sean said. "And yes, he does. I haven't seen him this perky in a while. Must be you, hon. You know how much he likes you. Loves you, even."

"You think he loves me?" Dennis thought he heard both gratitude and a touch of alarm in her tone, and his heart sank. He feared now that perhaps, in his very effort to embrace her and show his approval, he had in fact smothered and alienated her. Welcomed her to the family, in other words, a bit *too* graciously.

"Of course he does," Sean said, apparently either not having detected or simply disregarding that hint of discomfiture. "Why wouldn't he? You're going to be his daughter-in-law pretty soon, and I guess he's decided you're the one he's always hoped for, or should have."

"Should have?"

There was a pause here, and Dennis suspected Sean was already beginning to regret having said it. Women, he surely knew, loved nothing more than to trap a man with his own clumsy articulations, to find hidden meanings in every word. *To infer a tempest*, Dennis thought, *where there is barely rain.* When Sean spoke next there was a certain defensiveness to his tone. "All I meant was, the Dad I used to have would've probably asked me how we intend to support ourselves on two idealists' salaries, why I'm wasting my graduate degree on a public advocacy job and you're wasting yours helping irresponsible idiots avoid eviction and divorce spouses they should've never married in the first place. Then he probably would've proclaimed us both destined for financial ruin and washed his hands of the whole affair." Dennis winced at this.

"Jesus," Sarah mused. "He was that bad?"

"I'm afraid so, darlin'."

"Sometimes he goes a little overboard with it, though, don't you think?"

"Overboard with what?"

"Just, you know, how much he's changed in the past few months and how much he adores me, always lavishing me with compliments and telling me how glad he is that we met."

Sean's voice rose a little: "And there's something wrong with that?"

"No, no, of course not." Now *she* paused, perhaps seeing for the first time where the path of this exchange was headed, barring a quick correction in course. Perhaps she debated dropping the subject right there, but if so, she decided against it. "I'm just saying, I think sometimes he does it out of guilt, you know? Overcompensates for being so... well, whatever he was, in the past."

"An asshole, you mean?"

"I didn't *say* that, Sean."

"But it's what you meant, right?"

"No," she said. "What I *said* was, or at least what I *meant* to say, was just that sometimes he acts like I'm his daughter-in-law *already.*"

"Fine," Sean said. "Maybe he's a little overly affectionate sometimes. But if he is, it's only because he's afraid he won't be around to actually *see* you become his daughter-in-law, much less his grandkids and all the rest of it."

Dennis easily recognized this stage of the proceeding: what he often thought of as the "Minor Concessions/Redeeming Justifications" stage, where one party makes largely meaningless admissions of trivial fault solely to placate the other. Immediately thereafter, he effectively rescinds the admissions, or at least vastly dilutes their significance, by invoking usually unassailable humanitarian excuses for whatever he happens to be defending.

"Sean! We haven't even *talked* about kids yet!"

"Darling," Sean said, "I do believe that's beside the

point right now." Dennis had never heard his son sound so much like him; the similarity was eerie, and one he deeply regretted.

"Well, what the hell *is* the point, Sean?" At this he was struck with a potent bout of *déjà vu*, although he hadn't the foggiest idea what subliminal memory this might have aroused. Some semi-recent conversation with Rachael, perhaps.

"I don't know, Sarah, you tell me. You're the one who started this."

"I didn't start anything. I just said your father looks well and that sometimes he gets a little carried away with the whole... born-again thing. And now you're yelling at me."

"I'm not yelling at you. Calm down. Let's just go to bed."

"Fine."

Now there was a much longer lull in the conversation (*discussion*, Dennis's mind interjected, *this one's definitely at least a discussion*). He'd almost decided there would be nothing further, he could go after his glass of milk now, and had actually begun to turn away from the door when Sarah abruptly rekindled the dialogue. Except, what she actually did was to up the ante considerably: "He's not really dying, you know."

"Pardon me?"

"Your dad... he's not dying."

"How do *you* know?"

He didn't hear it, but Dennis was almost certain this elicited a sigh from her. "Nobody's that lucid if they're dying, Sean. Or that energetic."

"Energetic?"

"He practically jumped out of the bed when he saw me! Didn't you notice?"

"Yeah," Sean said. "I noticed. He was just excited, that's all. Trust me, before you got here, he had a very rough few days. I told you on the phone about how I called an ambulance for him this morning, didn't I, I was that worried about him? And how I found him sleeping on a cot in that shack out in the woods?"

"Yes, you did. But how could he perk up so much a few hours later if he's really as sick as he thinks he is?"

"I don't know," Sean said. "It comes and goes, I guess."

"So you believe him? Even though he's never actually been diagnosed - well, except by himself, for whatever *that's* worth - you just believe him when he says he's dying of cancer?"

Another long pause, then: "I didn't at first, but yeah, I'm starting to. Sweetheart, I've seen him throw up blood... *lots* of it. And what about the weight loss? He's dropped at least twenty pounds since I moved in here, says he's dropped almost ninety since last November. And he eats, Sarah. I see him. Not much, not usually, but enough that he wouldn't be losing weight like that unless something were seriously wrong. How do you explain all that, if he's perfectly fine?"

"Well, I never said he's perfectly *fine*. I just said I don't think he's dying."

"You're not a doctor."

"Neither are you."

"No, but I *am* the one who spends almost every waking hour with him, aren't I? So I think I'm in a much better position to judge his condition, don't you?"

His voice had risen again, and now she matched his pitch: "What're you trying to say, Sean? That I don't visit often enough? That I should quit my job and move up here and help you take care of him?"

"No, no, no. Stop twisting my words around. I *hate* it when you do this!"

"I'm not twisting anything. That's just what I heard you

saying. And you know I'd do it if I could, you *know* I would, but I can't. We need my income to live, Sean. And I can't get an extended leave like you can, because he's not my father. You know that. It's hard enough taking off almost every Friday afternoon to fly up here."

"Yes, Sarah, I know. I know all this. You don't need to tell me again. And you know damn well I wasn't *saying* that. You're just getting defensive and trying to paint yourself as the victim."

"The victim of what?"

"Never mind. I just wanna go to sleep."

Dennis heard the rustling of sheets and supposed that Sean had just rolled over, turning his back to her. It was a classic spousal (or near-spousal) maneuver. "No, tell me, Sean: the victim of what?"

"I don't know," he said. "It doesn't matter. To tell you the truth, sweetheart, I think all of this has a lot less to do with you thinking my dad isn't dying, and a whole lot more to do with how inconvenient it is that he's chosen to die up *here*."

*I'll see your fifty dollars*, Dennis thought, *and raise you the mortgage.* Then, rather dazedly: *Holy shit, son... you have no idea what kind of can of worms you just opened up.* He braced himself for a scream, maybe the sound of something smashing against the wall (another lamp, perhaps, just for good measure), but for a moment heard only silence. And then it came: the inevitable sobbing, at first hardly more than a murmur, then steadily climbing to an all-out, full-throated howl (what a writer like Thomas Hardy, Dennis suspected, might have called a *ululation*). Her chest was no doubt heaving forcefully.

"Sarah," Sean said, "I'm sorry. I didn't mean that." And there again was that terribly potent, somehow caustic feeling of *déjà vu.*

"Don't talk to me," she said.

"Sarah."

Dennis turned and walked quietly, very quietly, back to his bedroom.

He'd lost his craving for milk.

He stood, as in this dream he always did, upon the summit of a great mountain, head lowered and eyes trained downward. This time, instead of a pond or the usual snow-swept plain, at the bottom of the slope there lay only darkness, nothingness. It was awesome and terrible, unbounded. The face of the mountain tapered into it, became lost in the sprawling, swirling gloom. Above this there sat a thin sheet of mist. It did something for which Dennis did not quite know the right word. It rippled, he would have said, like a lake. A writer like Thomas Hardy might have said it *undulated.* What Dennis *did* know, however, instinctively, was that whatever penetrated that darkness died there, that the darkness was death itself.

He leaned forward a little, clad in his customary attire (burgundy cloth, affixed to his waist by a string), a strong gale whipping his face. He leaned forward, as if pulled by a magnet, and peered deeper into the abyss, transfixed by it. He leaned farther, farther, pondering the descent... as much as it *could* be pondered. In truth it was unfathomable, holding logic and order in blithe contempt. Perhaps it stretched on forever, such that even one who committed himself to the plunge would never quite reach it, the darkness itself, the death which dwelt infinitely farther down, mere surplusage. Perhaps the descent itself was death.

Or permanent madness.

He stepped back from the edge, very carefully, and hunkered down on the craggy rock upon which he found himself marooned. He wrapped himself in his arms to shield his naked flesh from the biting winds. He would not take the dive just yet.

He was, he found, unready to expire.

The next day he told Sean and Sarah that he wanted to have Molly Jeffords over for supper, and that, afterwards, he'd like to discuss something important with both of them. "I don't know," he said to them, "whether or not she has any children or other family, or whether, if she does, they live close by, or how often they might visit. But there's a good possibility she sits alone in that house all day long with no one to talk to and nothing to do except miss her dead husband, and I just can't stand the thought of that."

"That's very thoughtful of you, Dad," Sean said.

"I wish I'd thought to do it earlier. I've let it go too long."

"Better late than never, though. Right?"

Dennis nodded, and Sarah volunteered to prepare the meal. "We'll need to go shopping," she added, looking at Sean. "I assume."

"I'll take care of that," Sean said. "Just give me a list."

Dennis thanked them both.

Sean gave him an odd look, a hybrid of pity and concern. "Dad," he said cautiously, "you won't mind her seeing you... you know, how you are?"

Dennis smiled. His demeanor was somehow both flippant and earnest. "In my present condition, you mean?"

Sean blushed. "Well, yeah."

"No. It's about time she knew the truth, anyway."

"What will you tell her about Mom?"

Dennis had already considered this. "That she's away visiting her parents." He looked at Sarah, who was riffling through a copy of *Bird Watchers Weekly* which Dennis had bought at Cal's Cantina two months ago. Her interest in it, he suspected, was almost entirely feigned. Sean had hinted to him several times that his wholesale repudiation of Rachael did not sit well with her, that in fact she found it downright abhorrent. Dennis had gone out of his way never to mention his wife's name in front of her, as much to avoid upsetting himself as to avoid upsetting Sarah. The subject was one he had long ago trained himself to ignore.

"Okay," Sean said, looking distinctly uncomfortable himself. "So what is it that you wanted to talk with me and Sarah about?"

Dennis glanced between them. "That's for later," he said. "Dinner first."

He phoned her from Sean's cell phone, which got decent reception outside (inside the house, it seemed, even the most powerful signal fast deteriorated). She accepted the invitation with what seemed to him sincere gratitude and delight. There was something else Dennis thought he heard in her voice, as well, subtle and restrained but still detectable: it was relief, he thought, at the prospect of human contact. Perhaps his suspicion had been right; perhaps she really *was* all alone in the world.

"Before you come, though, Molly," he told her now, "I think it's only fair that I warn you about something."

"What's that, Dennis?" she asked. While pleasant enough, her voice had none of the old bubbly warmth that Dennis remembered. Her loss had dulled and rusted it, enfeebled her soul. Her every word laid bare her devastation.

"I'm not well, Mrs. Jeffords. Not well at all." He was unsure why he'd suddenly reverted to calling her by her surname, but she didn't seem to notice.

"I'm sorry to hear that, Dennis."

"And I don't look well. I'm extremely thin. I just didn't

want you to be startled or uncomfortable when you saw me."

"Have you seen a doctor? Not to meddle, of course."

"It's quite all right. And yes, I have. But I don't want to bother you with all that. Let's just have a nice, relaxing dinner, shall we?" He paused, considered, took a chance. "I feel terrible that I never invited you and Sam for dinner over the summer." He closed his eyes, waiting for her to burst into tears; he had quickly balanced his own need to apologize against the possibility of upsetting her, and was now sure that he'd misjudged the weight of both. When she simply replied that no apology was necessary, her voice remaining steady, he knew a profound relief of his own.

"Thank you, Molly. We'll see you at seven, then?"

"Sounds lovely."

"Great. Good-bye, Molly."

"Good-bye, Dennis."

He hung up, coughed violently, and went back inside.

Dinner *was* lovely, from start to finish. Except for one small incident before dessert (a delicious crème brûlée that Sarah had made from scratch, using a recipe from Rachael Ray).

"We had a lake house in Vermont," Dennis offered, in the course of a conversation about Sean's childhood. They were in the living room, sipping coffee while Sarah put the finishing touches on her creation. Molly had just finished explaining that Sam and a team of builders had erected the shanty in the woods, in the space of approximately three weeks, as a convenient place for Sam's foremen to sleep during the construction of Memory Cove. *That* one had taken a little longer, indeed, almost a year. She had no recollection at all, though, of having put fresh linen on the cot anytime in the recent past, was mystified by the whole affair. Nor, she'd said, could she understand why the door to the place might have been unlocked. In Sean's version of the tale, of course, he and his father had simply stumbled upon the structure one day while strolling aimlessly in the woods. "We went there every summer for nine years."

"No, Dad," Sean said gently. "It's in New Hampshire."

Dennis simply looked at him, his face utterly blank, eyes uncomprehending.

"The lake house is in *New Hampshire*," Sean repeated. He cast a reassuring smile at Molly, who then politely turned her eyes down to her plate.

"No, no," Dennis said groggily, as if battling an

encroaching stupor. "You grew *up* in Florida, outside Seattle, but the beach house was in Vermont. I remember it clearly. The porch, the lake. It was so pretty there."

"Dad," Sean said, now suddenly and deeply alarmed. "What's the matter?"

"Nothing's the matter," Dennis said. "We just have a disagreement of opinion here, that's all." He turned to Molly and said, "Nothing to get your knickers in a twist over, right?"

Molly nodded without meeting his eyes. Then she announced, "I think I'd best go help Sarah in the kitchen."

"That's a good idea," Sean said. There was an awful little quaver in his voice. He had seen his dad get confused before, his thoughts and memories muddled, but never quite so dramatically as this. "I'm sure she'd appreciate that. There was something I wanted to talk to my dad about, anyway."

"New Hampshire," Dennis said. "Of course." Then, to Molly: "Don't trouble yourself, Mrs. Jeffords."

"Really," she said, "it's fine."

"I'm looking forward to that dessert."

"Oh, me too. I can smell it already."

"It's one of Rachael's specialties."

Before she was even out of earshot Sean said, "Dad,

you're not doing this on purpose, are you?"

"Doing what, son?"

Sean looked at him, tears prickling the corners of his eyes. His jaw was working, his hands trembling ever so slightly.

"Doing what?"

"Dad," Sean said, and went to him, and put his arms around him.

"I'm fine," Dennis assured him, patting one of his arms. "I'm fine." He craned his neck to look up at his son. He was smiling, but his eyes were cloudy and distant, somewhere else. "New Hampshire, of course."

By the time Sarah and Molly emerged from the kitchen ten minutes later, Dennis had come round almost fully. His eyes were clear again, for the most part, and when he spoke he did so sanely, lucidly. He was *present* again, was how Sean thought of it, present and cognizant of the things going on around him. When Sean had asked him where he'd lived before moving to Oregon, he'd said Seattle. When he'd asked him what his profession had been, he'd said, "I was a lawyer. You know, one of them fellas who goes to court and uses fancy words." Though such humor was a little unlike his dad's usual, far dryer brand,

Sean was satisfied that he was merely being silly and not... well, unconsciously childish. And when he'd asked Sean why he was asking such stupid questions, Sean had simply laughed, breathing a huge, inward sigh of relief.

"Everything okay out here?" Sarah asked, rather gingerly, carrying a large ceramic bowl to the coffee table with oven mitts. Molly followed on her heels with two ramekins in each hand. The caramel glinted temptingly in the soft lamplight. The smell of the custard, ambrosial at least to Sean, wafted out from beneath.

"Yes," Sean said, "everything's fine. Dad just got a little... tired there for a minute."

"I'm not tired," Dennis said. "I wasn't tired. I'm fine. You worry too much, Sean."

Sean aimed a cautious, sidelong glance at the women. "Maybe I do," he said.

"Well," asked Sarah, "who's up for some dessert?"

As it so happened, they all were.

After dinner, after the three of them had seen Molly off, Sean suggested that Dennis simply go to bed and wait till morning to discuss with him and Sarah whatever it was he wanted to discuss. But Dennis refused, insisting on having the conversation right then and there.

"Let's sit," he told them, and they reconvened in the living room. Sean and Sarah sat on the couch, Dennis in the recliner beside it.

"So what's up?" Sean said, and for a moment Dennis imagined he was sixteen again, sitting next to him on his and Rachael's bed, during the storm, that terrible storm, listlessly awaiting his father's reason for summoning him.

*I've been having an affair*, Dennis thought. "I'm willing to see a doctor," he said.

"You are?" Both Sean's and Sarah's eyes went wide, more with relief, Dennis thought, than surprise.

"Yes," he said. "Any doctor you like, in Portland."

"When?"

"As soon as he can see me." He looked at Sarah, smiled. "Or she."

"Dad, I'm so glad you've decided to do this. I really think -"

"There's a condition," Dennis said.

Sean glanced briefly at his fiancée, then turned his eyes back to his father. "Condition?"

"Yes. Just one. But it's a big one."

"What is it, Dad?"

Dennis looked at them both. His eyes were intent, but not quite pleading. "I want you to have your wedding here, in my house, three weeks from tomorrow. Would that be enough time?"

At the exact same moment, their jaws fell agape. And at the exact same moment, they both turned to look at each other, as if to confirm that they'd heard what they had.

Dennis continued, undeterred. "You've had the plans on hold now for a while, haven't you?"

"Well," Sean said, as if talking in his sleep. "Yeah, I guess so."

"No church reserved yet? No preacher? No flowers or music or cake ordered and paid for?"

"Well, no," Sarah said, "but Dennis... here? In your house? With your being so ill?"

"That's why I want it here."

"But Dad," Sean said, finding his voice again, "we decided a long time ago that we'd just postpone the whole thing until you were better."

Dennis gave him a look which said unequivocally, *This*

*is no time, son, to be willfully asinine.* "I'm not getting any better," he said. "I'm only getting worse. I'm dying. Rather quickly now. If I make it even another six weeks, particularly without medication, it will be nothing short of a miracle." He had, at that very moment, a monstrous headache he was trying desperately to ignore.

"Dennis -" Sarah attempted to interject.

"No," he silenced her. "Please. You both know it's true. But you appear to need more proof than is evident to your own eyes. The doctor I see will give you that proof. And when he does, if we could put the whole matter to rest once and for all, and make the best of what little time I have left, I would be deeply grateful to you both."

They simply sat there, looking at him, their mouths still hanging open, incredulity etched onto their features. Dennis wondered if their faces mightn't get stuck like that forever, if they didn't change soon.

"And for you to have your wedding here," Dennis went on, "however small in scale it might need to be, would be the ultimate honor."

"Dad," Sean said.

"I'll pay for everything."

"Dad."

"The invitations, the cake, the gowns and tuxes, the pastor's commission. Or the judge's, if you'd prefer a secular ceremony. I even know a couple judges in Portland who might be willing to do it at a discount, maybe even for free. But, in any event, it's all on me. Every penny of it."

"*Dad.*"

"Yes, son?"

Sean looked at Sarah again, trying to gauge her reaction to all this, but her face showed only shock. Shock and bewilderment. "That's a really, really kind offer. And I think... I mean, I know *I'd* be more than happy to go along with it."

"I would, too," Sarah said, rather automatically. It was impossible to tell whether or not she meant it.

"But we'd planned to invite at least a hundred guests," Sean finished.

"We'll have it out by the lake," Dennis said. "Or the pond. We could easily fit that many people under a canopy out there. Wouldn't that be nice? Outside, on a pretty autumn day?"

"Well, yes," Sean said. "That *does* sound nice. Very nice."

"Then let's do it. Please. I want..." Dennis began to cry.

"I want more than anything to see the two of you marry before I die."

"Oh, Dad."

Sarah began crying as well.

"It's my last wish," Dennis said, wiping his eyes with the backs of his hands. "The last thing in this world that I want, that I could reasonably expect to have."

"But Dad..." Sean said, and trailed off, overwhelmed. All at once he looked as though he hadn't slept in days.

"What, Sean?"

He looked at Sarah, put an arm around her, pulled her close to him. The act seemed to steady him. He looked at his father and said, "What about Mom?"

Dennis had expected the question, and was ready with his answer. "She can come," he said. "Of course she can."

And though they did not just then actually agree to it, Dennis knew that, with those words, the matter was as good as settled.

## 39

They went to Portland three days later, in Sean's Subaru Outback. Dennis had made special arrangements with a doctor he'd once represented in a malpractice suit (successfully, of course). He was scheduled to undergo a chest x-ray, bronchoscopy, and a battery of other tests.

The mere thought of these things, of their intrusion upon his tranquil inner world, unleashed within him a furious dread, a revulsion as basic as it was irrational. He had never experienced anything like it, had no idea how to manage it; he had anticipated, instinctively, an unpleasant reaction - such was precisely the reason he had so diligently avoided seeing a doctor in the first place - but nothing on the order of this. He could only clench his teeth, literally, and abide it.

Sean and Sarah both sensed it, of course, his anxiety, and tried their best to alleviate it. Sarah spoke to him every few minutes, reassuring him, comforting him, telling him how proud of him she was, as if he were a child on the verge of having his tonsils removed or a stubborn milk tooth pulled. He was stretched out on the backseat, with a blanket and pillow. For most of the trip he kept his eyes closed, simply nodding when she spoke to him, just to let her know that he was holding it together, he hadn't gone off the deep end quite yet.

But he scarcely heard her; his mind was elsewhere entirely. And though he struggled mightily to turn it in a more genial direction, to guide it down a more hospitable path, it would not budge. The thoughts within it remained dark and haunted, hostages which refused to be rescued from their captor. They were content, seemingly, to suffer, the prospect of liberation somehow more terrifying than that of further confinement.

In all of it, the only solace he found was that the man who'd shortly be conducting the invasion was someone he knew, with a face he'd recognize.

This solace, however, quickly dissipated. Upon their arrival at the hospital, his reintroduction to all the sights and sounds he had come to loathe (the automatic sliding doors, the triage, the low drone of the television bolted high up on the wall), his disquiet redoubled and he actually began to shake. Whether mercifully or cruelly (and in the end he'd decide it was the former), only one event intervened to keep him there, else he surely would have fled: he was seen to immediately, Dr. Phillip Kowalski himself coming out to retrieve him. A hulking, broad-shouldered, barrel-shaped man, he towered over all three of them by at least half a foot.

"Dennis," he said, and at first he was all toothy, plucky

grin. Then he got a good look at his old attorney's condition, at how thin and frail Dennis was, and his grin shriveled up like a sun-scorched worm.

"Phil," Dennis said. His voice was a nearly inaudible croak. "How are you?"

Thirty minutes later, Dennis was laid flat on his back on an examination table, the anesthesia beginning to take hold. He had opted for general rather than local, having no desire to witness the procedure firsthand. His last clear thought before losing consciousness was, *Just let the bastard screw* this *one up and we'll see how much the jury loves him then.*

## 40

*He is almost awake, but not quite, not quite. He is groping toward it, some dim awareness of who and where he is, but for a while he fumbles, his hands falling through empty air, his eyes unable to penetrate the gloom. He stumbles forward, backward, maybe sideways. Space and direction are for him largely forgotten concepts, eluding him as cleanly as consciousness itself.*

*Is this the present? The past? When did time begin and when did it stop?*

*He thinks:* My name is Dennis.

*There is something called a "courtroom," and he goes to it - goes? goes? what is goes? - he goes to it a lot. He goes to it... what is the word? There are so many words. There are so many words he used to know.*

*He goes to it* frequently. *That is the word. That is the word he used to know, and now remembers.*

*He thinks:* My name is Arbaugh.

*There is water in the courtroom, and on the water, waves. There is an* ocean *in the courtroom, an ocean or a... the word is* lake.

*He thinks:* My name is Dennis Arbaugh, and I live on an ocean-lake.

*The jury is floating in a rowboat, twelve of them packed in tight, lined up like soldiers. They are drifting toward the... toward the...*

*His mind bellows: TOWARD THE JUDGE'S BENCH!*

*What is toward? What is present, what is past? The future is the one not yet. This much he knows. The future is the one not yet. It hasn't happened yet. It's still coming. It's not arrived.*

*Has* he *arrived? Has he passed?*

*He thinks:* With death comes sleep. Death *is* sleep.

*The jurors in the rowboat collide with the base of a mountain, a protrusion of terrific height, of awesome breadth. It's capped with snow, the frills of the skirt fluttering in the wind.*

*The wind is of the past. Wind is* from *the past. Wind is from the dream. The mountain is from the dream. The mountain is your death. You were always too scared to jump. The wind was always fierce. You always had to fight it. But now the wind is pushing you. Now the death below is calling you. The wind is from the past, and the mountain is your death.*

*He thinks:* My name is Dennis Arbaugh. I am an attorney. I am an attorney who lives at the beach, and I used to go to court *frequently.*

*The judge brings down his gavel, the jurors disappear, the rowboat capsizes on the tumultuous sea (is it a sea or a lake? a lake or a sea?), and then his eyes are open.*

*There is a white ceiling above, and hanging from it, a bright florescent light.*

*His throat is a corridor of fire.*

*He thinks:* This is my present. I have caught up with my present. The future lies just southward.

# PART VI:
# d i s c h a r g e

## 41

The call came three days later. Dennis was asleep in his bedroom when the phone rang. They'd activated the land-line the day before they'd gone to Portland, at Sean's request. He'd felt it was intolerably risky not to have a stable, reliable phone line with circumstances being what they were. Dennis, though unconvinced, had ceded the point to satisfy Sean. On the way home from the hospital, they'd stopped at the Radio Shack in Odell and bought a phone. It was stark white, with big, clear plastic buttons. It had rung only once before, when Sarah had called from her cell to test the line. It couldn't be Sarah this time, though, because Sarah was sitting on the couch, reading a book.

He lifted the phone from its cradle with a clammy hand and put the receiver to his ear. "Hello?"

"Is this Dennis's son?"

"Yes, this is Sean. May I ask who's calling?"

"This is Dr. Kowalski from Eastmoreland Hospital in Portland."

"Dr. Kowalski," Sean said. He'd lowered his voice, so Sarah wouldn't hear him. "How are you?"

"I'm fine, thank you. How are you, son?"

"I'm all right. Did the results come back?"

"Yes, Sean, they did."

Sean paused, looked at Sarah in the other room. She looked beautiful. Invincible. He cupped his hand around the mouthpiece. "Cancer?"

"Yes, Sean. I'm sorry."

The world retreated, diminished almost to nothing. "How... how far along is it?"

Dr. Kowalski cleared his throat. "He has a month left, maybe. Six weeks at the outside."

"Six weeks," Sean echoed.

"I'm sorry," the doctor repeated.

"Thank you, Dr. Kowalski."

"Sean, if there's anything I can do -"

"Yes. Thank you. And thank you for seeing him so promptly."

"You're welcome."

Sean simply held the phone for a moment, listening to the dial tone. Then the line began to beep, startling him back to reality. The world, a moment ago only a tiny, distant object, now rushed forward again, overwhelming him with its fullness, its sharp and vivid colors. He closed his eyes against it.

"Sweetheart?"

He opened his eyes. Sarah stood in the doorway to the kitchen, leaning against the wall of the arch. Her blonde hair cascaded over her shoulders, hung down over her breasts. For a moment it flashed brilliantly in the sunlight pouring through the bay window. "Are you okay?" she asked.

"He's dying, Sarah."

She went to him, embraced him. He put his head on her shoulder and wept softly.

Dennis had known desperation, and helplessness, had known truly gut-wrenching despair, but nothing, ever, like this. That which plagued him now, by whatever name it might be called, was of a breed wholly new to him, an immensity and intensity quite beyond him. Worst of all, he seemed utterly alone in it, in this terrible despondency that he knew, no matter who came near him or for how long, no matter how tenderly or earnestly she tried to reach him. He was unreachable.

He grappled with it, fought with it and clawed at it, battled it like a feral animal, a great, bronze-chested warrior, summoning in the act his final traces of mettle, his last gasps of resolve. But his mind ached and was bleary, his body a mere shell, and his valor proved no match for the grim pertinacity of his opponent. First dimmed by fatigue and finally crippled by exhaustion, he saw now that his exertions were in vain, and ceased to fight.

Such was wholly contrary to his nature, offended every instinct in his body, and it was in his surrender to death, far more than by virtue of his actual death itself, that Dennis Arbaugh perished.

He lay in bed with his arms folded across his chest, faintly but bitterly aware that he might be rehearsing for his final pose. A steady drizzle pattered the roof above his head. The whole room was enshrouded in darkness. He swam up for a moment from his haze, wrestled his way to some half-measure of lucidity. In a weak voice he called out for Sean, who reached over and placed his hand over his father's.

"I'm here, Dad."

Dennis turned and saw his son sitting on the chair beside the bed. "Sean."

"I'm here."

"I want to talk to you."

"All right. Are you sure you're up to it?"

Dennis gave a single nod of his head. "Yes."

"What would you like to talk about?"

For a moment he said nothing, but, incredibly, managed a waxen smile. "Everything," he said finally.

"Dad... that could take a while." Sean tried for a smile of his own, but in the long shadows of the room, with the rain drumming in his ears and a dull throb starting behind his eyes, his face felt too heavy to lift. He had barely slept since Dr. Kowalski's call two days earlier, and now a deep, debilitating fatigue was bearing down on him. But he must wait for sleep; for now, he knew, he must listen to his father.

"There's time," Dennis declared flatly. "Just enough. Maybe a bit more than enough."

Sean shrugged. "Okay. You start us off."

Dennis chortled and coughed, then chortled some more.

"What's so funny?" Sean asked, now smiling despite his weariness, despite his worry.

"This isn't... goddam *talk* therapy," Dennis said, and even with the mid-sentence wheezing his delivery was near perfect, the comedic effect complete.

Sean nodded, gave his father's hand a squeeze, and let go of it. "Point taken."

"But... in any case... why don't *you* begin?"

"I don't know what you want to talk about, Dad. This is your ballgame."

Dennis gave a feeble shake of his head. "No, no. I want, for one thing... to talk about *you*."

"What about me?"

"Hey," Dennis said. "You're defensive already."

"What? No, I'm not."

"Yes, you are. It's in your voice. I can hear it. It's on your face. Writ..." He wheezed again. "Written clearly. Giant letters. All caps."

"Why would I be defensive about talking about myself?"

"Because..." Dennis's face tightened. He leaned a little closer to his boy. "Because, Sean, you're *guarded*."

"Well."

"You get it from me."

"I get a lot from you, I imagine. You're my father."

"We protect... we protect our feelings... *fiercely*. In a way, ironically, that your mother never protected her own."

Sean said nothing.

"We protect them," Dennis went on, "as if... they were

the world's... most valuable treasures."

"Maybe they are."

Dennis nodded. "I've heard it..." He took a deep breath, as deep as he could, and his chest rattled in protest. There was so much oxygen in the room, he observed, and yet precious little he could siphon; he had might as well be in deep space, where the air was thin as toothpicks. "I've heard it said that the best guarantee... of unhappiness... is to keep your things and your feelings to yourself. To hoard what you get... and hide what you feel."

Sean was silent.

"And then... there's the other: the person who is truly generous with both... both his feelings and his things... is the happiest person on earth." Dennis's gaze had drifted. He found Sean's again, and spoke as forcefully as he could: "That person... knows true freedom."

Sean nodded. He began to say something, then thought better of it. Any comment he might offer would seem trivial and superfluous. The time for dialogue would come later; for now, he decided, he would simply listen to his father's prelude.

Dennis inhaled, and got more breath than he usually did. He seized immediately on his good fortune: "Most people in the world, Sean, carry around with them a great lot of heartache, a great lot of despair. Disappointments mount from one week to the next, or one month to the next, or, if they're lucky, one year to the next. But, however frequent, they build on one another, layer upon layer, and as the heap grows taller, the bottommost layers, all the sorrows of their youths... those layers grow firmer, ever solidifying... you might even say they *petrify*."

He was losing his breath again. "And at some point they get so hard, Sean, so firm, they form a... a permanent foundation. A permanent, unbreakable foundation... of unhappiness. And meanwhile, all the top layers, the newest disappointments, the freshest blows... well, they chip away at the soul, don't they? Bit by bit, steady as a river eroding a wall of rock, gnawing and nibbling, imperceptible from one day to the next but... stunningly visible... at life's end. They stand back... and survey the wreckage... and realize suddenly they can't recall a time... when life wasn't getting the better of them. Life gets the better of most of us, in the end."

Sean nodded. "I know what you're saying, Dad."

"The best protection... against that... is to be *generous*. Okay?"

"Yes, Dad."

"Generous with your things, yes, of course... in ways I myself certainly never was, never even... even *dreamt* of being. But more... more importantly..." He leaned in closer still, so that his face was mere inches from his son's. His hands were trembling; his feet were ice-cold; his whole body was a live wire, thrumming with humongous jolts of electricity, and something which lay inside him, the nearest kin to what others might call a soul, now howled frantically as it groped toward its own liberation. "Be generous with your *feelings*, Sean. Be generous with who you *are*."

"I'm not sure I understand."

Dennis raised a finger, signaling perhaps that understanding, at least deep understanding, was for the moment unnecessary. "People who are generous... with their feelings and their things... are the few people who don't carry... who don't carry around a lot of heartache and despair with them, everywhere they go. They are the few for whom... the luggage of their pasts... is light. A trail of disappointments stretches out behind them, too... reaches all the way back to childhood, more than likely, for most of them. No one... no one is exempt from life's... sundry horrors, Sean. But for such people those horrors are bearable. The weight of the cross on their backs is negligible, and some maybe don't notice it at all. Because, just as... as efficiently and... and *insidiously* as the disappointments of their lives... have corroded their souls, they have in turn, just as... as diligently... and fastidiously... repaired the damage."

Sean asked the question he sensed his father wanted to answer, although he suspected he could have answered it himself: "And how do people like that repair the damage, Dad?"

"By being generous," Dennis said, "with who they are."

Sean said nothing, simply mulled the comment over. He thought he understood it better now.

"They give themselves away, instead of keeping themselves... to themselves."

"They don't guard their feelings," Sean ventured.

"They guard them," Dennis said, "only as much... as is necessary... to guard other people's. But where there... there's no reasonable risk... of hurting anyone else..." He started to cough and held up his hand, so Sean wouldn't interrupt him. "Where that's the case," he finished, "such people treat their feelings... with reckless abandon."

Sean nodded.

"Do you know," his father asked him, "what is the root of all pain... in a human being's life? What lies beneath the surface... of any sadness... and feeds it, sustains it?"

Sean simply shook his head.

"Regret," Dennis said. "That's what."

"Regret," Sean echoed.

"Obviously... not every disappointment in a person's life... springs from something he has control over. There are unavoidable tragedies, plain and simple. I suppose... that's why I've never... never been able to accept what religions... what they teach about God and His benevolence. I simply can't accept... that a loving god... with the power to stop it... would let an infant die, or a child lose his mother... or a whole village be wiped out by a tsunami. Those with faith... say God has His reasons, which are beyond us. I say... He owes us a damned good explanation."

Sean smiled, waited for his father to continue.

"But the point is, even where the disappointment... comes from something like that, some unavoidable... tragedy." He paused, exhausted now. He let himself just breathe for a moment, grimacing at the whiny, strangled noise his lungs made, and at the powerful burning sensation in his side. For the past week or so, each time he'd glanced down at his body he'd half-expected it to be on fire. "Even then," he went on, "the foundation of the sadness is regret. Regret... that the tragedy happened in the first place, and that... nothing could be done to prevent it."

Sean nodded, rapt now, wholly absorbed. He was reminded of their conversation about a week ago, out in the shack in the woods behind the house. It felt to him now as if that conversation had occurred years ago, as if the whole world had been transformed in the interim. He supposed his own world had.

"But most sadness," Dennis continued, "most regret... originates in the choices we make, or at least *appear* to make. I don't know, Sean... if people really do have free will, because I don't know... what it would feel like... *not* to have it."

"There's the philosophy major in you," Sean observed quietly, with a soft grin.

"But supposing we *do* have it... and we make free choices every day... that's where most of the regret comes from. That's where most of us... fuck up big time. But not so much when we choose *to* do something... as when we choose *not* to. When we choose to hide ourselves, to be stingy with our feelings. That's where fear comes in. Fear's even bigger than regret... even more fundamental.

"Because the most direct cause of regret itself... is fear. Fear stops us from doing what we want to do... but it also stops us from doing... what we *need* to do, in order to be happy and bring happiness... to others. It makes us timid, dilutes our vitality, clouds our... our judgment. It stifles our every impulse, Sean... the good and the bad. And that's what it's there for, to keep bad impulses... in check. But in most people it takes a stranglehold, comes to dominate their decision-making. At that point, fear controls them almost completely... and there's no courage left, no stubborn insistence... on being happy, to challenge its rule. It becomes a dictator... and dictates their every choice. Sometimes it's obvious. Sometimes it's... it's subtle. But it's always there, lurking in the background... tightening its grip... clamping down harder still, robbing more life... erasing more opportunities to be happy."

Sean said nothing.

"The story of my life," his father told him, "has largely been one of regret." He looked at his son, saw the tears pricking the corners of his eyes. "With two major exceptions."

"Those being?"

"Marrying your mother," Dennis said, "and having you."

Tears streamed now down Sean's face, but still he said

nothing, for once again there was nothing to say.

"Do you want to know, son, why I was unfaithful to your mother so many times?"

"No," Sean said, his voice muffled and watery, much as it had been on the evening, some nine years earlier, that Dennis had first confessed to him his adultery.

"Because I was a selfish hedonist who couldn't bear the thought of his own insignificance in a universe, frankly, where insignificance is the fate of us all."

Sean just looked at him.

"If I could have these women, I thought to myself... then that must make me important. That must make me special. It was food for my ego, Sean, nothing more. I wanted... to feel better about myself, in greater control of my destiny. There is perhaps... no more banal or uninspired motive... for any human behavior. Nor more common."

"I won't argue with you there."

Dennis nodded. "And those who recognize that fact early on, before life... can sink its claws in too deep, hurt them too badly... and remain vigilant of it, of how stupid but powerful the temptation can be... no, *is*... they can more often than not avoid that pitfall altogether, and stand a decent chance... of being happy."

Realizing that his father's prelude was finished, at least for now, Sean said the only thing he could think to say: "I forgive you for what you did to her, Dad. For what you did to Mom."

"Don't," Dennis said. "Don't forgive me. I don't deserve... your forgiveness, as much as I want it. Just avoid... the mistakes I made. Don't be stupid and insecure. Don't try to make yourself... feel more important or special... by hurting other people. This is advice we're all taught... or most of us are taught... as children. But somehow we forget it... not long after. Or willfully ignore it. Because life's disappointments add up."

He inhaled, exhaled. Inhaled, exhaled. The sound of his breath was the sound of a train whistle, fading into the distance. "They build on one another, wearing us down... chipping away, bit by bit... robbing us of life. And before long we're too jaded and miserable to give a shit... too scarred by it all to do what we know... is right. Too hurt and angry and scared... to heed the advice we were given as children. We might remember it for a moment, reflect on it... for a fleeting instant. We might recall a conversation... just like this one. But then the heartache and despair rear up and... obliterate our good intentions. And then, in our waning days, we're like me: weak and frail and filled with regret, barely able... to look other people in the eye. Even... our own son."

Sean replaced his hand on his father's, gently squeezed it. He held back a sob. "Okay, Dad."

"Be generous with yourself, Sean. And be generous with your things. Things are just toys, anyway. Without people to share them... share them with, they're meaningless. And even when shared, they're still just... distractions. No matter how shiny they are... or how much... how much noise they make. They can't fill voids. Some people... it takes their whole lives for them to learn that. They spend millions... trying to fix what's wrong with them. They fill their lives with trivial diversions... and still wake up miserable. I did it myself... for so long. I accumulated great wealth, Son... for naught. I am grateful... that I was able to provide... for you and your mother, to give you... comfortable lives. But beyond that... I regret having spent a dime of it. I could've saved untold lives with... the money I wasted. We didn't need... our mansion in Seattle. I didn't need... this lake house. I should've moved into that shack... in the woods... out back. I should've..."

He'd exhausted himself. His face was paper-white. He slumped into the bed, his head lolling on the pillow. Beads of sweat had sprung on his brow. He clenched his teeth, unclenched them; wheezed noisily; shuddered with fatigue. And then he simply lay there, Dennis Arbaugh lay there perfectly still, with his son in the chair beside him, gazing into empty air with vacant eyes, all his features awash in agony, the meager remnants of his intellect, once exceptional and acute, now a mere thoughtless void. There was in his countenance, in that terrible instant, no semblance whatsoever of his former self, the man he had once been, with all the potency of a giant, all the promise of a newborn infant, untainted by disappointment, unmarred by despair.

"It's okay, Dad," Sean said. "You don't need to say anything else. I understand now. Everything's fine." He stroked his father's cheek, hot and rough as a desert landscape. His own cheeks were moist with tears. The rain had slackened, the pinging on the roof intermittent now. The sun had at last penetrated the clouds. Through the curtains over the bedroom window spilled the faint, reddish-purple glow of twilight. "Everything's fine now. You don't need to regret a thing. You did what you thought was right. You made the best decisions you could."

His father groaned.

"I'll be generous with myself, Dad. And with my things. I promise."

Dennis slept as his son, young and strong and handsome, sat hunched over in the armless wooden chair, sobbing quietly to himself.

## 42

The wedding, originally scheduled for Saturday, October 6, was expedited to Saturday, September 23, in order to accommodate Dennis's rapidly failing health. Consequently, many of the guests originally slated to attend were unable to, those who actually showed numbering in the tens rather than the scores. Nevertheless, and despite the extraordinarily bleak circumstances, it was a festive affair, everyone, even Dennis, having a good time. Judge Earl Gardener, Dennis's friend from Portland, had gladly agreed to preside. And though nominal Catholics, neither Rachael nor any of Sarah's family had raised any objection to the ceremony's being wholly secular. Under the circumstances, of course, such objections surely would have sounded petty.

It was held, as planned, on the shore of Lost Lake, under a warm, early autumn sun, beneath a dazzling canopy of blue sky, with soft music and sweet birdsong and the faint, merry din of distant boaters to fill the air. Only one boat passed by during the ceremony, and those on board, no doubt well lubricated and reveling in the beautiful weather, this rare northern Indian summer, honked their horn and blatted well wishes to the bride and groom.

At this Dennis smiled, and there was none of the usual envy or self-pity to spoil his pleasure. He supposed that, on this of all days, nothing could: he had been granted a twenty-four-hour respite from all his suffering, it seemed, all the ugliness and sorrow his life had become, that he might fully relish this day, this day he had anxiously awaited for some twenty-five years - and do so without the bitter aftertaste of woeful yearning, of wistful and crippling regret.

With Dennis's approval, Rachael arrived on Thursday the twenty-first.

He was in bed when she came, though not asleep. Sean knocked on the door, asked if it was all right if they came in. Dennis told them it was, struggling to make his voice audible.

The door opened and they entered, Sean first and then his mother, Dennis's wife, estranged now for nearly five months.

She looked at him and burst into tears. He had expected nothing less.

"Sweetheart," she said to him.

"Rachael," he replied.

"I love you," she said.

"I love you," he said.

She smiled through her veil of tears. "It's so good to see you. You look..."

"Awful?" Dennis asked, a devious little smirk touching the corners of his mouth.

"No," she said, shaking her head in vigorous denial. "Not awful at all. You look... *dignified.* And handsome. Very handsome."

"Rachael," he said, grinning wider, "you were always... so full of shit. I think... that's why I fell... in love with you."

She laughed, still crying, and embraced him. Much as when Sean had first hugged him at the concert, he felt now a terrific weight lifted from him, a spiritual tumor dissolved.

*Maybe you have to be dying*, he thought, *before everyone you ever hurt will forgive you. And maybe it's not really about how much you deserve it, either. Maybe it's just the fact that soon you won't be around to receive their forgiveness, and their sudden realization that, for all they know, you were never free to do otherwise in the first place. Maybe, deep down, we all sort of just know, without consciously admitting it to ourselves, that nobody can ever do other than he does, that our so-called choices are prescribed long before we ever make them, that our lives are written for us long before we even get here. Or, at the very latest, the moment we show up.*

He hugged her back, hard, and whispered in her ear, "I'm so glad you came, Rachael. And I never should've walked out."

That, of course, only got her crying harder. He had expected nothing less.

The other guests trickled into town, if one could call it that, on Friday night and Saturday morning. Those who arrived on Friday night (including Dennis's sister, Hope) mostly lodged at the single motel in Odell, except for Sarah's parents, who opted to stay at the Holiday Inn in Hood River, and Rachael's parents, who slept in the Sunrise Room. Rachael herself slept with Dennis.

He slept on his back, and she on her right side, with her left arm stretched across his chest and fingers buried in his ribs, precisely as they had slept almost every night for twenty-seven years. Dennis snored, as he always had, and although Rachael had taken early in their marriage to wearing earplugs to bed because the sound too often kept her up, tonight it didn't bother her in the slightest. In fact, although no longer accustomed to it, she told him the next morning that she'd slept better, more soundly than she had in years.

"Think of it!" he exclaimed to her, himself feeling unusually well rested. "The night before your only child's wedding, and you sleep like a rock!"

"I guess it was being with you," she said, stroking his arm with her fingers.

"I'll take the credit," he said, "but I suspect it belongs more rightly to Sean. When was the last time you slept in the same house with him?"

"I don't even remember," she said.

"But you always slept better when he visited from college. Remember?"

"That's true."

"It's a mother's instinct," he said. "Having her young

close, tending to her nest."

"I'm not a bird," she said. She was smiling.

"That's too bad." He wriggled his fingers, smirking, and thrust his hands around her ribs. "Because I was about to tickle your feathers."

"No!" she protested, laughing helplessly as he goosed her. "Stop it, Dennis! We have to get moving. Now stop it!"

But of course he ignored her, and of course she wanted him to. He could almost believe things were okay again, could almost believe that being back with her had obliterated his cancer, forestalled his demise. And maybe he would have, just for today, if not for the sight of his own bony arms and sallow flesh and sunken cheeks, and the deep burning in his lungs. These things, for both of them, were impossible to ignore.

But they would do the best they could, he knew, despite them.

And they did. From start to finish. The wedding ceremony, by all accounts, came off without a hitch (save for that, of course, between bride and groom). So did the reception held under the vinyl canopy they'd erected on Dennis's thin slice of lakeside beach, except for a partial collapse of the canopy about a half-hour into it. This had been easily remedied, however, simply by burying the support pegs deeper into the sand. Besides, nearly everyone's reaction to the incident was one of inebriated amusement, bride and groom included. Even Dennis, who'd allowed himself to imbibe a little against his doctor's firm advice, chuckled heartily at the sight of Sarah's family almost diving for escape.

At sunset, while the reception was in full swing, Dennis kissed his wife on the lips. He kissed his wife, whom he had many times considered divorcing, mostly to spare her further heartache and embarrassment. She kissed him back eagerly, enthusiastically, ugly and shriveled as he'd become, as deeply as he'd hurt her. None of the women who'd ever kissed him had done so with such tenderness or affection; none had ever done so as unreservedly or satisfyingly. He could taste the wine on her lips, the oysters on her tongue; he could smell the perfume on her neck, the soft aroma of her hair, like nectar. Beneath his hands her skin felt soft and cool, smooth as ivory. He pulled her in closer, let her hold him up, his fragile and wasted body, and held her tightly, as tightly as he could.

Behind them, the evening's last sliver of crimson sun disappeared from view.

## 43

It was Sunday, October first. Rachael's birthday was on the third. He would last until then, he told himself. He would do her that final courtesy.

She was downstairs, with Sean and Sarah. Sarah was about to leave for the airport in Portland, having to get back to Los Angeles for work on Monday. She had exhausted all of her leave and could now visit only on weekends. Rachael and Sean, of course, would be there for the duration.

Dennis lay in bed, staring out the window, recalling images of the wedding. How nice it had been! How truly perfect.

He heard the front door close, and then, a minute later, a trunk and a car door closing. Sarah's rental (some manner of truck, Dennis thought) sprang to life. For a moment the engine just idled, its driver no doubt getting situated. Then he heard the crunching of tires on gravel, and listened as the sound of the engine grew softer, as his new daughter-in-law drove away, toward the city.

A moment later, the sound of footsteps on the stairs. Just one set. Rachael's, he knew.

His bedroom door opened. She came in, lay down next

to him on the bed. Put her arms around his neck. Kissed him on the cheek.

Without either of them uttering a word, they both fell asleep, together, in broad daylight.

He awoke to the sound of a familiar tune: "Catch the Wind," by Donovan Phillips Leitch. It had been one of his favorites as a teenager, Donovan himself one of his favorite artists.

*In the chilly hours and minutes, of uncertainty, I want to be, in the warm hold of your loving mind.*

Dennis wasn't sure where the music was coming from, how he was hearing it, but didn't care. He just listened to it and enjoyed it, savored its gentle, soothing rhythms, its hauntingly pretty lyrics.

*To feel you all around me, and to take your hand, along the sand, ah, but I may as well try and catch the wind.*

Then he saw Rachael, standing by the window in nothing but a bra and panties. They were black, probably cotton. He had seen them before. He remembered them fondly. Perhaps he had bought them for her, maybe for her birthday one year. He had told her, he thought, that she'd look sexy in them. And she had. Oh my, had she ever!

*When sundown pales the sky, I wanna hide a while, behind your smile, and everywhere I'd look, your eyes I'd find.*

They stirred in him now the tiniest flicker of carnal yearning. She arched her back now, ever so slightly, and the flicker grew, caught flame. Sick as he was, frail as he was, God help him, he wanted her.

*For me to love you now, would be the sweetest thing, 'twould make me sing, ah, but I may as well try and catch the wind.*

She turned and looked at him, her face gorgeous in the sun, whole decades washed clean away. There were no wrinkles in her cheeks, no bags under her eyes, none of the pain and loneliness he'd seen there for too long. She looked nearly as she had when he'd first met her, in that weird way that he had, all those many years ago.

*When rain has hung the leaves with tears, I want you near, to kill my fears, to help me to leave all my blues behind.*

She went to him now, understanding without needing to be told, as silent as she was resplendent. Still, all day, they had not exchanged a single word.

She bent down and put her hands on the bed, began to

crawl up it, toward him.

*For standin' in your heart, is where I want to be, and I long to be, ah, but I may as well, try and catch the wind.*

She pressed her mouth against his, kissed him, and slowly slid the covers off his body.

"I want you to ask yourself, Sean: 'How often... in the course of a day... do I contemplate the plights... of others? And how often... do I dwell... on my own?'"

"I try so hard not to be self-consumed, Dad. I really do. But God knows I don't always succeed."

"And you never... will... all the time. But please... just do... the best you can."

"Of course I will."

"Don't give in... to the temptations... that I did. And please... don't quit caring. About other people. Everyone... even strangers... but especially... the people who love you."

"I won't, Dad."

"Because... if nobody gives a damn... about anyone else... we'd might as well... just call it quits."

"Yes."

"Let the whole world... expire."

"Yes."

"Remember," Dennis said, "every day... to ask yourself: 'Have I stopped... giving a damn? Is it all... about me now? How many times... have I stopped to ponder... the plights of others... today?"

"I'll try, Dad."

"And please never... deceive yourself... into thinking you couldn't..."

Sean waited a moment, then prodded him: "Couldn't what, Dad?"

"Do more," he said.

"Okay." Sean took a deep breath.

"And please remember," his father told him, "to appreciate... when you're happy. To appreciate... rare moments. Moments... when everything's right. Moments... with the texture... of silk. That taste... like milk... and honey. When your world... is painted... with dazzling colors, lit... with brilliant, colored lights. When... when you are young... and the world... belongs to you. When *you*... have the better of *it*. Those are moments, Sean... those are the moments... and there are not many of them... but dear God, my son, if you... if you really stop to enjoy them... they will leave you... breathless."

"Okay, Dad. I will. I promise you I will."

"I love you, son."

"I love you, too."

Sean held out a bowl of slowly cooling chicken noodle soup. "Ready to eat now, Dad?"

But his father was already asleep again.

It was Monday, October second. The temperature had dropped dramatically. The weather forecast on the radio was calling for snow the following weekend, at least at high elevations.

Dennis was all but delirious. He had been mumbling incoherently all day, referring to people Rachael and Sean had never heard of, describing events which perhaps had never occurred. At one point he asked if Tony was coming to dinner. Rachael, holding back tears, told him he wasn't sure yet. Later Dennis inquired if someone had remembered to take the soup off the stove, because if not they might have a fire on their hands, and then, before either Rachael or Sean could respond, observed that Peter had never seen an ass he didn't like. This elicited a wan grin from Sean and more tears from Rachael.

The day wore on. Dennis initially refused all the food he

was offered. Eventually Rachael coaxed him into eating two spoonfuls of blueberry yogurt, telling him that Sean would bring him a present if he did. Sean held up his end of the bargain, delivering a radio to his father's bedside. It was the one Dennis himself had purchased in Odell.

"Put the game on," Dennis told him.

"There's no Mariners game tonight, Dad. Sorry."

"Put it on!"

"Dad. There's no game. I'm sor -"

"We'll put the game on, sweetheart," Rachael interjected. "Here, Sean, let me see the radio."

Sean handed it to his mother. He watched as she turned around, blocking Dennis's view (not that he likely would've noticed), and slipped a tape into the tape deck. A moment later, the sound of Simon and Garfunkel's "Bookends" filled the room.

"He likes this one," she told her son.

"I know he does," Sean said.

"Is that the game?" Dennis asked.

"Yes," she told him. "It's the game, honey. The Mariners are winning."

"What's the score?"

She looked at Sean. "Four to two," he said, "bottom of the eighth."

Evening fell. Rachael played more music for Dennis, all his favorites: the Beatles, the Stones, Beethoven and Mozart, Bob Dylan, Chuck Barry, Miles Davis, Roy Orbison, Eric Clapton, Dire Staits, Bach and Schubert and Pachelbel. Throughout most of it Dennis slept.

Rachael had brought the tapes from Dennis's study at their home in Seattle. She had also brought the gold chain and crucifix his father had given him shortly before he'd passed away, himself from cancer, twenty years before. Dennis had never worn it, both because he'd despised his father and because he had always flouted organized religion. But he had not resisted Rachael's placing it around his neck the day after the wedding, and had worn it since without complaint. She knew he'd let her do it entirely to appease her, but she didn't mind; his acquiescence, she'd decided, was a victory in itself, and a sufficient display of humility, surely, to appease any other interested parties as well.

Around the time it started raining, Rachael fell asleep herself. Sean, meanwhile, sat in the rocking chair in the Sunrise

Room, thinking about Sarah, hoping she could make it back in time to be with him once... once it happened. He would need her.

There in the rocker, though, he felt oddly at peace.

Rachael's birthday began with a nasty scare: Dennis, seemingly, could not be woken. She shook his shoulder, gently at first and then harder, repeating his name with increasing urgency, tears rushing to her eyes.

Then his own opened slowly. He turned his head and looked at her with total recognition. "Hey, sweetheart," he said. "How are you?"

"Oh, Dennis!" She sobbed. "Oh, God. Jesus!"

"What's the matter?"

"Nothing," she said, shaking her head, hiding her face. "Nothing at all."

"I love you," he said.

"I love you, too."

And then, incredibly: "Happy birthday, sweetheart."

She was forty-eight years old.

*   *   *

Sean, somehow, had actually managed to buy his mother a gift. It was a framed photograph of the three of them, he and his parents, together on the porch of their New England retreat. The photograph itself was about twelve years old, had been taken by a neighbor. Sean had been thirteen then, and in the picture was grinning from ear to ear, holding his fishing pole in his right hand. Dennis was wearing a burgundy sweater and slacks, Rachael an old, flower-patterned dress she had bought not long after starting her teaching gig. Dennis had teased her about it, she remembered, telling her it made her look like an old school marm. They had been happy back then, all three of them. But perhaps she especially.

She cried, of course, when she unwrapped it. Sean had expected that, but the sight of it still panged his heart with sadness.

"Don't cry, Mom," he told her.

"It's okay," she assured him.

"I wanted it to make you happy."

"It did," she said. "It *does* make me happy, son. It's just..."

"I know."

She rose from her chair and hugged him. He hugged her back, planted a kiss on her cheek. It was warm and flushed. "Here," he said, taking the photograph from her, "let's show it to Dad."

"Okay."

Dennis lay perfectly still in the bed. More still, Sean thought, than ever. "Dad?" he said. The word barely made it off his lips.

"He's just sleeping," his mother assured him. "He gave me an awful fright this morning when he looked that way. But he's just sleeping, don't worry."

Sean went to his father and put the back of his hand to his cheek. He waited a moment, then bent down and pressed his ear against his chest.

"He's just sleeping, isn't he, Sean? Tell me he's just sleeping, son."

Sean did not reply, just kept his ear to his father's chest.

"Sean." She was hysterical now. "Sean!"

Sean lifted one of his father's hands from the bed and touched his thumb to the center of his wrist, held it there for perhaps five seconds, and lowered it to the bed.

"He's just sleeping," Rachael said, her voice tiny and

words anemic, rife with desperate, stubborn disbelief. She had grown unsteady on her feet. "I know he is."

Sean went to her, meaning to grab her before she fell, and fell himself. He fell to the floor and pulled his knees up to his chest, as if to keep his heart from bursting, as if to quell his torrential sobs. Eventually, some eternity later, his mother helped him up.

## 44

*Retreating into his thoughts, he pictures blue skies like the ones he's seen so many of in the last few months, blue skies with nary a cloud to mar them. He pictures the forest behind his house, and the lake, and the mighty Columbia River along which he drove to find this quiet paradise. He pictures the birds that sail over the lake with wings spread wide, effortlessly, diving low before rising again, headed nowhere and everywhere at once. He marvels at the stillness of the earth itself, too often missed for the noise and business of its creatures. He pictures also the deer which crept up so bravely to the window in his kitchen nook, and regarded him as if reading his thoughts with perfect comprehension. Its eyes were sad and beautiful, and he wept at the sight of them. Having perhaps accomplished its goal, it then fled.*

*These thoughts give him great comfort, inspire a terrific calm within him. He thinks them over again, chases them as closely as he can without actually catching them; he does not want to catch them, for he knows that, once caught, such treasures quickly fade. Such treasures are far more valuable sought than owned.*

*His thoughts turning finally to Rachael and Sean, somewhere very nearby, slumber finds him once again and he welcomes it.*

# EPILOGUE:
## d i a g n o s i s (ii)

## 45

Not long after the Christmas holiday, a middle-aged woman appeared at the Legal Aid office in Los Angeles, California at which Sarah Arbaugh, now six weeks' pregnant, was employed. This woman was also named Sarah, and was originally from Kirkland, Washington, just outside Seattle. For years she had worked as a waitress, but had recently quit her job and moved to LA to open a restaurant of her own.

Shortly thereafter, however, she had met a man with whom she had instantly fallen in love - or for whom, at least, she had felt an immediate lust. Within a matter of weeks this man had become controlling and verbally abusive toward her, she told her attorney. Not long after that, he had begun to grab her or push her whenever she made him mad. Finally, two days earlier, he had punched her in the face with a closed fist, blackening her left eye. She had never been in an abusive relationship before, she explained, so she'd been rather caught off guard by the whole affair and woefully oblivious of the warning signs. Now, she confessed, she was virtually bankrupt, homeless, and living for the moment at a local shelter for victims of domestic violence. She had a grown daughter, but had not yet been able to bring herself to call and tell her what was happening.

"I don't think you need me to tell you, Sarah," her attorney said, "that what he did to you is not your fault, that *none* of it's your fault. You didn't ask for it, and you didn't deserve it."

"I know."

"There are enough good men in the world," her attorney continued, "that you never have to settle for assholes like that." She blushed a little, not having meant to be profane. "If I can speak bluntly, that is."

"Of course you can. And I know there are. I know I don't. It's just -"

"But even if there weren't," Sarah Arbaugh said, "you still wouldn't have to settle for that crap, because it's always better to be alone, free, and unhurt than somebody's prisoner and punching bag. Right?"

"Of course," the ex-waitress said. "I'm not like the other women you probably help. I'm not... you know."

"Not what?" She waited a moment, giving Sarah the waitress a chance to reply. "Stupid? Insecure? Masochistic?"

Sarah from Seattle said nothing, just lowered her head as if ashamed of her comment.

"It's okay. You don't have to feel bad. A lot of them aren't geniuses, that's for sure, but plenty of them are damn smart enough that you'd think they'd know better. Only, it's not *about* knowing better. It's not about what you know, or think you know, at all. It's about having the courage to say no, to turn your back on him and walk away. Because for *him*, it's a control thing, plain and simple. Some men, some *people*, aren't happy unless they're controlling other people. Physical abuse is just one of the more extreme symptoms of the disorder, that need to control."

Sarah the ex-waitress nodded.

"You know," said Sarah the attorney, swiveling in her chair to face her computer, "you're lucky you didn't come in *last* week."

"Oh? Why's that?"

Sarah Arbaugh opened a program on her computer and began entering case notes. "Because we hadn't gotten our new funding yet, and I may not have been able to help you."

"Oh. Wow."

Sarah the attorney nodded and turned back to her new client. "Yes. It was looking pretty grim for us. We were down to being able to accept about ten percent of potential clients."

"But the government came through? Gee, that's a first."

Sarah Arbaugh shook her head. "Nope. Not the government. An individual, actually. He made a very generous posthumous donation, naming all the Legal Aid offices in California, jointly, as the primary beneficiary of his life insurance policy. He passed away in early October, but the paperwork didn't go through until just last week. Our office alone got close to five hundred thousand dollars."

Her client's eyes widened a bit. "Really? Who was it, some rich guy?"

"He did well for himself. But he was a very generous man."

"Sounds like. But what about his family? Didn't he leave anything for *them*?"

"Oh," Sarah Arbaugh said, and waved at Sean, who'd just appeared in the doorway to her office. "He left plenty for them, too."

"Sounds like a good man."

"He was."

"Is this a client of yours?" Sean asked, hovering where he stood. "Should I come back later?"

"Yeah. I don't think we'll be too much longer." Sarah

the attorney looked back at Sarah the waitress and said, "Sorry about this. That's my husband."

Sarah from Seattle turned in her chair and regarded the young, handsome man who stood in the doorway. "Hi," she said. "I'm Sarah."

"Hey," Sean said, stepping gingerly into the room. "Same name as my wife. How cool." He extended his hand and she shook it, smiling sheepishly.

"Yeah, that's what I told her." She hesitated a moment, looking at Sean more intently now. "My goodness," she said, "you remind me so strongly of someone."

"Who's that?"

"I don't know," she said, putting a finger to her temple, still regarding him closely. "I can't quite place him. But you're basically a younger version of him. You could be his son, in fact."

"Hmm," Sean said. "Interesting. Maybe it'll come to you later and you can tell my wife."

"Yeah, maybe," Sarah Arbaugh interjected. She smiled, and looked beautiful when she did it. "Now scram. You're killin' our confidentiality here."

Sean laughed, told Sarah the waitress it had been a

pleasure meeting her, and scurried out of the office. "Meet you in the lobby of the building in ten," he called to his wife on the way out. "Or twenty, whichever."

Both women chuckled. "He's cute," Sarah the waitress said. "You're lucky."

"Yes," said Sarah Arbaugh, "I am. *Very* lucky. But so are you."

"Because of that rich guy's donation?"

"For one. And for another, because you're alive. You got away from that son of a bitch who hit you, and probably, eventually, would've killed you, given the right opportunity. A lot of women aren't so fortunate."

"Oh."

"So now you can start over."

Sarah the waitress nodded. "That's all I *want* to do."

"And it's what you *will* do. With my help."

"Thank you."

Sarah Arbaugh turned back to her computer and began typing again. A bright winter sun broke through the clouds, dousing the office with warm, lovely light. Her hair and eyes flashed brilliantly.

Her new client, meanwhile, sat and contemplated her

situation, which before had seemed so frightening and onerous but now felt possible to beat, to overcome. She could get up and over it, she realized, get the better of the damned thing. Put the whole mess behind her. Move on. Open that restaurant, achieve her life's dream, find some happiness after all. It wouldn't be easy, not by a long shot, but she could do it, if she tried. She felt it in her bones. And she realized, all at once, that she really *was* lucky, that what her lawyer had said to her a moment ago had been more than just empty consolation. It was, as a matter of fact, the honest-to-God's truth.

Smiling a little now, she pondered, too, the kindness of strangers, of the woman behind the desk who'd offered to help her, and of the man, whoever he was, who had apparently cared a great deal about people he'd never met, enough to give so much as he had to them at the end of his life. She hoped that one day she'd meet a man as kind as that, sure that she could love him no matter what he looked like or where he came from or what he had. For such people, she decided then, were life's most valuable treasures.

*March 6, 2006*
*November 15, 2008*
Morgantown, WV
Charleston, WV

Made in the USA
Coppell, TX
29 July 2020

31924171R10256